DEADLY VENDETTA

DEADLY VENDETTA

DONNA SCUVOTTI

For information about this title or to order other books and/or electronic
media, contact the publisher:

Donna Scuvotti
www.donnascuvottiauthor.com
info@donnascuvottiauthor.com

ISBNs:
978-1-7371576-3-2 (hardcover)
978-1-7371576-4-9 (softcover)
978-1-7371576-5-6 (eBook)

Printed in the United States of America

Cover and Interior design: 1106 Design

For all of you who think you're not good enough.
It's never too late to follow your dream.

CONTENTS

CONTENTS

ACKNOWLEDGMENTS

Starting out on this journey back in September 2021, when I published *Just Jonathan*, I knew very little about getting a book out there. Fast forward to September 2022 and I still have a lot to learn but one thing I've stumbled upon is the importance of having people in your corner.

Who would have thought I would have found that in the Instagram writing community? The friendships I've formed will last a lifetime and most I will cherish forever. The vast amount of knowledge I've come across is unmeasurable. And the support is like no other. Thank you one and all from the bottom of my heart for embracing me and my journey. I can never repay you for your kindness and acceptance.

Helen Aitchison my bestie from the UK you deserve a medal. You have unselfishly listened to me rant about my characters and offered me invaluable advice in my quest to make *Deadly Vendetta* the best that it can be. Thank you a million times over again. Your friendship and many talks mean the world to me. #pocketloveforever

Harriet (Harry) Pearce you are an angel. Not only did you spend hours combing through *Deadly Vendetta* giving me insights, but you helped me so much with the ins and outs of marketing. I would be remiss not to mention you're a creative genius when it comes to book reels. Thank you my Kiwi friend for the many talks we've had and the help you've given me.

Liz Kraus you are a lifesaver. Your vast knowledge of the ins and outs of the English language helped me tweak my blurb, to what I hope is catchy and leaves everyone wanting more. Thanks friend.

Thank you to my husband, Tony for putting up with me when I get into the writing "zone." It can be self absorbing, but you never complained, well almost never!! Your support and love make me a better person and I can't think of anyone else I'd rather do this life with.

To the team at 1106 Design, once again you hit it out of the park. From the cover design to the editing, not to mention all the steps in between, you continue to be the best at what you do. Thank you Michele, Ronda and Frank for helping me shine.

Many of you reading this will not know what an ARC is but I have many and they are my core of book loving, review writing, content sharing, all around fantastic people. It stands for Advanced Reader Copy and the people that I share my book with prior to launching it, are paramount in its success. Thank you one and all. You know who you are. I love you and your support.

Lastly but most importantly, thank you my readers. Without you I wouldn't be me. I strive to give you content you enjoy. Your kind words and wonderful reviews have humbled me more than you know. It continues to warm my heart knowing I have created characters you find endearing and also a little scary. Here's to many more years of jumping down rabbit holes together, hunting the bad guy and living a life through my characters.

Sundays are my favorite day of the week. I had never given it much thought until recently, when it just hit me: It's genius, actually—like a do-over if the past week was crap. I have been having a lot of those lately—crap weeks, that is.

Mainly because I can't seem to focus, at least not today, anyway. I have been working on a case that involves a thirteen-year-old whose parents are in the midst of a divorce. I keep finding myself becoming lost in a daydream, remembering when I was a misplaced soul, thirteen years old, drowning in suffering and trying to come to terms with the loss of my beloved Mom. The year was 2019, which seemed like a lifetime ago, but, in all actuality, it was only two decades ago. How was it possible that twenty years had gone by and, just like that, it was now 2039? Another year of turmoil and unrest. But I digress.

I guess it's true what they say: One minute you're here, the next you're gone. I would eventually come to learn that the older you get, the faster time seems to fly. To date, I haven't met a single person who can tell me otherwise. The time between birthdays or Christmases in the innocence of youth felt like an eternity. Now, it's the blink of an eye, where January and December seem to merge as one. One could only imagine how it would be as I aged—hopefully, gracefully and filled with love and acceptance. But all I really cared about was being given the opportunity to age. I wanted to look back at my life with awe and excitement and be able to tell my grandchildren about my escapades and stories from my worldly travels.

Life isn't a given. We are merely passengers on the wheel of time. It's the unknown, the fragility of it that makes me feel so strongly about it. My poor Mom, whom I still miss desperately, was not granted such luxury. She was taken from me, from this world, at thirty-nine years of age, by a drunk driver. She deserved so much more. To think that, when she died, she was a mere six years older than I am now puts life into perspective. So much life left to live. So much love left to spread.

Not many things anger me more than people who take life for granted. My motto has always been to *get the most out of each day*. Live clean, love hard, and respect all is how I aspire to live my life. In the aftermath of such a tragedy, looking back, I can see just how that day molded me into the man I am today. I have learned to cherish each day to its fullest and express myself. One is never promised tomorrow, so it's best to let others know how much they mean to you. As a child, I was very sensitive. Not much has changed in that department. I still feel things deep within my soul. I would be considered "in touch with my feelings," which has caused me to shed a tear here and there. My friends kid me about that, but I've come to accept that's who I am. I'm proud to say I wouldn't change it for the world.

Just as I was making my way down the dreaded rabbit hole, I was shaken from my funk by a loud, urgent, demanding knock on my door. My immediate impulse was to pretend that I was out for the afternoon, but my melancholy mood wouldn't benefit anyone—least of all me—so I answered.

"Come in," I said, halfheartedly. "The door's open."

Brie, my personal secretary/paralegal, stumbled in, looking like she had been trapped in a cat fight and lost. Her characteristically coiffed appearance was nowhere in sight. Her blond hair was in a top knot that was half falling out, her make-up was viciously smeared, and her pale-blue blouse was missing a couple of buttons, next to a massive red spot that looked like fresh blood. The sight of her immediately made my heart start to pound. Needless to say, she was frantic when she spoke.

Barely audible, she managed to stutter, "Mr. Elliott, I um . . . I" before her mouth formed into a grimace. A puff of air escaped her lips as she, once again, tried to speak, and then she collapsed abruptly on the floor next to my desk.

I immediately ran to her side, knocking over my chair as depositions went flying here and there. I'm pretty sure I yelled at the top of my lungs for help, because, within a matter of seconds, my office was filled with confused fellow attorneys as well as other staff members. All hell broke loose, and the next hour or so was a bit of a blur as chaos ensued. Through all the noise, I heard someone frantically call 911, and, as we waited, I bent down to check for a pulse.

Her once-beautiful blue eyes were rolled back in her head, and a mixture of spit bubbles tainted with blood was forming around her lips. Her pulse was weak and slowed but still beating rhythmically. Her breathing was shallow; anybody could tell she was in dire straits from each slow rise and fall of her chest. She was in such a bad way that I was afraid I would be witness to her last breath, and this alone terrified me. Death was not something that I ever cared to witness again after watching my Mom take her last breath. It still haunted me.

In desperation I could see Brie was trying to talk. Cradling her head gently, I begged her to please hold on—help was on its way. I lowered myself next to her and put her freshly manicured hand in mine. I couldn't help but notice her hand had fresh scratches, and a bruise was already beginning to form. Two of her nails were broken, and all that was left were jagged, sharp edges. As I put my ear next to her mouth, the scent of her Jo Malone perfume I had grown accustomed to was intoxicating.

She let out a shallow, panicked breath and whispered to me something that sounded like "*hard kiss*," but, through her slurred speech, her words made no sense. Just as I was trying to get her to repeat what she had just said, the paramedics burst through the door. She took one last, heaved breath, and she was gone.

CHAPTER TWO

My heart was racing, and my fingers began to tingle; I was sweating bullets. I loosened my tie and took a sip of water, but it was all in vain, because I was starting to feel the telltale signs of a panic attack. I hadn't experienced one in years, but now I remembered the feeling all too well.

"Mr. Elliott, can you hear me?"

Yes, I wanted to say, *I hear you—I just can't respond.* I tried my hardest to remember how I coped with the ever-present anxiety after my Mom's death. Slow, even breathing should have done the trick, but this was more than just a panic attack. I felt like my chest had a four-ton elephant sitting on it. And then I blacked out.

It was like I was having an out-of-body experience, or at least what I suspected it would feel like when you're in nowhere land, floating above your own body, watching but not understanding. In some strange twilight state, I could vaguely comprehend what was happening, but I was still not totally aware. Definitely not aware enough to respond when asked questions. Or was I being asked questions? I wasn't even sure at this point. All I really knew for sure was that I was in a room that was sterile and white, with people running around like someone's life depended on it. But, whose could it be? Certainly not mine—or was it?

Did I really remember reading once that, when you die, before your spirit flies off to heaven, you "hover" and watch yourself taking your last breath and have a feeling of peace? I was *anything but* at peace—panicked and on edge instead. Hopefully, that meant my current state wasn't as sorry as I suspected.

I tried to ignore the hustle and bustle going on around me: footsteps sounding loud and hurried as they made contact with the tiled floor, doors creaking as they opened and shut, voices whispering. Maybe I was subconsciously shielding myself from what I had just witnessed. Did Brie actually die in my office, or was I dreaming? My mind wasn't thinking clearly, making it impossible to figure out what was a figment of my imagination as opposed to reality.

Fading in and out of a mindless fog, I heard two women in scrubs, who, I assumed, were nurses, huddled together, talking about me. And Brie. Was I hearing correctly when they said Brie had died and I had suffered a heart attack? At thirty-three, was that even possible? Well, I know anything's possible, but I thought it rather unlikely. Or so I hoped.

My thoughts wandered to Brie, my trusty right hand. She had always joked about her name when she met people and would say her name was just like the cheese. Now, all I could think about was her lying on a slab in the cold, sterile morgue just like a piece of cheese on a charcuterie board. The image repulsed me, and I leaned over and retched. Vomit hit the white tile floor and beaded up in crazy patterns, resembling all kinds of nonsensical things. Was I looking at a clown, balancing a cow with one arm, while riding a unicycle?

Just the thought of this made me start to hyperventilate. I tasted something salty and realized it was my own tears streaming down my face. The constant rhythmic beeping of machines close by was oddly comforting to me, and I felt my breathing slow in cadence with the sounds. And then I must have blacked out again, because the last thing I remember was someone in a white lab coat and a stethoscope hanging loosely around his neck, calling out my name . . . "Jonathan, Jonathan Elliott—can you hear me?"

CHAPTER THREE

I was floating in the ocean on a homemade raft that had been battered and beaten by waves and a storm that had just passed. Black clouds looked ominous as they drifted off to the east, blown by a gust of wind that almost blew me off my raft. I was lost. Far from home and scared of drowning. My mouth was parched. Looking around, I was trying hard to get my bearings, when I saw a ship on the horizon. *Hallucinations must be taking over my brain*, I thought, *because I could swear it was a pirate ship.* I could distinctly make out the outline of the sails, cannons that adorned the ship, and what appeared to be pirates hanging over the side, drunk and disorderly. A loud bang sounded in the distance, and I woke up with a start.

Vivid dreams and many nightmares had been a thing of the past for me until now. To say I was not too happy to have them return is an understatement, but unlike the thirteen-year-old me, I was much more in tune with reality as an adult. Was it due to the trauma I'd just experienced watching Brie die? I was constantly haunted for about a year and a half by nightmares after I witnessed my Mom's death. Those were trying times for me, but I came out on the other side stronger and in control of my destiny, so to speak—as much as a teenager could be, anyway.

As I looked around, my limbs couldn't move. I was paralyzed and confused. My mind started to race. Where was I? I saw people in white lab coats and multi-colored scrubs moving swiftly, here and there. It was almost like they were all on a clandestine mission or being timed to see who would come in first and win an invisible, fictitious race. I heard a strange, never-ending beep and realized it was coming from me. Or at least a machine that was attached to me. My legs and arms were beginning to regain feeling, and I opened my mouth to speak. An unrecognizable croak emerged that sounded foreign to me. I calmed myself with a couple of deep breaths and tried again. "Water, please," I managed to say before the radiating pain stabbed at my flesh once again.

Then, out of nowhere, the best sight in all the land appeared. My Dad and Luke were by my side, looking like they hadn't slept in days—or eaten, for that matter. My Dad's blue Oxford shirt was a wrinkled disaster, and his salt-and-pepper hair was standing on end like he had been raking his fingers through it, in a subconscious effort to soothe himself.

His brow was furrowed, causing deep creases in his forehead, and his eyes appeared bloodshot and weary.

"Dad, are you OK?" I managed to say.

A genuine concern was growing in me because my father had always been meticulous on all accounts. Since he'd become sober two decades ago, I'd watch him fine-tune himself into an amiable and respectable man. No words can describe how proud of him it made me to see him rise from the ashes. A man once tainted with a brush few come back from flourished into the man I now felt honored to call my father.

A smile that lit up the room broke through his pursed lips.

"Welcome back to us, son. You had us both scared half out of our minds with worry!" he exclaimed, beaming from ear to ear.

Before I could respond, Luke seized my hand as tears ran down his face, soaking my fingers. This did not come as a surprise to me, because he'd always been in touch with his feelings and worn his emotions on his sleeve.

Luke—my other Dad and best friend—had been my savior and partner in crime for years, the man I had always described as having a heart of pure gold. That hadn't changed through all our years together. He was a gem of a good person, emotions and all, and I, for one, couldn't have been happier at this moment to see the two most important people in my life. As my eyes began to focus, I took a second to take a long, hard look at Luke before I spoke again. There was something off. He was smiling and seemed genuinely happy, but there was something lurking behind his eyes that spoke differently. His eyes showed worry and sadness; this concerned me, and red flags started waving everywhere. He immediately looked down and broke eye contact. He knew I was onto him. We had shared so much through the years, and I knew him better than I knew myself. What I knew with one hundred percent certainty was that he was worried and hiding something from me—something that had the potential to derail my life.

Ever since I was a child, I had experienced an oddly preternatural intuition nobody could explain. Not altogether full-on ESP, but more like a sixth sense that appeared out of nowhere. One thing I had to come to realize through the years is that I needed to pay attention and heed its warnings. It had never before let me down, and I felt fairly confident that this time would be no different.

Just as I was about to inquire about what was going on with Luke, a doctor appeared at my side. He, too, was all smiles as he came to shake my hand and welcome me back. He was a small, grandfatherly man, with Harry Potter-type glasses perched on the tip of his nose. When he spoke, it was warm and gentle, like he had wrapped me in a warm blanket on a cold winter's day.

"You sure gave everyone a scare around here, Jonathan. You have been in and out of consciousness for almost a week now. It's good to see you fully awake and coherent," he said. "My name is Dr. Owens, but you can call me 'Gus.'"

Time stood still for the next hour or so while I was submerged into the world of medical gibberish. To me, all of it sounded like a bunch of mumbo jumbo that went in one ear and out the other. All I really needed to know was that I hadn't suffered a heart attack, like everyone seemingly thought. What was surprising, though, was that I had pneumonia, causing fluid to build up in my lungs' air sacs. That, coupled with the anxiety more than likely brought on by the trauma of watching someone I had grown to love and confide in die in my arms, all mimicked a heart attack. Flashbacks from my Mom dying in my arms tipped me over the cliff of pure panic. Come to think of it, I'd been feeling a bit under the weather, but in pure Jonathan fashion, I carried on thinking I was indestructible like every other like-minded thirty-three-year-old.

Complete bed rest after a couple more days in the hospital, mostly for monitoring, was ordered. Dr. Gus, along with my two Dads, left me to ponder what had just transpired. Within a short period of time, I had witnessed a death, I had blacked out for almost a week—and now this. I started thinking that I needed to evaluate my life, but first things first. Was Brie's death a murder? And if so, by whose hands? What really needed my immediate attention was Luke and why he seemed so concerned.

CHAPTER FOUR

Luke was a mildly complicated man with a very colorful backstory. The gods had intervened years ago when we'd met haphazardly while investigating strange happenings in the forest near our Pacific Northwest homes. What started out as what I would describe as me being scared shitless of him turned into the most wonderful of friendships—one that I would cherish above all others.

He was a gentle giant of a man, a Gulf War veteran, and an alcoholic. He had stared those demons in the face and been alcohol-free for more than twenty years now. To say he'd been instrumental in getting me through some of my darkest days would be an understatement. He was the one and only person who had been there every step of the way, showing me how to come to terms with my Mom's death. His support never wavered, showering me with all the love and guidance I needed to move on. He was the epitome of what a true friend looked like. I trusted him with my whole being, and I knew that he wasn't just troubled—he was *deeply* troubled.

"Dad, do you mind taking a jaunt to the cafeteria? All of a sudden, I'm ravenous. You know I'm famished if I'm craving hospital food," I joked. In truth, I really wasn't hungry at all, but it was all my mind could muster in the fog. I desperately needed to get some alone time with Luke.

My Dad was more than eager to help and almost took off in a full sprint out the door. I could hear him telling everyone as he ran down the corridor that I'd woken up; applause broke out. I must've been in a bad way. I'm glad I don't remember the worst of it. The human body is amazing in the way it shields your memory from the worst by making you black out and get some healing sleep.

"Okay, old man—what's going on?" I affectionately pleaded with Luke.

"I don't know what you mean, Jonathan. I was overcome with emotion when you finally came back to us. You must have mistakenly read that as something else," Luke replied, the denial strong in his voice.

Unconvinced, I probed more. Luke had always prided himself on his honesty, so I knew the best tactic would be to take him on a little trip down memory lane. It tripped him up every time and usually was the quickest route to get him to spill the beans. I knew my Dad would return soon, and my window of opportunity would be lost, so time became of the essence.

Quickly I reminded Luke of all our heart-to-hearts, sitting in front of a roaring fire at his cabin adjacent to the forest, where we had spent many bonding moments. His cabin had always provided a home away from home, where I felt the most comfortable and at peace. It is also where we collectively hatched the plan to bring down the Mount Sierra killer. One thing was for sure: nobody could ever deny that the bond Luke and I had formed was unbreakable.

After what seemed like an eternity, Luke caved, just as I knew he would.

"Jonathan, I don't know how to tell you this, because it hurts me to know the pain this will cause you, but I know in my heart of hearts you have the right to know."

I held my breath and braced myself for what I was about to hear. While Luke seemed to be struggling internally about what to say, I waited patiently. The noticeable twitch in the corner of his mouth that he displayed only when he was stressed to the max appeared. My senses seemed to be keener. I homed in on the smell of the disinfectant that made my eyes water and on the sound of the clanging of dishes being loaded onto carts from breakfast. The ever-present beeps that had lulled me to sleep earlier was now irritating me and driving me more than a little loony. He hesitated. A lone tear cascaded down his cheek before his mouth opened to speak. "Jonathan, your Dad is . . ."

Before he could say another word, my Dad barreled through the door with more food than a small army could devour.

"**M**y Dad is *what*?" I wanted to scream, but, when Luke shot me a death glare and mouthed for me to keep my mouth shut, it made me think twice. The last thing I wanted was to upset Luke any more than he clearly already was. It had to be something major. Was my Dad dying? Did he have some horrible disease that he had been keeping from me? Had he lost his job again? And then it hit me. *He must be drinking again.*

Why had I not recognized the signs? I had chalked it all up to worry and lack of sleep when I noticed my Dad's sorry state. He looked like an unmade bed with his wrinkled shirt, unkempt hair, and bloodshot eyes. This was huge, and it would definitely account for Luke's concern, apprehension, and his overall hangdog look. Luke, after all, was my Dad's sponsor in Alcoholics Anonymous, and, knowing him like I did, he would feel like a failure—a failure to himself, my Dad, and myself. My Dad was an awful drunk. It turned him into an abusive, volatile, and angry man with little regard for others. The damage caused by his toxic, liquor-fueled behavior had taken us years to repair. Why would he sacrifice all we had built? Was this something new, caused by my being nonchalant about my own health, or had I been too consumed by my job to pay him the attention he needed?

If this was, indeed, true, it concerned me very much, but, just like when I was younger, I was mystified about how to address it. I was a grown man now and should have been able to confront him, but it was complicated. Alcoholics could be devious when they hid the truth and acted defensive. After all, it wasn't like he hadn't lived with the damage he'd caused for decades. He had to know the ramifications of going down that path again, didn't he?

I feigned tiredness and an overall sense of malaise so that I could be left alone. I had some thinking to do, and the last thing I needed was two hovering men—although they had my best interests at heart—watching my every move.

The minute they left the room, sadness consumed me. I had to deal with my Dad, and the sooner the better, but what was I to do about Brie? My mind played back all I could remember of that dreaded afternoon, and I was positive there was foul play involved. *That*, I was 100% certain about—that and the fact that, knowing myself so well, I wouldn't be content until I got to the bottom of who or what was responsible. Justice for Brie was paramount and would take precedent now as soon as I was on the mend.

Just thinking about getting justice for Brie got me hyped up. I loved seeking adventure and intrigue. My life had become too mundane as of late, and in a very strange way I can't describe, my soul craved the hunt. Just as I was concocting a plan for what my next step might entail, an odd feeling that someone was watching my every move caused me to become agitated, making me question my sanity. I looked around but couldn't see anything except beeping machines and a white, sterile environment.

Convinced I was being paranoid or just overcome with tiredness, I put it on the back burner. *Surely, my mind is playing tricks on me*, I thought to myself as I drifted in and out of lucidness. Eventually my eyes caved, and I fell into a fitful sleep. In my dream, I was frantically searching for Brie. I could hear her calling my name over and over again, urgently begging me to save her. As I meandered up through the dark alleyways that smelled of cat piss, stale beer, and barf, my panic grew. Rats scurried up my pant leg, and I swatted at them. I opened foul-smelling dumpsters that contained rotting food and the remnants of other gross stuff I couldn't even begin to identify. Every turn I made brought me back to the same spot, like I had been searching in vain. *Where was she?* The calls from Brie grew louder, and I ran toward the piercing sound, tripping over a body. In the dark, dreary alley, crouched over, holding a bottle of gin, I heard an all-too-familiar groan. I looked down, straight into the bloodshot eyes of my Dad. He returned my gaze with a blank stare and brought the bottle up to his mouth, taking a long swig before a loud belch escaped his lips. He wiped his mouth with his filthy sleeve, saying nothing. As I brushed myself off, I couldn't get the constant beeping out of my head, echoing like a garbage truck stuck in reverse.

Before my Dad could talk, my eyes snapped open as sweat beaded on my brow and ran down my back. Somehow, I'd made my way out of my bed and tripped over a chair, which had caused two nurses to rush in. Flat on my back, the floor as my bed, my legs were coiled haphazardly in the chair. I'd somehow managed to pull my IV out, and machines were screaming for help. *Ugh*—the nightmares were back after years of absence, and I was more convinced than ever it had to be from witnessing Brie's death.

My nightmares seemed always to manifest themselves out of what was going on in my life, which gave them an even-more-eerie quality. I made a mental note to first address the drinking situation with my Dad before starting my dive into Brie's life. I knew nothing would be right until these two things were addressed. I wouldn't escape the torment every time I tried to get some shut-eye. Needing to uncover information I clearly knew nothing about and knowing there was no time like the present gave me focus.

Luckily—although, quite frankly, I'm not sure luck played any part—I was able to squeak by without any more crazy-ass dreams and was discharged two days later. Dr. Gus was downright adamant that I come for a follow-up examination but, most importantly, made me promise to take better care of myself. "Burning the candle at both ends never benefited anyone," he cautioned.

I had become a bit of a workaholic lately, mostly because I loved my work. Becoming an attorney had been my dream for years, and, now that I had fulfilled that dream by graduating *magna cum laude*, I was eager to prove myself. A major drawback to this was that it left little time for a social life. I had always been an introvert, with only a select group of friends, but I vowed to change that. As soon as I was declared well, I planned on joining a gym and getting back into soccer, another passion of mine I had let die. This illness might be just the wake-up call I needed.

Being discharged from the hospital was the highlight of my month. The best part was that I got to go back to the cabin with Luke. It actually was more like he *insisted* that I convalesce at his cabin so that he could keep an eagle eye on me. No complaints were heard from me, though. His place was my happy place. There was something about home-cooked meals made with love and being in the presence of animals that did the body and mind good. I loved animals, and, years down the road after retiring from law, I planned on opening an animal sanctuary for unadoptable, senior, and disabled animals. Every living thing deserved to feel loved. Putting the daydreaming out of my mind for now, I needed to get my mindset in place before I plunged headlong into my investigation. Once that started, it would be all-consuming.

The best part about being here, though, was the company. I loved my time with Luke and his golden retriever, Autumn. Ever since Luke had been honorably discharged from the Army forty-eight years ago, he had endured a battle with PTSD and depression. Through the years, he'd found solace in his therapy dogs. I loved them all like they were my own. Sydney, the golden retriever he had twenty years ago, when we met, had been every bit as instrumental in my recovery as Luke had been.

Luke still lived on about ten acres of land adjacent to the dreaded forest where the Mount Sierra killer had undertaken his killing spree. In Luke's cabin, we spent hours orchestrating the plan to take him down and prevent him from using the forest as his personal playground. We spent countless days and nights digging around, finding evidence. That piece of land still held a very special place in my heart, and, when I needed to escape or do some deep thinking, I often went there. There was something about the dense trees and the untouched, still air that gave me the solitude my soul craved. My best thinking could be done sitting on a pallet of pine needles, breathing in the damp-earth smell, and becoming one with nature. In order to uncover the mystery of how Brie had met her fate, I had a feeling I wouldn't be leaving Luke's place anytime soon, desperate to get to the bottom of it.

After I got settled, Autumn curled up at my feet and gave me nonstop, affectionate kisses. I was surprised there wasn't a permanent imprint of my butt cheeks on the couch after all the time I'd spent on it, beside the massive rock fireplace, which spread the entire width of the wall. I pressed Luke on what was bothering him, now that we were alone. Free from the constant eyes and bustle of the hospital, his pained expression and concerned look hadn't dissipated. The twitch in his mouth still trembled uncontrollably, and, when I looked at him up close, I could see the sweat dripping from his forehead.

"Come on. What is it?" I begged, concern overwhelming me.

He was huge in stature, by anyone's standards, but he looked like he had shrunk in an effort to withdraw into himself. His shoulders sagged, his head bowed, and he refused to meet my gaze. He knew his time of avoiding the inevitable had come to an end and drew in a deep breath.

"Okay, Luke—enough with the woe-is-me persona. I think I've already figured out what has you so distraught, and, if I'm right, it's not the end of the world. Has my Dad started drinking again?" I inquired.

He glanced at me before opening his mouth to respond, but, before he could, a loud *bang* echoed through the cabin, like a shotgun or a car loudly backfiring. We both jumped a foot in the air and almost knocked each other over as we collided, running to the door.

As we threw the front door open, my Dad was standing there, looking white as a ghost, clutching his arm, as blood trickled down his fingers before pooling on the ground. As I reached for him, he collapsed at my feet. Out of the corner of my eye, I saw a flash of black run into the forest. My first impulse was to chase after whoever it was, but my Dad wasn't in a good way and needed my immediate attention.

My adventurous spirit normally would have gone after the alleged culprit, but, instead, I dialed 911 and prayed my Dad wasn't seriously hurt. As Luke bent down to scoop my Dad up, we heard another shot fired that sounded close. The way it ricocheted off a pine tree caused a scream that pierced the night, a sound like a wounded animal. With all the racket, the forest had come alive. Owls had become agitated and began hooting loudly. I longed to investigate and feel the earth under my feet, as I listened to the trees sway and whisper secrets of the horrors of times past and present.

Pleading with my Dad to hang tough while he was clearly in shock was like telling a person not to breathe. After getting my Dad as comfortable as possible, I assessed the wound and was reasonably confident it wasn't life-threatening. Feeling helpless waiting for the paramedics to arrive, I let my mind wander to why and who would have done this. Luke lived off the beaten path, so I was reasonably sure this wasn't a random act of violence. Someone had deliberately sought him out. Or had my Dad been in the wrong place at the wrong time? Maybe it wasn't him they were targeting but more the location. Millions of thoughts swirled through my head, and they all led back to one question. I didn't think there was any doubt, but could this shooting and Brie's death be connected?

Coincidences are something I'm not a big believer in. They just didn't happen. Not often, anyway. And I felt very strongly that my Dad was the target of a carefully thought-out plan. Maybe not him, specifically, but the bullet had an intended target, and it was someone on Luke's property.

Random shootings were, unfortunately, getting way too commonplace, with assault rifles being so easy to buy, but that was another whole topic that I couldn't allow myself to think about. This wasn't a random shooter out for target practice. This, I was sure about—and my intuition rarely failed me.

Running scenarios over in my mind and remembering the constant, uneasy feeling I had while in the hospital that someone was watching me made me more confident than ever I hadn't been imagining things. At the time, I'd chalked that up to being out of it, but, now that I was thinking more coherently, I knew I was onto something. But what? The one scenario that kept coming to the forefront was the correlation between Brie and myself, but, no matter how hard I tried, I couldn't think of anything that would warrant *this*. A case we were working on? A lover gone mad? Ties to the mafia? The possibilities were endless. And how well did I really know her?

Brie and I had first met when I had been hired as an attorney at Maddox, Kline, and Patterson. It was a well-known, prestigious law firm in Portland, Oregon, that dealt with a variety of aspects of the law, which was rare. Most firms choose a specialty, but we run the gamut from criminal law, to wills and trusts, to family law, and everything in between.

I loved being part of such a diverse group of individuals. My own practice primarily dealt with family law, just like my Dad. Like father, like son. As fortune would have it, I had landed the position right out of law school, and, in the four years since I had signed on, life had been great.

Living in Portland was a dream come true. The Pacific Northwest had always spoken to me, with its breathtakingly beautiful landscape, wide-open trails, and its world-renowned chefs, hundreds of food carts, and craft breweries. There was never a shortage of things to do. I loved the outdoors. Becoming one with nature was instilled in me as a young child, camping numerous times with my family. That was always where I did my best thinking, and, on any given weekend when I wasn't working, you could find me hiking many of the endless trails, followed up with a cold brew on the deck of my condo.

I was having a difficult time wrapping my head around how, in a matter of a week, my life had been turned upside down, and I wasn't about to let whoever was responsible get away with it—or cause any more issues, God forbid another death. I was assuming a lot at this point, and that wasn't like me. As an attorney, I dealt with facts, not assumptions. Honestly, the law had a lot of gray areas, but I was getting off on tangents, and I needed to focus.

Red lights were illuminating the sky and bouncing off trees, creating cartoonish figures, as sirens blared. The ambulance pulled up in front of Luke's cabin, just as I was going over case names in my head, trying to see if any sounded close to *hard kiss*, the last words I thought Brie had uttered.

Paramedics rushed in, assessing the wound and asking a slew of questions we didn't have answers for. Unfortunately, we had very little to tell them, because we were as much in the dark as they were. After they loaded my Dad into an ambulance and gave me extra assurance that he was in good hands, they told me to stay put and concentrate on getting my strength back. My protests fell on deaf ears, so, instead of going with the paramedics to the hospital, I asked Luke to go and to keep me posted on any new developments. I trusted him with my life, so I figured he could be trusted with my Dad's.

As everyone drove away, I was left all alone with just my thoughts—and Autumn, of course. That was not entirely true, though, because Luke had a variety of animals that lived on the land. When I was younger, I spent hours feeding the horses an unlimited supply of carrots and apples. I could always get clarity on my issues by being with them and letting them snuggle my neck as I stroked their velvety snouts. Even as an adult, the pull was undeniable. This gave me an idea, and I raided the refrigerator before making my way to the stable. I had a lot to figure out, and this might be just what the doctor ordered.

CHAPTER EIGHT

Surprisingly, in the stable, it was as if time had stood still. The horses proved as therapeutic now as they had decades ago, and I was able to start putting a semblance of a plan together—one that would require me to be back at work. I was not a patient person, but I guess there's truth to the statement *Good things come to those who wait.* I needed to go through all my files, ongoing cases as well as any that had been completed. Had there been any disgruntled clients I had forgotten about? There had to be someone that had an axe to grind, unless I was totally going down the wrong path. Maybe it was not work related in the least and was a personal issue involving Brie. But to kill someone and shoot another? There I was assuming again, but I was positive that the two incidents were related; it would have been too coincidental for them not to be.

Lost in thought, I didn't notice the movement behind the barn until it was too late. The horses quite possibly saved my life, because they neighed and started pacing around, which brought me back to the present. A man, quiet as a ninja and dressed in all black with a ski mask to shield his identity, was upon me. He took a swing with some type of pipe that connected with my jaw, and I felt something crunch. Pain radiated through my face and dropped me to my knees, and then he kicked me in the ribs while I was down. I gasped for air as he towered over me. My life flashed before my eyes, and, just as I was thinking my end was in sight, one of the horses came from behind him and kicked him hard, right smack in the ass.

I watched him stumble and heard him yelp in pain as he ran as fast as he could straight toward the forest. As I scrambled to my feet, searing pain racked my body. Somehow, I needed to make my way back to the cabin, but the thought of it was too daunting, and, instead, I curled up in a ball on a pallet of hay to try to, once again, form a plan, but, instead, I either blacked out again or fell asleep. Either one was in the realm of possibility. I woke up confused and scared, not only for me but also for my loved ones. Something needed to happen soon; I was beginning to think anyone I came in contact with was in jeopardy.

The pain was intense, and I knew I needed to get to the cabin to call for help. Why had I been so foolish as to think that the attack on my Dad was an isolated incident? Now, more than ever, the danger was palpable, and I was a sitting duck, out in the open. I found a shovel in the barn and decided to use it as a crutch. As I hobbled slowly to the cabin, blood filled my mouth, and, as I spit it out, two teeth flew out and landed in the dirt. Scooping them up—for what reason I wasn't sure, but I thought I remembered reading once to save them and immediately put them in milk. Walking for what seemed like hours, feeling stabbing pain with each step I took, I finally made it to the cabin. Approaching the front door, I saw something nailed to it. It was a torn piece of paper that had a message scribbled in red on it. Was that blood? As I made my way up the steps, panic coursed through my body when I read . . .

YOU'VE BEEN WARNED!!!!!
Back off, Counselor, if you know what's good for you!

Holy shit, who and what kind of madman was I dealing with, and what had Brie gotten me mixed up in?

Finding my cell phone was no easy feat. I wasn't thinking clearly; that, coupled with the fact that I didn't know where it had been misplaced, was proving to be near impossible. But first things first: I made my way into the kitchen for milk. I washed my teeth off in the milk and submerged them in a glass. My curiosity got the best of me, and I swished my tongue around in my mouth and felt more than two empty sockets. I must have accidently swallowed the others and not even noticed, as I was crippled with pain. I made myself vomit in hopes that they would come up, without considering the pain this would cause. The pain was for nothing, because all that came up and splashed in the sink was bile. I was reasonably sure I had broken ribs and perhaps a punctured lung as well. I had assumed my lack of air and raspy breath were from my pneumonia, but now I wasn't sure anymore. There I go assuming again.

My hunt for my cell phone ended when the theme song from "The Good, the Bad, and the Ugly" blasted out from underneath the plaid couch that sat nestled in front of Luke's massive fireplace. Thank God Luke had decided to give me an update. After hearing that my Dad was going to be fine and they would be home soon, a split-second decision had to be made on what I wanted to tell him. He had enough on his plate without me worrying him any further, but I felt he needed to know what had happened in his absence. I decided to rip the Band Aid off and just go for it, bracing myself for his response.

"Luke, I don't want to alarm you, but I was attacked and need to call an ambulance, so hang out where you are for a while till I get there," I mumbled.

Needless to say, this went over like a turd in a punch bowl because he freaked out on the other end, asking a million questions all in one breath. I promised answers would be coming soon but that I needed to free up the line to call for help. I left the part out that it was pure torture to move my jaw to talk. Some things were better left unsaid.

Arriving at the emergency room was a fiasco. Mayhem ensued as the paramedics jockeyed for a spot among gunshot cases and other trauma. Who would have ever guessed the quaint, quiet town of Mount Sierra would become a Mecca for crime? Paranoia was starting to set in, and I trusted no one at this point. If someone even so much as gave me a passing glance, I thought I saw an outline of a gun hidden within their pocket. I heard people plotting my demise, when, in reality, there was nobody there. I wasn't an unstable person, but I was starting to doubt my own sanity. Hopefully, it was my physical state that was causing my mind to go places that it didn't belong.

Reeling with pain and confused beyond words, I saw my Dad and Luke approaching me, with concern clouding their otherwise jovial faces. They had every reason to be concerned. I was, too. A lot. I just kept thinking about this latest development setting me back even further. I needed to start my investigation before someone else got hurt or, even worse, killed. That made me shudder, which Luke misread as pain. I watched him practically tackle the nearest nurse, demanding I be seen immediately. Luke, having no children of his own, took our relationship very seriously. He had told me years ago that I was like the son he never had; his wife had died of a brain aneurysm early in their marriage. The papa bear in him was out in full force, and I feared for anyone who was caught in his wake.

Minutes turned to hours as I lay waiting. I managed to convince Luke, who had become enraged, that it was time to see the positive. I had been triaged, so even though I looked a fright and felt even worse, my life must not be in danger. We adopted a hurry-up-and-wait approach while we watched in horror as trauma after trauma hurried through the doors. I had been given something for pain, so I actually felt quite content and one with the world as I drifted in and out of hazy sleep.

Sweat poured down my back, soaking my yellow T-shirt as I was dodging in and out between the ginormous pine trees. I was being chased by not just one person but what seemed like an army of them. Every turn I took, there was someone new laughing a menacing laugh and shouting obscenities. The pine needles were relentless and painfully jabbed me as I frantically made my way out of the forest. As I emerged, the sun was shining and warm. I instantly felt safe, and I allowed myself a moment to take in a deep breath to calm myself and soak up the sun rays that warmed my soul, until I looked down and saw a growing red spot that was drenching my shirt. Then I collapsed.

Squawking relentlessly, machines woke me out of a drug-induced deep sleep. I managed to open an eye to look at the clock on the wall. Hours had passed, but I had finally made it into an examining room, where bright lights blinded me and bathed the room in a strange aura. A warm blanket had been tucked in around me as I tried to get my bearings.

"Mr. Elliott? Mr. Elliott? I'm Dr. Jacobs. I am your attending physician. Are you able to answer any questions?

There are some Sheriff's deputies here who would like a word with you," he said.

The doctor looked like he had just stepped out of *GQ*. Tall, debonair, and very handsome, with surfer-style blond hair that swooped to a tight curl in the front and the whitest, unnatural-looking teeth. The very last thing I wanted right now was to talk to the authorities. I was still holding a grudge against the Sheriff's department twenty years later for their inept handling and cover-up of the Mount Sierra murders. Murders, *plural*—twelve in fact, had gone unsolved, which I found a total disgrace to any law-enforcement agency. I doubted anything I could tell them would help, mostly because I knew nothing. Being blindsided can have that effect on you.

Opening my mouth to say "No" proved harder than I imagined. Dr. Hot Stuff must have seen my pained expression because he put a firm-but-gentle hand on my shoulder and assured me he would take care of it. Relief washed over me. Luke and my Dad were nowhere to be seen, but knowing them both the way I did, I knew they were probably just a stone's throw away, waiting not at all patiently and wearing paths in the emergency-room carpets as they paced back and forth. The methodical rhythm of a heart monitor sounded soothing against the backdrop of the constant urgency of the ER. I tried to keep my eyes open, but they felt so heavy. I felt like I hadn't slept in days, and my eyes wouldn't stay open any longer—no matter how hard I tried to convince myself it was imperative to save my life. The paranoia that had started to set in earlier had shown up to the party and had taken over my every thought.

My release from the hospital in Portland was short-lived, because I was once again lying flat on my back with tubes attached to who knows what at the local hospital in Mount Sierra. Mount Sierra was too far away from Portland to be considered a suburb but still close enough to reside in the same section of the Pacific Northwest. It was a very touristy town, with Mom-and-Pop shops that sold souvenirs on Main St. and the most magnificent scenery one would ever lay eyes on. People from all over flocked here in the summer for the stellar fishing. In fact, our high school mascot was a rainbow trout, and, as a kid, I'd always wanted to be the boy behind the costume. In the winter months, people came in droves for the top-notch ski slopes. I was born and bred here, and it would always have my heart, but my life was in Portland now—mainly because that's where the opportunities were.

Mount Sierra was a small town, and my dreams were bigger than it could offer, hence, my life away from *home*.

Previously, I'd been told I could recuperate on my own, but this time the doctors were adamant about me staying for a while. My room looked like a clown had thrown up in here. It was so colorful, with multi-colored balloons, numerous vases of every flower imaginable and banners begging me to get well. I had come a long way in the friend department. After my Mom's unexpected death at the hands of a drunk driver, I had shrunk into myself, withdrawing from everyone and everything. Mostly thanks to Luke and our many heartfelt one-on-ones, I was able to heal and come to accept what couldn't be changed. I had come a long way from being a tormented shell of a child. I was now a successful, confident, easy-go-lucky, adventurous spirit. I was touched that so many people cared about little ol' me.

Luke and my Dad sat on each side of me as I listened to the doctor explain in depth what damage my body had sustained this time. My broken jaw had been wired closed, but, unfortunately, the teeth I had soaked in milk had been for nothing. Although it was no walk in the park, it proved to be the least of my problems, since my other injuries were more severe. I had three broken ribs and a punctured lung, which was troublesome, since I still had the pneumonia. No wonder I felt like shit.

As the magnitude of what I had just been told sank in, I couldn't help but feel vulnerable, like I was waiting for the other shoe to drop. I was jumpy and on edge. In my mind, shadows turned into would-be killers, and I was certain that every person who walked into my room was going to inject me with lethal poison. To say I was looking forward to getting out of here and locking myself away in Luke's cabin was an understatement. Even though I was a grown man, I still craved the peace and comfort Luke's cabin supplied. It had a way of making me feel protected and loved. It was going to be torture for a while though, because Luke was a marvelous cook, and it seemed like I would be eating my meals through a straw for a while.

My Dad looked a little worse for wear himself. Actually, he looked worse than that, but I gave him the benefit of the doubt. It had been a rough day, and I was hoping that the worst had already reared its ugly head. Assuring me he was fine, he made me swear that I wouldn't worry about him and concentrate only on myself. I'm grateful he and Luke had the foresight to see that I was wiped out and needed to sleep—if for no other reason than to escape reality. My reality sucked right now.

Within minutes of them begging out, I fell into a fitful sleep. It was dark—so dark, it was as if I had my eyes taped shut and I had been put into a cave, inside the forest, where it was *always* pitch-black and cold. I wanted so badly to see what was going on, but when I put my hands to my face, I felt a bag tied over my head. I tried to scream, but I couldn't open my mouth, and all that emerged was a pathetic, feeble squeak. Waves of nausea flooded over me from being jostled around so much. Where was I, and why did I feel so cold? I could hear voices whispering to each other to be careful not to kill me because the boss needed me in one piece.

Cold water was thrown on my face, and, when I opened my eyes, I immediately regretted it. Thinking I had woken from a nightmare, I now realized I hadn't been dreaming at all. Staring straight at me were two men I didn't recognize. They both looked to be in their twenties, with tattoos from head to toe, a week's worth of stubble and scraggly hair that looked like it hadn't been washed in days. They smelled like weed mixed with patchouli soaked in sweat. It was anything but pleasant. I was sitting inside a hospital laundry cart, and my hands had been tied behind my back. I tried to scream but was warned to keep my mouth shut. Ordinarily the irony would have amused me, but since I was feeling like death, my sense of humor was nonexistent. Chastising myself for not listening, I tried to open my mouth again and was immediately injected with something that made me warm and tingly before I lost consciousness.

CHAPTER TEN

As I came to, I was confused and disoriented. I had the worst taste in my mouth. It tasted like blood with undernotes of barf and an underground sewer. It was disgusting, and the taste alone made me dry-heave. My mind was spinning a million miles a second, wondering how I'd allowed myself to get into this predicament. Whoever was behind this wanted to shut me up in the worst way and would go to great lengths to make sure that happened. I was determined not to let them.

My head was pounding, and the more I tried to make sense of everything that had happened in the past week, I was left dumbfounded. Was it a case of mistaken identity? Mulling this over in what lucidity I had left, I decided it was highly unlikely, since my Dad had been attacked as well. But a person can hope. That sure would simplify things.

Much to my surprise, my hands had been untied. I took this as a good sign. Either they didn't see me as a threat, or they had been instructed to make me as comfortable as possible. That was going to be near impossible, because I ached all over. My jaw was throbbing, and my chest felt exactly as I would expect it to feel for having broken ribs and a punctured lung—not to mention the pneumonia. Not only had my prescribed drugs worn off, but so had whatever they had given me. Surprisingly, I found myself wanting an injection of any type so that I could lose myself in sleep and, hopefully, have an epiphany.

Wherever I was, it was really cold, with a creepy vibe going on. I sat up as best I could and peeked out of the cart. I wasn't alone. Everywhere I looked, I was surrounded by tables with bodies completely covered with sheets. Toe tags were attached to all of them, and the smell of decomposition mixed with formalin, used to preserve organ and tissue samples, hung in the air. It was obvious that I was in a morgue, and I panicked. No matter how I tried to reason with myself and get it together, I started to hyperventilate. Methodical, slow breaths while I massaged the hollowness in my collar bone to slow my heart rate was doing little to calm me. I didn't want to die and end up on a slab like these poor souls.

Thoughts of me dying alone and never seeing my Dad or Luke again gave me a shot of adrenaline. My situation looked dismal, but being a quitter wasn't in my blood. So, with every ounce of strength I could muster up, I cautiously and painfully climbed out of the cart. Standing on very unsteady legs, I took inventory of my surroundings and tried to formulate ideas on what would be my most productive plan of action. The room was bathed in darkness, but I could make out faint images. Besides the bodies, I saw an assortment of scales and instruments I suspected were used on a daily basis in the job of a medical examiner. It was imperative I find my way out, even though every step I took shot jolts of pain through my body. My breathing was ragged, and I felt a rumbling in my chest that hadn't been there before.

Either it was the most complicated labyrinth of morgues, or I was just so disoriented that it appeared that way. Weaving around tables, I saw a door on the east end of the room. This gave me hope, and I almost allowed myself a moment to celebrate when I saw him. One of the tattooed men from before was sitting next to the door. His head was cocked back, and I heard snores emerge from his partially open mouth. He was holding a machine gun on his lap, but, besides that, he looked harmless in his napping state. I wasn't dumb enough to believe that, though, and was quite aware of the danger I was in.

Slowly making my way around the perimeter of the room, I discovered that was the only exit. I armed myself with a couple of scalpels and approached him like a little kid does when seeing Santa Claus for the first time. Tiptoeing and holding my breath, I was so close to him I could smell his body odor. I was starting to feel halfway decent about life, when the door opened, and the whole room was illuminated in light.

Relieved but highly skeptical, I quickly looked around feverishly for a hiding spot to observe if the stinky tattooed guy and this new person were in cahoots. The only place I could find was under a sheet next to a body. A dead body! This gave me the creeps, but my choices were that or nothing, so I painfully hopped up and tried not to think about the companion I was sharing the slab with.

As I cautiously peeked from under the corner of my sheet, I watched as a tall, balding man with a clipboard under his arm and a pager attached to his belt walked in like he owned the place. He had bulging eyes, a pencil-thin mustache and a deathlike pallor that one gets if they don't ever get to see or feel the warmth of the sun. He must have been in the twilight zone not to get the vibe that he was not alone. He set his clipboard down as he made his way over to the sink, where he commenced to wash his hands. He meticulously scrubbed beneath every nail and all the way up to his elbows before wrestling into some latex gloves.

Amazingly, the tattoo guy was still sleeping. Or was he? I took a long, hard look at him, checking for any movement, and that's when I saw him move his head very slowly toward the man, who I assumed was a medical examiner. His movements were almost undetectable as he very slowly picked up his gun and positioned it toward the unsuspecting bald man. I had a split second to make up my mind on what to do. I could either keep myself hidden and quiet, or I could yell to spook Mr. Tattoo, trying to divert him long enough to potentially save the bald guy's life. I chose the latter, but yelling proved to be challenging. When only a barely audible squeak came out of my mouth, I threw one of the scalpels toward the other side of the room.

I watched as Mr. Tattoo turned toward the noise as the scalpel skidded across the white tile floor. It proved to be just the diversion Baldy needed, as he turned on his heel like he had just been cattle prodded in the ass, fear washing over his face. I stayed hidden and watched the whole confrontation unfold.

"Who are you, and what do you think you're doing here?" Baldy demanded, while Mr. Tattoo looked like he had been caught with his pants down in the middle of Times Square. I wanted to scream, "Watch out for the gun," but the second I was about to, I saw a glimmer of recognition in Baldy's eyes as he had an "Oh, shit!" moment. They both threw a punch at the same time, and, if I were a betting man, I would have put odds on Mr. Tattoo—but I would have lost my shirt, because Baldy proved to have a vicious uppercut. Mr. Tattoo folded like a deck of cards.

Seeing this as my chance to make a run for it, I jumped down, slipped on something wet, and landed on my bare ass on the cold floor. My hospital gown ended up around my neck as I scrambled to cover myself. I must have made quite a racket because, as I managed to stand upright, Baldy approached me with apprehension. With raised eyebrows, he looked at me like I had woken the dead, and I was one of his corpses come to life. He steadied himself as a slight bit of color returned to his almost-ashen complexion. Fearing that Mr. Tattoo would come to any second, I took off like a bolt of lightning and ran like I was in the Olympics, competing for my life.

Hugging my arms close around my body to try to alleviate some of my rib and chest pain, I made my way to the elevators. I managed to grab another gown as I passed by a housekeeping cart situated in the middle of the hall. As I scrambled to put it on backwards so my ass wasn't mooning everyone as I ran by, I avoided stares from people who were casually going about their business. I had absolutely no clue what time it was, let alone the day. For all I knew, I could have lost another week of my life. All I really knew was that this was bigger than I could have ever imagined, and I needed to get out of here—and the faster the better! My life depended on it. *That* I knew with 100% certainty.

Luck was on my side, as the elevator doors slowly opened, and I was all alone. Strange, but true, I love empty elevators, because there's no awkward silence or worrying about where to avert your gaze. There was no piped-in elevator music, so I was forced to listen to my own breathing. I wasn't thrilled with what I was hearing. My breathing was raspy and my gasps for air hurt deep in my chest. I knew this wasn't a good sign, but I had bigger issues weighing on my mind right then. As the elevator descended at a snail's pace, I took inventory of myself. My feet were bare, with dried blood between my toes, I had a nasty gash on my left cheek that was dripping fresh blood, and it felt like my hair was standing straight up. I tried to check out myself as best as I could on the elevator wall, but what stared back at me was nobody I had ever met. My throat was so dry that I felt like I could drink the equivalent of a whole pool full of water in one sitting. As the doors opened, I peeked down the hall and saw a whole slew of Deputy Sheriffs wandering in and out of my room. Clearly, one man was in charge, barking orders on where to look and what to do once I was found.

For a nanosecond, my mind contemplated taking the elevator down to the ground floor and making a run for it. Truthfully, it would be more like a crawl, but an escape nonetheless. I wasn't the most trusting of souls to start with, and I was doubting if these deputies could be of any help. Or, for that matter, had my best interests at heart. Conjuring up some energy, I had decided *What the hell, let's throw caution to the wind and see how far I can get.* Then, I was spotted, and the decision was out of my hands.

CHAPTER ELEVEN

All kinds of people rushed to my side. I must have looked absolutely dreadful, because no one was able to hide their shock before they looked away. Even though my room was about twenty yards away from the elevator, a wheelchair was rushed to my side, and I was forced to take a seat. I have to admit—I didn't protest too loudly, and it felt like heaven to take a load off. I was worn out.

As a person in scrubs wheeled me to my room, I was greeted by my Dad and Luke. Even they looked shocked at my appearance, and this was saying a lot, because they had both seen me at my worst. With my curiosity piqued, I hobbled into the bathroom to take a gander. Who I saw staring back at me was frightening—so frightening I looked over my shoulder, half expecting to see a stranger lurking in the background. But no, I was alone and scary looking, indeed.

My normal cornflower-blue eyes were so bloodshot the whites were pink with a tinge of yellow, suggesting jaundice to add to my growing list of maladies. They also had dark circles on top of puffy bags. Dried blood was crusted all around my mouth, and my left cheek had a gash inside a blue bruise. As if that weren't bad enough, my nose must have been broken because it was swollen, crooked, and oozing a trail of blood, soaking my gown.

I decided to leave unwell enough alone and not inventory the rest of my body, because I was scared of what I might find. Everyone was shooed from my room as the doctor was called in to evaluate the newest trauma I had sustained. I was pleased to see Dr. *GQ* walk through the door, although being in the same room with him in my present state made me feel more nervous than ever. I watched closely as he examined me, looking for changes in his facial expressions. He remained stoic. This must be something that's taught in medical school: Facial Expressions 101. If so, he got an A+.

"Luck must be your middle name! By looking at you, I would have thought you were headed to the ICU straightaway, but if we can get some protection posted outside your door, I'm okay with you staying put," he exclaimed. I guess miracles do happen, because my morgue adventure proved to be more taxing on my mind than on my body. Ten stitches later in my cheek and a setting of my nose, I was on my way to healing. I wish I could say the same about my mental state. Upon inquiring about the date, I was delighted to learn that

I hadn't lost another week of my life. My morgue adventure had taken up only hours and not days.

I kept playing back in my mind the ordeal that had taken place, and I was repulsed by sharing the slab with a dead body. I was feeling lucky to escape semi-unscathed, even though I wasn't entirely sure luck had played a huge role. I was positive if "they" wanted me dead, I would be. Not to say that wasn't their long-term goal, but for now, they clearly only wanted to scare the shit out of me and beat me within an inch of my life. For some reason I hadn't figured out yet, they wanted to put the fear of God in me and play mind games. Now I was being a tad melodramatic, but it had been a rather adventurous week, and I felt entitled.

After putting all my modesty aside, I allowed two nurses to help me shower. The warm water beating down on me hurt but also was a little slice of heaven. For the moment, I let the water wash away my troubles and my fears down the drain. It felt good to have a clean body and spirit for the time being. Exhaustion took over, and I couldn't ever recall being this wiped out. Drying off, I lay down on the fluffiest cloud of a bed. I had to stifle a laugh, because the thought of me welcoming a hospital bed and thinking it felt soft and inviting was crazy talk. Nothing about being in the hospital was ever comfortable or relaxing—quite the contrary. Just as I was on the brink of sleep, two Deputy Sheriffs walked in.

They were both tall in stature, and their presence cut the feel of the room in half. Their presence should have offered me a sense of security, but I was agitated as soon as they opened their pompous mouths. I couldn't help but wonder if they were holding a grudge of some type against me for an incident that had happened twenty years earlier. All Luke and I had done was shine a light on the corruptness of the department. It really had been one of my finest moments, and I was only thirteen when I helped bring attention to their inadequacies. The fact remains, though, it *was* twenty years ago, so what had crawled up their asses?

On the verge of asking why they seemed so agitated, I took a glance at their names, since no introductions had been made. That, to me, was rude on its own merit, but now I had my answer. Or so it seemed. Standing in front of me, a man every bit of 6'3" with sandy blond hair and a toothpick poking out from between his lips, covered by a bushy, unkempt mustache, opened his mouth to speak at the same instant I noticed the name etched on his uniform: Deputy Osborne. *Holy shit—what were the odds that this deputy could be related to the infamous Sheriff Dan Osborne from twenty years prior?* That would be too coincidental, and we all know how I felt about coincidences. This most surely would explain the attitude.

Sheriff Dan Osborne had been a corrupt sheriff, running an even shadier department, failing to do their jobs properly. Mount Sierra had been besieged by numerous murders at the hands of a serial killer twenty-five years earlier, and I, with the help of Luke, had solved the crimes and brought down the Sheriff's Department. It was a small price to pay, because, in doing so, we were able to bring justice to the victims and surviving family members—and make Mount Sierra a safe place to raise a family once again.

"By any chance, are you related to Dan Osborne, the ex-Sheriff of Mount Sierra?" I questioned.

Time stood still as he glared with hatred boiling in his steely brown eyes, while the toothpick made its way from one side of his mouth to the other in jerky movements. Looking away would show fear on my part, so I met his gaze and held it. Although it had been a long time since I had seen the Sheriff, his image had been etched in my memory for eternity, and I already knew the answer before Deputy Osborne spoke. Sweat formed on his brow, and he began nervously tapping his foot and wringing his hands. I felt like I could see the wheels turning in his brain before he answered, wondering if he would tell the truth.

When he spoke, hatred dripped from his words. "What's it to you? You obviously didn't care two hoots about my estranged father years ago, so why would you care now?" He looked like he was contemplating throwing a punch as his hand tightened into a fist.

"I wasn't aware that the sheriff had fathered any children, so I was just wondering," I managed to say, keeping any emotion out of my voice. Truth be told, I was scared shitless. Things had not ended well between the Sheriff and me, and, if this guy had an axe to grind, I was in no shape to protect myself. Of all my crap luck, I *would* get the only deputy in the department who had it out for me. So much for getting any protection from these guys!

Before any more was said, Luke burst through the door with the most humongous bouquet of sunflowers and purple hydrangeas I had ever seen. If I could have, I would have jumped up and hugged him. I was so happy to see him. Luke always had the most impeccable timing. I could tell by his expression, turning from pure joy to one of confusion, as he sensed friction in the room. Not only was his timing impeccable, but his intuition was always spot on as well.

"If you're done here, I think Jonathan needs to get some much-needed shut-eye, so leave now, please," Luke demanded. The deputies started to protest but thought better of it when Luke shot them a *Don't mess with the papa bear!* look. Even though they were big guys, Luke was bigger and a formidable opponent. They turned to leave with their tail between their legs and made a promise that they would return tomorrow to get a statement. Not if I had anything to do with it, they wouldn't!

CHAPTER TWELVE

L uke demanded answers the second they were out the door. As I explained what I thought the connection between the deputy and Sheriff Osborne was, he had to pick his jaw up off the ground. He hadn't noticed the name on the uniform and was as shocked as I was that the Sheriff had any offspring. As far as we knew, the Sheriff had a family that he had left behind when he was sixteen and never looked back. It had to be the Sheriff's son. This was huge—in more ways than one. As we contemplated the ramifications this created, we were left without answers on how to handle the situation.

The deputy clearly had a problem with me, but did I think he was behind the attacks? We mulled this over for a while but came to the conclusion that, although it was *plausible*, it wasn't very likely. For one, why would he wait twenty years to get his revenge when he would have had plenty of opportunities when I still lived in Mount Sierra? He looked to be about twenty-five, so he would have been a small child at the time of his Dad's demise. He had, after all, said *estranged* father. Was it possible that the Sheriff never even knew he had fathered a child?

Two things were for certain: the first and obvious one was that I needed to be discharged from the hospital immediately. Maybe I was wrong, but I felt pretty certain that the longer I stayed there, the more danger I was in. Secondly, I couldn't count on the Sheriff's Department to protect me. As much as I didn't want to talk to Deputy Osborne, I needed facts. My gut was telling me I needed to clear the air. I needed the help of the Sheriff's Department, and I knew that, as long as Deputy Osborne saw me as the enemy, that would be impossible.

Luke was adamant that he spend the night in my room, for protection. It didn't take much convincing on his part, because I didn't want a repeat from last night. The thought of any more dead bodies or threats on my life was unfathomable. As he settled in, the lawyer in me immediately started forming an argument for Dr. *GQ* on why I was better off recuperating at Luke's. With all the charm I could muster up, I was hoping I could persuade Dr. *GQ* to discharge me. After all, I was a lawyer, so I could plead my case. It might be the most important case of my life.

Luke wanted to talk, and I didn't. I was a quiet man by nature, but when it was a topic that interested me, that was a whole different story. I could plot and scheme for hours, but, now, I just wasn't in the right mindset. The reason was none other than I was hurting all over. My nose and mouth were both throbbing, and my body felt like I had been used as a human punching bag. My nose vibrated every time I made so much as a peep. It was a weird feeling—one I was not fond of in the least. I was finding it difficult to breathe properly, since breathing through my nose packed full of a ton of gauze was out of the question, and having my mouth wired shut was making it a challenge as well. I was a mess.

I pleaded with my eyes in hopes that he'd gotten the message. We had always been in tune with each other, but, for some reason, his judgment was clouded, and he continued on. He was keyed up, throwing out scenario after scenario, looking for answers. His problem-solving skills had always proved to be spot on, but this time, he kept running into a brick wall at one hundred mph. Ordinarily, I would have welcomed the brainstorming session, but I needed to get my argument together for the doctor in the morning. I was leaving—with his blessing or without!

Faking sleep did the trick, and he got the hint. I only meant to rest my eyes but fell immediately into a deep sleep induced by drugs and trauma. Darkness surrounded me. I sensed that I was in a closed space, and I started to freak out. I was not a fan of closed spaces and would wager to say claustrophobia was right at the top of my list of things you never needed to know about me. As I moved my hands up to my face, they hit something fluffy. Almost like a pillow of sorts, but different. I felt around me, and all my hands came in contact with was more pillowy substance. I was unable to roll over, as I was lying flat on my back. The air was still and heavy, and, as I moved my head to the left, I saw a couple of small pinholes—just enough to realize I was in a cemetery, being buried alive! I tried to scream, but my mouth had been taped shut.

My funeral was taking place, and, as I lay unable to tell the world I was still alive, I hovered over my coffin, invisible to those around me. Luke, my Dad, old college pals, and colleagues from the firm were gathered around, weeping silently. Sheriff Dan Osborne was conducting the eulogy, telling everyone I was not the man they thought they knew. I was the devil reincarnated and was better off dead. As they lowered me into the ground, I watched as shovels of dirt were being thrown on top of me by the two tattooed men from the morgue. And then I woke up frantic and gasping for air.

Sweat poured down my back and drenched my hospital gown. I was in a total panic as I strained to get my bearings and take in a deep breath. Both of these things were proving to be impossible, which made me panic even more. Thank God Luke had stayed the night, because he was there in a flash, bringing me back to reality. Through the years, he had always had a special way of calming me, with not just his presence but a firm, reassuring pat with his warm, massive hand, but it did little to calm me now. I was spiraling, unable to catch my breath, when a warm sensation from my IV flowed through my veins, and I relaxed enough to gain control.

CHAPTER THIRTEEN

Next thing I knew, it was morning, and the sun was peeking through the curtains in the corner window of my hospital room. I still felt like death warmed over, but whatever had been given to me last night in my state of panic had worked like magic. My head was still a bit groggy, but I wasn't on edge anymore, which meant I could plead my case to the doctor when he made an appearance today. In the meantime, I urged Luke to go snooping around. I needed to know what had happened in the morgue after I'd made my sudden departure yesterday. Luke was skeptical, but he wasn't one to tell me "No." So, he took off to solicit answers.

I was on pins and needles waiting for answers, so I turned the television on for some mindless background noise. A commercial was advertising a company called Sonic Airlines. Their claim to fame was non-stop travel between the west coast of the United States to Europe in two hours. That was pretty impressive, and I marveled at modern technology. Visiting Europe was on my bucket list, in particular, Amsterdam, but I hadn't gone, simply due to the fact that I didn't like to sit still for that long. But a two-hour flight was totally doable. I caught myself with the first smile of the day on my face dreaming of the possibilities before me. Then I took the time to write down reasons for why I needed an immediate release. I knew it was going to be a tough sell, given that my condition wasn't the best.

Number one on the list was that my life depended on it. Number two on the list was that my life depended on it. Number three on the list was that my life depended on it.

All my reasons pointed to that one equation. The doctor was aware of what had physically transpired in the morgue, but not to the extent of how much it had impacted me mentally. To heal physically, I needed to be in the right headspace, or I would be climbing an uphill battle on all fours, only to slide down at every curve, getting nowhere fast.

With Luke away, my paranoia took it upon itself to return. I looked at every person with skepticism and trusted no one. I didn't like this about myself, but this was no time to let my guard down because I was certain the second that happened, the next attack would come. Next time, I might not be lucky enough to live to tell the tale. I loved life too much to let that happen and also had worked way too hard to graduate at the top of my class in law school to let some thugs take me out.

But the attacks had changed me. My mind now seemed to be playing tricks on me, focused on seeing the evil in the world instead of the joy. I almost threw a punch at the male nurse who came to take my vitals—all because he had tattoos on his arms. I needed some fresh air and sunshine to rein in my thoughts of doom.

So, I scribbled a note to Luke that I would be in the solarium. I edged my way out of bed, wincing in pain. After putting on my hospital booties with the rubber appliqués on the bottom to keep me upright, I painfully moved toward the door. The only part of me that didn't hurt was my pinky. I ached all over. On my way out the door, I took a quick glance in the mirror and was horrified. I looked like a zombie, my skin drained to a light-gray pallor, straight out of that old TV show, *The Walking Dead*. This, for some reason, made me laugh. I laughed so hard I couldn't catch my breath, and I doubled over, wheezing through metal and gauze. If you can't laugh at yourself once in a while, a reality check on what kind of heartless monster you have become needs to happen.

Every step was a challenge, but I kept my head down and inched my way outside. The sun was high in the sky, as a slight breeze rustled the leaves on the Bigleaf Maple tree offering shade in the far-right corner. I looked up. The sky seemed bluer than normal, and billowy clouds were moving in precision to an imaginary song. Life almost felt normal, full of promise. That was, until I gingerly sat down and became racked with pain, which turned into stomach spasms. I tried to get to a trash can before I heaved, but I tripped on a tree root and crashed face first onto the mosaic-bricked ground. I learned fast that throwing up with your jaw wired shut was on the list of things you never want to do. I managed to roll over, and, as I tried to get up, Luke appeared in just the nick of time. His impeccable timing was never more welcome.

"What, may I ask, do you think you're doing out of bed?" Luke inquired. As I peered at him through a half-open eye, I laughed again. Belly laughs consumed me, and tears ran down my face, stinging the cut in my cheek. At that point, it was all I had, and, if I didn't laugh, I would have broken down and fallen into a depressed, sorry state. I refused to feel sorry for myself—even in this unfortunate situation. Life was throwing me curveballs, but I had showed up to the game and was ready to play. Or, at least, I was at bat, and, hopefully, I wouldn't strike out.

Finally controlling myself, I managed, with lots of help from Luke, to get upright again and find my way into a chair. I was dying (bad choice of words) to know what, if anything, he had found out. "I'm not kidding, Jonathan—stay put. I am off to find you some peppermint tea, and, when I get back, I don't want to find you anywhere but in this chair. Do you hear me?" Luke sternly said. Peppermint tea had always been my drink of choice when my gut was doing flip-flops. I had consumed copious amounts after our many trips into the forest, discovering the gruesome souvenirs the serial killer had left behind. I was flattered that Luke had remembered.

CHAPTER THIRTEEN

I was soaking up some rays with my face to the sun when something caught my attention. It was a noise that sounded like the crumpling of paper, but, as I opened my eyes, I saw no one close by. Looking around, I saw a wad of paper down by my feet. Knowing this hadn't been there before I'd closed my eyes, I jerked my head to and fro, looking for the culprit. Up above, on a catwalk, looking down from a window to the solarium, stood one of the tattooed men, staring down at me. He raised his hand and made a motion across his throat that indicated he was going to slit my throat. Flashbacks from twenty years ago flooded my mind as I had seen Sheriff Osborne make the same, exact gesture. Shivers ran down my spine, and I felt a coldness sweep over me.

As I reached down to pick up the paper, Luke appeared like an angel. He must have sensed the tension I was feeling, because he placed his hand on my shoulder and gave me a pat. "You know I'll always have your back, no matter what, don't you, Jonathan?" he said warmly, as a reassuring smile spread across his face. Not doubting this for a second, I let him know we were in this together. My main concern was that I feared this was even bigger than the two of us. We may have just met our match, and if we didn't start acting fast, we might not get the chance.

I was afraid to open the note. I hated that fear had become a part of me, consuming my every thought. The paper was written on nondescript, everyday lined notebook paper, but what was unusual about it was that it appeared to be written in blood. Scribbled in childlike writing, it said . . .

CONSIDER THAT YOUR FREEBIE!!
YOU WON'T BE SO LUCKY NEXT TIME!!

How much stock could be put in this, I was unsure, but I wasn't one to tempt fate. Luke and I sat there for a moment, in silence, both lost in thought. Not being able to help myself, I took a glance up to where the man was before, but he was gone. I swept the room, half expecting him to be standing in the corner, laughing at me, but, everywhere I looked, unfamiliar faces stared back at me like they had seen a living, walking corpse. "Luke, could you please help me back to my room? I'm feeling self-conscious." I whispered. So much for the sun warming my soul.

Making my way back to my room, even with Luke's help, proved to be laborious. I was out of breath and crippled in pain but determined not to succumb to whoever was behind this madness. Right when we were rounding the corner to my corridor, we ran straight into a man dressed head to toe in surgical scrubs. As I excused myself, I locked eyes with the tattoo man. I would know those evil eyes anywhere. When I looked at them, they were filled with vile wickedness. I eyed Luke, and confusion washed over his face as Mr. Tattoo took off in a full sprint toward the stairwell at the end of the hall.

CHAPTER FOURTEEN

Wheezing, I tried my hardest to run after him, but my legs refused to cooperate. Reading my thoughts, as usual, Luke yelled to me to stay put and call security ASAP. I watched as he disappeared around the corner. I could hear heavy footsteps and Luke yelling, "Enough is enough—give yourself up, or else." *You tell 'em, big guy,* I whispered to myself and said a silent prayer that he wouldn't get hurt. I would never forgive myself if something happened to him while he was trying to save my sorry ass from who knows what. Another reason to get better—so that I could start an investigation on my own before another death occurred. This was getting out of hand faster than I could blink an eye.

When the security for the hospital showed up, Luke had already made his way back to my room. Not being able to keep up with Mr. Tattoo, he had been left in his dust. The hospital security, up to this point, had been pretty much non-existent, but I was still holding out hope. I asked them, with the best smile I could muster up, if they would at least go investigate the stairwell and surrounding areas for any evidence. I had nothing of any substance to go on, and I was as bad as Luke, hitting brick walls about who could be wanting to cause me harm. I didn't hold out much hope that they would find anything, but it was worth a shot in the dark, since I was grasping at straws at this point.

With me tucked back in bed, Luke sat in a chair by my bedside. I urged him to tell me what he'd found out in the morgue. But first things first. Questions about my Dad needed answers. Had he, indeed, gone back to drinking—and where the hell was he? After my introduction twenty years ago, Luke and my Dad had become the best of friends. They were almost inseparable, and, with Luke as my Dad's Alcoholic Anonymous sponsor, I knew he would know all the dirty details. I was almost 100% positive that I knew the answer, but I needed to hear it straight from Luke's mouth. It felt like a punch in the gut when Luke affirmed my suspicions.

Needless to say, I was devastated but not the least bit surprised by this news. We had come so far as a family finding our way back to one another after my Mom passed that I was bound and determined not to let gin take over his life again. Seeing that I was upset, with good reason, Luke assured me he had it under control and to concern myself only with getting well enough to find the lunatic who was bound and determined to cause me harm. As far as where the hell he was, Luke couldn't shed light on that subject. That led me to believe that Luke really didn't have things under control and that I should, indeed, concern myself, reassurances or not.

"Tell me—tell me what happened in the morgue." I inquired with bated breath. Just as Luke opened his mouth to explain, Dr. *GQ* peeked around my curtain. He was dressed to the nines and smelled like he had just jumped out of a cologne advertisement in a magazine. I'm not gay, but if I were, I would have jumped his bones on the spot.

He allowed Luke to stay as he did an exam, for which I was thankful. It was weird, but I was a tad uncomfortable being alone with him. Is there such a thing as being so good-looking that you're intimidating? I think I felt inadequate, due to my present state. Let's face it: I was more than a disaster. My latest fiasco in the solarium had left me with a new gash on my left eyebrow and scuffed-up knees. It didn't bode well for me getting sprung from here, but I pled my case anyway. For what little good it did, because I got a big fat *NO, absolutely not, no way, no how!!!* I got the message loud and clear.

It looked like I was stuck in here for the long haul, but one thing was for certain: I was not going to let Luke out of my sight. I'm not normally superstitious, but every time I was left alone, bad things happened, and my body couldn't afford any more of that. I desperately needed some good news, but, when Luke began explaining what had happened, I knew it wasn't going anywhere promising. His eyes didn't have that twinkle in them that he got when he was excited. He picked at his left thumbnail and hung his head like a dog that had just gotten in trouble for stealing food off someone's plate.

"Oh, gosh, Jonathan—you know I never want to disappoint you. With much trepidation, I wandered from room to room, but there was not a soul in sight, none that were alive anyway. When I came to the door marked "Morgue," I held my breath, and my knees buckled. The door squeaked open, and I was greeted with the grim reality that there were many sad people out there mourning the death of a loved one under one of the sheets. It was eerie, cold, and downright depressing, and I admit I wanted to run to the elevator as fast as I could, but, instead, I called out for anyone to answer. I was greeted with stone-cold silence. The room was illuminated with bright fluorescent lights casting shadows under the slabs—that creeped me out. I wanted so desperately to get answers for you, and I'm truly sorry I let you down."

I could see in his eyes that he'd been destroyed by this. As sad as he was that he couldn't get answers, I was equally bummed out. I had been having good vibes that he would find some answers, but, instead of answers, he hit, yet another, dead end . . . great!!

As I was dozing, hospital security came in with more bad news. Surprise, surprise—they'd found nothing! I had a sneaking suspicion that they hadn't even looked, but, on the off-chance they had, I didn't want to accuse them of something and risk pissing them off. I had enough enemies already, so it seemed. I was due some good news since I'd been living in

Doomsville, but that wasn't in the cards, because in walked the deputies from yesterday. Well, at least one of them. Right from the get-go, they had me on edge. Deputy Osborne was back in all his glory, but he had a new guy along for the ride. The new guy was a pipsqueak of a guy, or it may have seemed that way since Osborne was a Goliath of a man. He looked like he was hiding a secret and wanted to blurt it out in the worst way. I, on the other hand, didn't give two shits about what he had up his sleeve. And I told him so. When had my hospital room transformed into Grand Central Station?

It was clear he didn't care how I felt and was too busy taking great satisfaction in keeping me on edge. I rolled my eyes and went on making small talk with Luke. It wasn't like me to be rude, but I wasn't into mind games—plus, I was still feeling like death!

Deputy Osborne spoke first. "As much as I dislike you and would much rather spend my time elsewhere, I have something that needs to be discussed."

He was downright gloating, which now had my curiosity piqued. What kind of bullshit had he dreamed up? With a smirk on his face and a look of contempt laced with hatred, he proceeded.

"There's been an accident. What appears to be a firebomb was thrown through your Dad's window at 11:30 p.m. last night, and, to my knowledge, there were no survivors."

CHAPTER FIFTEEN

I was noticeably shaken. If my jaw wasn't wired shut, I would have had to pick it up off the floor. A million and one questions swirled in my mind, but before I could verbalize any, the deputies were out the door. I could hear them giving each other high fives and laughing as they walked down the corridor. I looked at Luke, and he looked as if he had seen a ghost. The color had totally drained from his face, and tears had already formed in the corners of his eyes.

Before I could say anything, he jumped up so quickly his chair flew across the room, landing on its side and snapping in two as he rushed toward the door. I heard him running down the hall yelling at the top of his lungs for the deputies to stop because we had questions. And lots of them. And then there was silence. I cringed as I swung one leg over the side of my bed. Damn, I was wrecked—and not just physically.

The emotional roller-coaster I was on had me upside down. Knowing I couldn't lie there and wait for answers, I continued to maneuver my broken, bruised body slowly to an upright position. Was Osborne playing games with me, or had my Dad perished last night while I lay here wallowing in self-pity? This sure would explain where he'd been.

It was totally out of character for him not to be by my side. Drinking or not, he would be here. As I peered around my door, Luke was making his way back to my room. His head was hanging as his shoulders trembled. He reached up and wiped tears from his eyes before he saw me staring at him. I didn't care that I was a grown man—I wanted to run into his arms and plead with him that this wasn't true. But, instead, I started firing questions at him. One after the other, not even waiting for answers. I was afraid to stop because I feared reality would slap me in the face when I did. Knowing I couldn't deal with the loss of my Dad made me continue as I made my way back to my room, reeling in pain. "Did you talk to the deputies?" I pleaded. "Did they find his body?" "Do you think there was foul play on their part?" "Is the house still standing?" "Do you think they're making this up?"

Luke had his suspicions, and this gave me hope, even though my gut was telling me something different. Catching up to the deputies, he was unable to get more information. Either they didn't know or they were making the whole thing up. I wanted to believe it was the latter, but I knew in my heart that would be wishful thinking. Bastards. I was convinced that they knew the whole story, but to find that out would require Luke to go in search of answers, again leaving me in more of a vulnerable state than I was at the present time. Without him here, by my side, I'd be alone and a sitting duck. We both decided this was their plan and went searching for answers elsewhere.

Even though I now lived in Portland and had been away from Mount Sierra for some time, I had maintained friendships back here. As luck would have it, one of those friendships happened to be with the editor of the local newspaper, the *Pacific Sun-Times*. As the phone rang, I started to feel anxiety creep in. I wasn't sure I was ready to hear the truth—at least, if the truth was what I feared to be true. Luke had gotten up and began pacing back and forth in my tiny room. I was about to flip my lid when my call was answered after three rings.

"*Pacific Sun-Times*, a newspaper, not a snooze paper. How may I direct your call?" Her voice was much too chipper for the way I was feeling, and I wanted to yell at her to stop being fake, but I knew I was being unrealistic, and it wasn't her fault I was tense and anxious.

"Tom Watson, please," I managed to say on the verge of tossing my cookies. I leaned over the trash can, just in case, while I waited an eternity for Tom to answer. "Tom Watson here. How can I be of assistance?" I froze, and no words came out when I opened my mouth to speak. "Hello, hello. Is anyone there?" I heard Tom ask.

Knowing it was now or never, I answered, trying to sound cool and collected while feeling the exact opposite. "Hey, Tom, old pal—this is Jonathan. Jonathan Elliott from Mountain View High. Long time no talk," I managed to reply.

"Wow, Jonathan—it's so great to hear your voice, although you sound a bit muffled."

Should I go into all the gory details of my latest shitshow of a life? I thought better of it, for no other reason than I didn't have that kind of time. Best to be left for another time. I did plan on keeping Tom in my back pocket, though, because, after all, he was a *news guy*. Those kinda guys had a lock on the happenings that were worth knowing about.

"Hey, I heard about your attack out at the Travers' farm. Are you okay?" he inquired.

He sounded genuinely concerned, so I dove into a tad of my backstory just to get him up to snuff. Saying it all out loud made it sound scary as hell—and to think I was living it!! After my *Reader's Digest* version of my past week or so, I divulged that the real reason for my call wasn't just to reminisce about the good old days, although it was nice to catch up.

It was nice to get a bit of normalcy in my life, as I told him about my life in Portland. It hardly seemed possible that, two short weeks ago, I was living the good life, without a care in the world. Or so I thought. How naive had I been? Little did I know my life was about to take a turn into the Twilight Zone. I still had the question swirling around in my head and gaining momentum about how Brie's death was the start of all of this mess. Or was it?

"Tom, did your paper report on a fire that resulted in a death from last night?" I managed to blurt out.

I was shaking and all consumed with fear that his answer would be "Yes," and he would proceed to tell me the gory details, not knowing it was my Dad who had been burned alive. I held my breath and braced myself for bad news. Luke looked half-crazy as he paced and mumbled to himself.

I felt as if the weight of the world was on my shoulders, and I knew Tom's answer would determine my next move. I would either crumble or rejoice. I had to stifle a nervous laugh, thinking *If he only knew how close I was to losing my shit, he might decide to hang up the phone and never look back.* But, thankfully, he didn't know, and he spoke.

"Are you talking about the firebomb that was thrown through a window on the land adjacent to the forest? From my knowledge, there was a casualty, but we haven't released the name yet. I do know the home was destroyed, but I don't have any other details besides that," he casually answered.

It was obvious he still didn't know this was potentially my Dad who had been charred alive and, surprisingly enough, didn't question why I was asking. As he put me on hold while he checked with the reporter in charge, I was held captive to random music from a couple of decades ago. I remember this song well—"Don't Worry, Be Happy."

It used to hold a special place in my heart, but today, at this very instant, I felt anything but happy, and trying to tell me not to worry was the same as telling me to enjoy filet mignon in my present state. Both were utterly impossible to accomplish. It didn't look good, but I was holding onto a sliver of hope that it was another poor soul who had met their maker. I was on pins and needles waiting for answers, as Luke looked like he might barf. We might have to fight over the trash can.

Even though Tom was gone only a few minutes, I was positive I had aged ten years and had twice as many gray hairs. "Sorry, Jonathan, but all I could find out was what I told you before. The name has not been released yet, pending notification of next of kin. If there are new developments, I will be sure to share them. In the meantime, let's grab a cold one soon and catch up further." I told him that sounded like a great idea as soon as I was up and able. I was not interested, to say the least, but sometimes you have to tell small white lies and deal with the consequences if or when they present themselves later.

The only thing I was positive about right now was that something was screwy. An inchworm of doubt was wiggling its way into my brain, and I needed definitive answers ASAP, or I might lose my mind. As I replayed my and Tom's conversation with Luke, I watched a myriad of emotions wash over his face. He first showed disbelief and shock that quickly turned into anger, followed by sorrow and pity. I felt the same way, but I also felt hatred—the kind of hatred that makes you think bad things.

Frustration got the best of me, and I threw Luke's lunch across the room. I watched as spaghetti sauce splattered against the white wall, leaving ambiguous, meaningless splotches. It looked like a Rorschach inkblot test. I sat mesmerized while the spaghetti slithered down the wall like a parade of worms on a rainy day. It would have been more dramatic to throw my own lunch, but liquid wouldn't have made the same impact. Add that to one more thing that I was frustrated about. A person does need the satisfaction of chewing once in a while, not to mention the taste of food.

I loved to eat and was pleased to admit I had become a decent cook through the years. All the years of Luke cooking for me had piqued my interest, and I had taken some classes to hone my skills. I was missing not only eating right now but cooking, too. It was very therapeutic, and I did some of my best thinking when I was concocting new recipes.

Although wallowing in self-pity was justified, I knew it was a waste of my time. Too many bad things were coming at me fast and furious not to react, but my hands were tied, figuratively speaking. Not only did I need to get out of medical jail, but I needed to get better. My mind was still so damn foggy from the drugs that I hadn't been able to use my brain, and that was one of my better assets—another trait I thanked my Mom and Dad for passing on.

Luke was not himself. He had always been a shining light for me and had been upbeat in the darkest of days, but he was anything but that today. He was trying to busy himself cleaning up the mess I had created but succeeded only in creating a bigger one. The wall now looked like it had been painted red. He let out a big sigh, waving a white napkin in the air, admitting defeat. "Penny for your thoughts?" I casually asked. He didn't answer, but he didn't have to. His demeanor and face spoke volumes. If there's one thing we had in common, it was our intuitiveness. And it's the one thing I would change right now, too.

We sat in silence for a minute, both lost in our own thoughts. I didn't want to talk. Everything going through my mind right now led back to things I didn't want to accept or express. Was my Dad actually gone? I glanced Luke's way, and he had his head bowed, quietly mumbling to himself when I saw a tear land on his jeans. It just sat there, refusing to be absorbed by the denim. I was fighting back tears of my own when there was a loud knock on the door, announcing the entrance of my nemesis.

CHAPTER SEVENTEEN

Walking in was Deputy Osborne and one of his cohorts. It wasn't the small guy from last time, but someone entirely different. The new guy didn't share the pompous-asshole attitude Osborne had. His name tag read "Deputy Titus," and when I looked him in the eye, I saw compassion and sorrow. Thank God he was the one who spoke. Hearing what I was anticipating would make it easier to hear from anyone but Osborne. I didn't want him to have the pleasure that I was certain he would get from making me squirm and burst my happy-family bubble. The air was suddenly suffocating—but with a chill—while we waited for the other shoe to drop.

"Jonathan? Jonathan Elliott?" he questioned. I could see in his eyes that he was wrestling with how to form his next sentence. He hesitated before he began. "What I have to tell you is troubling, to say the least. The Sheriff's Department got a call early this morning to respond to a fire on Prescott Lane. When we arrived, the Fire Department had extinguished the fire, for the most part. We are suspecting arson, and the preliminary reports point to a firebomb that was thrown through the front window as the cause." He paused, asked if he could have some water and braced himself. "Unfortunately, we had the displeasure of finding charred remains within the house and have recently been given positive ID through dental records." He stopped talking, right when I was going to find out my Dad's fate. I wanted to scream "Come on, Buddy—what the hell?" but instead I sat patiently waiting while butterflies were fighting in my gut.

The deputy opened his mouth a couple of times to speak, but only a slight trail of spittle emerged. Finally, noticing the problem Deputy Titus was having, Mr. Asshole-in-the-Flesh sneered, "Payback's a bitch, Elliott. Karma always has a way of coming back tenfold, and you got yours! I'm sure your Dad suffered a painful death, and you only have yourself to blame for the rest of your sorry existence." Was he threatening me? The only other time I had witnessed such a villainous black-hearted person was when I had dealt with his father. It was clear the apple had not fallen far from the tree.

Before Luke and I could even begin to form a semblance of a meaningful question, they both stormed out, leaving the curtain around my bed fluttering in their wake. Deputy Titus at least had the decency to turn before he walked through the door. He mouthed *I'm Sorry* and then was gone like a puff of smoke.

The pain and anguish I had felt when my Mom passed years ago was back. What had just happened? How could my life have taken such an evil, twisted turn in the matter of ten days or so? I wasn't even sure what day it was anymore, nor did I care. All I cared about was getting to the bottom of this and getting justice for my Dad. I hadn't even gotten to say "Goodbye," and that was unacceptable. I was afraid this was going to stir up a plethora of emotions I had since buried, and I foresaw more nightmares coming my way.

Luke was staring at me with a look of shock mixed with heartbreak in his tear-filled eyes. For the first time since I had met him, I could tell he was at a loss for words. What do you say to someone who had just become an orphan? Not only had I lost my Dad, but he'd lost his best friend, and I knew he was going to blame himself. That was who he was. He took the weight of the world on his shoulders, and, as my Dad's Alcoholics Anonymous sponsor, he would feel like he'd let us both down.

I broke the ice and addressed the elephant in the room. "Luke, please don't blame yourself for this," I pleaded. "If anyone is to blame, it's me, but I can't go there right now because, honestly, I don't have the first inkling of an idea or where to start." As anguish consumed me, all I could think about was I wished I could turn the clock back. Back to when there was no evil in the world and people loved one another, but, then again, I wasn't even sure a time like that had ever existed.

Tears streamed down our faces for the man who was so much to so many people. But most importantly, he was my Dad. We had been through hell and back after my Mom passed, and I loved him with all my heart. The thought of him suffering was more than I could wrap my head around, and I paged the nurse into my room to temporarily put me out of my misery. Maybe that was a cowardly thing to do, but I wasn't in the right headspace to deal with *anything* right now.

My eyes felt like they had tiny weights attached to their lids, pulling them down and making it near impossible to concentrate or keep them open. As I drifted into a drug-induced sleep, I started fighting demons I thought had been buried years ago. My Dad stood before me but not seeing me. His brow furrowed as he scratched his head. To say he looked concerned would be an understatement of major proportions. He was self-absorbed in a conversation he was having with two men, who had their backs to me. They were both tall and dressed head to toe in black. Hoods adorned their heads, and gloves covered their hands. One was standing totally still, while the other appeared to be doing the talking, as he became animated. I noticed a gun in his right hand. I crept closer so I could hear what was being said. They were all standing in front of my Dad's house, so I took cover behind some overgrown shrubs. Note to self: Help my Dad get some gardening done before I return to Portland.

As I moved in closer, there was something about the man doing the talking that seemed familiar. Where did I know him from? He was pissed and warned my Dad that, if he didn't get me to back off, there would be hell to pay. My Dad stood looking confused. He was pleading with them as he rubbed his face in frustration. I was bound and determined not to let them have the upper hand and freak my Dad out like this, so I took matters into my own hands. Or so I thought. I jumped out from behind the bushes and yelled, trying to sound intimidating but feeling anything but. "Hey, thugs—whatever beef you have with me, I'm here. Now leave my Dad alone, and back off with the threats." Nothing. Not a bat of an eye or any type of recognition. They went about their conversation with details on what would happen if things didn't change in their favor. I cried out to leave my Dad alone. Still nothing. I reeled back, and, with every ounce of energy I could muster up, I punched the tall, animated one square in the jaw. It went through him, and that's when it hit me that I was invisible.

I woke up drenched in sweat, swinging my arms in the air like I was in a fight. Luke had nodded off but was jolted awake and now on top of me in a flash trying to gain control before I hurt myself. It was like I was thirteen years old again in his arms, being comforted. I was wailing incoherently about threats and men clad in black before I realized I was awake and despondent.

The reality of the present situation was beginning to set in, and I was losing my shit. I lay there being comforted by Luke, feeling completely hopeless and helpless. I still didn't have the first clue as to who was behind these dastardly attacks, and I was in no shape, mentally or physically, to find out. I said a silent prayer that my Dad had been wasted out of his mind and unconscious, so he hadn't felt pain or was not aware of what was happening—the only time I can ever recall that I actually wanted my Dad to be drunk. That was saying a lot, if this is what it had come to.

Luke looked like I would expect. Someone who had just lost their best friend. He had noticeable bags under his eyes, and the twitch that he got in the corner of his mouth had returned. I couldn't blame him. I was afraid to look in the mirror at what might stare back. I was positive it would be frightening. As I lay there heartbroken and hurting, I couldn't stop thinking about my dream. Why did one of the black-clad men look so familiar? Was he the one responsible for my father's death and behind all the latest craziness? How was Brie's death related—or was it?

My mind was spinning out of control with images of the past two weeks. So many things had happened, but nothing had really changed—at least pertaining to the fact that I was at square one and perplexed about which way to turn to find answers. And I needed so many of them, because my mind was in overdrive with questions. My mental state was so fragile that I was afraid if I talked about my Dad, I would cry, and I didn't want to cry. I found crying cleansing for the most part, but I was fighting it back mainly for the reason that I knew once the floodgates were opened up, there would be no closing them.

I could tell Luke was torn as well. He was wrestling with his own inner demons and blaming himself for not protecting my Dad, even though I had told him he was not to blame. I knew Luke as well as I knew myself, and, for that reason alone, I knew he would hear what I said but not really listen. As I was about to gingerly approach the subject of my Dad, the bedside phone rang and scared me half to death. I was semi-getting used to the inner sounds of the hospital, with its beeps and clanging drowned out by a cacophony of wailing ambulance sirens at all times of the day and night, but this sound was foreign amongst all the others.

I cautiously answered, bracing myself for more bad news. I was getting more pessimistic the longer I stayed here. Not being a fan of the new-but-far-from-improved me, I nervously answered. "Jonathan Elliott here." I held my breath as Luke looked on with eyes the size of saucers. I visibly exhaled when I was greeted on the other end by my friend Tom Watson, the editor from the *Pacific Sun-Times*. The lighthearted chipperness was gone from his voice as he regrettably informed me that a positive ID had been made. He offered his heartfelt condolences and promised he would be around to help in any way that I needed. I had never felt so alone. I knew that, technically, I had plenty of people to help me, but I no longer had my Dad. Or Mom. My *new normal* was a punch in the gut.

After much begging on my part and using my Dad's death as leverage, I got Luke to go investigate. I needed to know what the crime scene looked like and if there was still a house left to salvage. I also needed him to make a positive ID. And, above all, I needed to get out of here so I could man up and do these things myself. I knew this was asking a lot of him, but, out of everyone in my life, he was the only one I trusted explicitly. He reluctantly left, not making any promises but an affirmation that he would do his best. His best had always been pretty damn good, so I wasn't worried he would let me down.

I had a fire burning in my belly, and I wasn't going to allow anyone a chance to mess with me, so I pompously dared any of those jerks to come try while Luke was away. Even though I was physically still a disaster, I was pissed. What was the saying, *Hell hath no fury like a woman scorned*? Well, I felt that way, except I would change it to *Hell hath no fury like a man disrespected.* They had gone too far this time, and if it was the last thing I did, heads were going to roll.

CHAPTER NINETEEN

Waiting for Luke proved to be insufferable. My eyelids were so heavy, but I didn't dare go to sleep, fearing my demise in my sleep, never to wake up again. I eyeballed with cynicism every person who set so much as a toe into my room. The distrust I had for people was borderline paranoia, and I knew it was only a matter of time before people began to question my sanity, but I didn't care or give a crap what anyone thought. Even Dr. *GQ* got the once-over, and I was reasonably sure he could be trusted.

I was starting to think someone's chain had been yanked in a major way. Bad enough that karma had my name on the top of what I assumed was a very long list. Was I ever going to get good news again, or was I doomed for a life of disappointments, heartache, and watching my back? As I was wallowing in self-pity, Dr. *GQ* walked through the door for his afternoon rounds. "Well, Jonathan, against all odds, you have been making some good progress. You still have a ways to come, but I'm encouraged," he said with a big smile that almost blinded me. If it was physically possible, I would have jumped for joy and celebrated with a big juicy burger, but instead I tried my best to smile around the wires and thanked him profusely. He made a promise to return in the morning and made me pinky-swear I would stay put and not get into any trouble. I just hoped that I wouldn't have to go back on my word.

Luke returned as I was peering out the window. I always found it ironic that life carried on at such a fast pace, no matter the struggles someone might be facing. There was a massive billboard to the left from *Adventure Seekers* advertising space travel as your next travel destination. I wasn't sure that would be something I would be interested in, but I still found it intriguing that it was available to everyone now. I watched as a young child skipped to an imaginary tune, while his mother trailed behind, preoccupied by her phone. Flowers were in full bloom and vibrant pinks, yellows and purples welcomed the sunshine and a promise of better days. As much as I was still a mess mentally and physically, the sight of the flowers cheered me up to the point that a smile had formed on the edges of my mouth when Luke pulled up a chair.

He looked like he had aged ten years in the past twenty-four hours. His ever-present, jovial smile had turned into a perpetual frown, and the bags under his eyes had multiplied and become trunks. As he took a load off, he exhaled the weight of the world. I was eager to hear what he had found out, but at the same time, I didn't want to know. Ignorance is bliss, so they say. He took a long, hard look at me—the type of look that stares straight into your soul and can see your deepest, darkest thoughts and fears you didn't even know you had. And then a lone tear escaped before he could turn away. I wanted to tell him everything was going to all right, but I wasn't a liar. I wasn't sure it was going to be okay ever again, so I remained quiet and waited for him to speak.

He was having trouble formulating a coherent sentence, so, instead, he stood and wrapped me in one of his infamous bear hugs. "I love you, son, and will do everything in my power to protect you. You have my solemn promise." I'd never doubted that for a second, but it was heartwarming to hear, nonetheless. He was wrecked, and I was reluctant to ask what he had found out. It almost seemed selfish of me, but curiosity got the best of me, and I blurted out, "Well, do tell before I lose what's left of my mind!"

He was wrestling with what he wanted to say. I could see it in his eyes, and I saw the wheels turning in his brain. Honesty had always been at the forefront of our relationship, and I knew no matter how much he struggled with what to tell me, he would eventually spill it all. He started slowly and then got into a rhythm, while I sat perched on the edge of my chair, wishing I could change what was coming next. If only I could turn the clock back at the very least to say goodbye.

"Jonathan, you know I've never lied to you. And never will, but I want you to know that this pains me to my core to have to tell you what I saw today." He didn't have to tell me this, because it was etched on his face. He had been destroyed, and I wasn't sure if we'd ever be able to find ourselves in a place of happiness and security again.

"First of all, the house is toast. It will have to be gutted and rebuilt if that's what you choose. There were numerous investigators walking around, looking for evidence, but it's clear to me that, whoever planned this had done their research and knew what they were doing." He paused for a second, wiped his eyes, and took in the longest, deepest breath I had ever heard. "I sincerely doubt they will find any evidence, but I've hired our own private investigator. I think you and I know that, no matter how awesome of a team we make, we have met our match. This is bigger than us, and the thought of losing you is more than I can handle."

This didn't shock me, and I was in full agreement. We had met our match. This by no means meant I wasn't going to get to the bottom of this fiasco, but now I would have help—much needed and welcome help. The wisest thing you can do for yourself is realize your limitations, and I knew mine. I knew that this didn't mean that Luke was throwing in the towel by any means. Nor was I. Looking at him, the poor guy was begging for affirmation with his eyes, hoping that I wouldn't think less of him. How could I? He was only thinking of me, as usual, and I couldn't have loved him more right now. As I reached over and wiped tears from his eyes, I let him know I agreed a thousand times over again that we had met our match.

Unfortunately, the news about my Dad's house was just the beginning of the dismal news. Luke wasn't sure if it was his present mental state that made him imagine things, but he could have sworn he saw a man dressed in all black peeking from behind my Dad's garage as he looked for clues of any type. He yelled out to him but got no response. Shocker. Was Luke "catching" my paranoia, or was it valid? More than ever, I needed out of here because I've always felt like there was safety in numbers, and, as long as I was here, not only was I a sitting duck, but so was Luke. Yet another reason to keep Luke here with me until we could return together to the cabin.

CHAPTER TWENTY

earing about Luke's trip to the morgue was more than I was prepared for. Not knowing what to expect, I should have been smarter and given it some thought in advance, so that the actual commentary wouldn't destroy me. And to think what Luke must be going through by seeing my Dad burned to a crisp with his own eyes—that accounts for his acting so broken up and shattered. "Jonathan, the only thing good about you being in the hospital is that you didn't personally have to see your poor Dad lying there, totally unrecognizable. It's bad enough that I had to see it, but I wouldn't want that etched in your mind forever. It's all I can see, and it haunts me. I can only hope it will fade in time."

Luke excused himself and limped into the bathroom. Although the door was closed, the walls couldn't contain the uncontrollable sobs that I heard, followed by repeated retching in the toilet. I was feeling more than guilty now, because I was the one who had asked him to go make a positive ID. I could tell he was uncomfortable about it when I asked him, but he didn't want to tell me "No." Now that I've given it some thought, he'd *never* told me "No." In our twenty-plus years of knowing each other, he had always been so agreeable and supportive. What had I done to deserve him?

When Luke emerged from the bathroom fifteen minutes later, I could tell he had tried to pull himself together, for my sake, but had failed miserably. He was hunched over, adding a decade to his appearance. His face was flushed and his eyes bloodshot and puffy. His whole demeanor was one of a wounded puppy. If he had had a tail, it would have been tucked tightly between his legs. I was at a loss for words, because a simple *I'm sorry* seemed highly inadequate. There had never been uncomfortable silence between us in the past, but I couldn't say that any longer, because, now, we both sat in silence, lost in our own thoughts. I wanted to tell him I was sorry for whatever I had done to bring this black cloud upon us, but I was still at an extreme loss to what it was that had set this wrecking ball in motion.

There was no denying in my mind any longer that Brie had been caught in the crosshairs and lost her life because of me. Not only her, but my Dad, too. I was solely and ultimately responsible for their deaths, and I wasn't sure I could ever come to terms with this. One thing I was certain of was, if it was the last thing I did, I would get to the bottom of this and bring whoever was responsible down. They would pay dearly, and I wouldn't rest until they did.

My head was pounding from stress and crying. I hadn't had much of an appetite, which was good, I suppose, but all of a sudden, I had the strongest craving for a neopolitan shake. They had always been my Dad's favorite, and I not only wanted but *needed* to have one in his memory. The only problem was I wasn't about to let Luke out of my sight, for his sake as well as mine. As I was weighing my options, in walked my old pal Tom Watson, the editor of the *Pacific Sun-Times*. Ordinarily, I wouldn't have welcomed a guest, but I almost jumped for joy when he appeared at the door.

Taking this as a good sign, I quickly sent Luke out to buy the shakes my Dad craved, while I entertained my guest. Tom had changed a lot since high school, but, at the same time, not at all. He was taller, and his voice was lower, but his face still had the round cherub look, although it now sported a goatee. The oversized tortoise-shell glasses he wore gave him a studious air and fit perfectly with his occupation. Age hadn't caught up with him yet, and he still was as skinny as a string bean. The awkwardness that comes from not seeing someone in years, coupled with totally different career paths, made for what seemed like an eternity of small talk. It became abundantly clear that we had nothing in common anymore—or ever had, for that matter. One can only talk about the weather for so long, and, when Luke peeked around the curtain, I was relieved and ravenous.

Tom took this as his cue and beelined for the door faster than you could say *boo* and made promises to return later. Luke looked shell shocked. I waited for him to give me more bad news. I was getting accustomed to things going south on a regular basis, but he remained tight lipped and dove into the juiciest-looking burger I had ever seen. I was envious, and I had to wipe my mouth as I salivated. It was encouraging that we both were getting our appetites back, even though it would be better for me if mine stayed dormant for the time being.

"Turns out these hoodlums aren't done messing with us yet, Jonathan, because when I was out, I was being tailed. At first I thought I was imagining the black sedan trailing two car lengths behind, but when I turned into the burger joint, they sped by waving the finger in my direction, yelling to *watch my back*." Luke was not one to shy away from danger, but he looked spooked. Hence the shell-shocked look when he had returned.

Physically, I was feeling a little better, and the meds were working their magic, making my pneumonia better. The broken bones would take time, but I was starting to feel halfway human, so I turned down my nightly meds. I needed—now more than ever—to clear the cobwebs out of my brain. It couldn't have been clearer that, until I got some information about who or what was behind this, we both would have to watch our backs.

I must have fallen asleep discussing ideas with Luke, because, the next thing I knew, there was a nurse taking my vitals and Luke opening the blinds. Sunshine poured through the window, making shadows bounce across the wall. It instantly felt warmer, with the promise of a new day. I knew that I was going to have to make funeral arrangements, but, for some strange reason, with the sun shining, I knew it would be easier than if there had been a dark gloomy drizzle falling. My Dad wouldn't want me to mourn him but instead celebrate his accomplishments and our solid, loving relationship as father and son. I was finding this difficult to do because I had a hollowness where my heart was. I hated more than anything that I hadn't been given the chance to say goodbye.

Right when I was wiping a tear off my cheek, Dr. *GQ* walked in, smiling like he had just won the lottery. *Dear God, I hope he has good news* was all I could think as he gave me the once-over. "Well, Jonathan, I think you can leave today. I'll get your discharge papers together and have someone call to set up your follow-up appointments," he cheerfully said. Finally, a prayer had been answered. I hoped this was the start of a new trend.

CHAPTER TWENTY-ONE

Sitting in a wheelchair, soaking up some much-needed sun, I patiently waited at the entrance of the hospital for Luke to bring the car around. I was ecstatic that I was blowing this joint. Even though I was feeling good enough to leave, I was far from healed. Much to my dismay, I'd been informed that my jaw would have to be wired shut for about six more weeks. I was already planning in great detail the meal I would devour the day I was cut free, most likely resulting in stomach cramps, but that was a risk I was willing to take.

Just as Luke pulled up, a figure came running toward me in a full sprint, covered from head to toe in black. A ski mask covered the face. That was the last thing I saw before I was knocked over. As I lay on the ground, the wheelchair haphazardly twisted around me. I was shocked that someone would attempt this blatant act of violence in broad daylight, with people around. I was in no shape to give chase, so I lay there confused and completely clueless as to how my life had taken such a wrong turn. I was also a little mortified as hordes of people ran to me, trying to get me upright. Although I was embarrassed, it did my soul good and renewed my faith in mankind that there were still good people in the world. I, unfortunately, had gotten on the radar of some bad ones. It felt like I was sitting straight smack in the middle of a bullseye, and they wanted to use me for target practice. I wasn't in the mood to play.

Luke left the motor running and was out of the car faster than I would have expected for someone his size and with disabilities. One thing I could always count on was his ability to be there for me, no matter what the situation. Thank God for that, because, sadly, it was looking like these bastards were a very determined bunch.

Leaving the hospital is always a euphoric feeling. After being cooped up in a sterile environment with the funky smells, moaning people, and the white walls, everything smelled and looked beautiful and cheerful on the outside. As I settled into the front seat, I bid a fond farewell to the staff and told them, "Nothing personal, but I hope to never see you again." They all chuckled and wished me well. I sure was hoping this was the leaf I needed to turn over to get the upper hand I so desperately needed.

As Luke drove through town, I was enjoying being on the mend and "free." Everything seemed more alive to me.

Losing my Dad and having my life turned sideways and upside down lately made me realize how precious life was. I saw little girls with bright pink bows tied around pigtails, happily skipping, holding tight to their mothers' hands and young boys dodging in and out of storefronts, playing hide-and-seek. Oh, to be young again.

Of late, I'd been feeling like the weight of the world rested on my shoulders and that I was the only one who could get to the bottom of this whole mess. Knowing I had Luke was reassuring, but, somehow, I needed to take a leap of faith. We had always made a great team, but, now, learning how to trust others as well was going to be paramount for solving this mystery.

Pulling up in front of Luke's cabin, after stopping to get more shakes, I was overcome with emotion. The last time I was here, things had been much different. My Dad was still alive, and his house was still standing. Thankfully the acre of land where my Dad's house sat was tucked on the outskirts of Luke's ten acres of paradise, so it couldn't be seen from the cabin. I had decided I needed to get in a different mind space before I ventured over there. The horses were calling my name, and I needed a much-deserved visit to the barn to see the animals. I craved alone time, but the last time I was in the barn was when the attack had happened, so I asked Luke to accompany me. I had voiced my opinion to Luke numerous times about how I felt about guns, but I also was not stupid, so I agreed to let him bring a rifle as well as a pistol. I was bound and determined not to have a repeat of my last visit.

Opening the front door and feeling the love that lived within these walls brought out an avalanche of emotion. I was going to try my hardest not to lose my shit and cry, but it was taking a great deal of willpower to hold it together. I sat there trying to get a grip, as Luke looked on with concern. He knew what a sap I was and left me alone to contain myself. The loss of my Dad was finally starting to sink in, and I knew there would be bad days ahead as we put him to rest.

Finally getting my shit together, I wandered into the kitchen. This was one of my favorite rooms in the house because it was so cozy. The view from the window over the farmhouse sink looked out to the barn and corrals, where the horses were happily frolicking. Luke was such a great cook, and he always had something either baking in the oven or simmering on the stove. As I sat down at his knotty-pine pedestal table, I wasn't surprised to see a bouquet of flowers, picked from his garden, arranged in a vase I had made for him in crafts class my freshman year—the last time I had attempted anything crafty. I quickly learned I was better off using my mind, rather than my hands. What I was surprised to see was a note addressed to me.

I reached down to pull it out from under the vase and immediately recognized my Dad's handwriting. I ran my fingers over the letters, willing him to come to life, knowing in my heart I was asking the impossible. Luke looked over my shoulder, and, realizing what I had in my hand, patted me on the shoulder and quietly walked out of the kitchen to allow me time to myself. I wanted to read it in the worst way, but I also knew that once I had read it, I wouldn't have anything new from him again. So I sat quietly, holding it close to my heart and saying a silent prayer.

CHAPTER TWENTY-TWO

Finding the strength to dive in and open it proved harder than I thought. My mind went places that I thought I had buried long ago. Memories flooded my mind and heart with our many vacations as a family, time spent camping and becoming one with nature. Saturdays we had spent during our "daddy and me" bonding dates that we had when I was growing up. Next thing I knew, an hour had passed, and the letter was stained with tears. I put my head down on my folded arms and let it all out. The tears, the heartache, the loss of what would never be as well as what had been.

There was no holding back, and, after I'd composed myself, I had a bit of a clearer head. I needed this but had been fighting it—for too long, actually. I remember crying a lot after my Mom passed and as I struggled for months, trying to help my Dad out of his alcoholic funk. But since my Dad had been killed, I had allowed tears only here and there. Not full-on pouring your soul and heart into it where you couldn't even catch your breath. It was the cleansing cry I needed, and it gave me the courage I needed to open up the letter.

Dear Jonathan,

Where do I begin? I have loved you since I first laid eyes on your little squishy body swaddled in your blue blanket knitted with love by your Mom. I had dreamed about you for years, but, when you finally arrived, you were a miracle. A miracle I've cherished and loved more than life itself.

I have failed you over the years, and, although I have apologized, I feel like I owe you more. You have never once given up on us through the darkest of days. You were a constant beacon of light, and I thank you for being the son I never knew I was worthy of having.

When we found our way back to each other years ago, I made a promise to you, one I had every intention of keeping until I didn't. I still love you more than I can put into words and will protect you with everything I have, but I have not remained sober. That was part of my promise, and I broke that promise to you. I feel like a failure and a liar, not to mention a coward.

I can't even look you in the face and tell you this, and I'm sorry for not being the man you thought I was. I was weak and so worried about you that I had a beer. Then another. As you very well know, that's all an alcoholic needs to fall completely off the wagon. I didn't just fall, I crashed. And hard. It's been near impossible for me to look you in the eye. Luke has remained my steady rock and has promised he will help me. And you.

Please accept my deepest apologies, from the bottom of my heart. I couldn't be prouder of the man you have become, and I promise, again, that I will overcome this and be the Dad you can admire and respect.

I love you to Pluto and back,
Dad

Wow! That hit me hard, and I sat there, trembling and sobbing. I thought I was crying before, but that was nothing compared to this. Dammit, why had I never been allowed to say goodbye and to tell him one last time how much I loved him? I hoped that, when he took his last breath, he knew how I felt.

Luke appeared out of nowhere and wrapped me in his arms. He patted my back and reassured me we were going to get through this. He had seen me struggle for years, but this was one of the darkest days I'd had. Knowing he was there to help me and the rage I felt toward the people behind these vicious attacks would get me through. I was sure of that. I just wasn't sure how to go about starting over, yet again.

Pouring cold water on my face, I loaded my pockets with apples and carrots and ventured out to the barn. I was more determined than ever not to wallow in self-pity. To me, there was no better medicine than the horses. Luke, right by my side, kept quiet, turning his head to and fro, acting as my own personal bodyguard. The private investigator that he had hired was set to have a meeting with us tonight, but, for the time being, Luke was acting as my eyes and ears, ready to pounce on a moment's notice.

No matter how therapeutic the horses were, there was an ever-present danger that hung in the air. Neither Luke nor I could relax. We both kept hearing twigs snap or voices that weren't there. Or were they? I could have sworn I saw a figure crouched behind the barn, but when we both investigated, guns poised and ready, there was nothing. Not even footprints—no evidence that there had been anyone. We were both too on edge to thoroughly enjoy ourselves, so we cautiously made our way back to the cabin. I was dragging ass anyway and needed some rest. The letter had taken its toll on me, and this was the first time in more than twenty years that the horses hadn't been able to soothe me.

Luckily Luke and I made it back to the cabin unscathed— we were both a ball of nervous energy but in one piece. I gingerly made my way up to the loft, with Autumn eagerly following behind, and got comfy under the weighted blanket with a lavender-scented pillowcase for a much-needed nap. I was instantly transported back to the time Luke and I had spent thirteen days on a stakeout, waiting to catch the Mount Sierra killer. Luke had sprayed my pillow nightly with lavender essential oils to keep me calm. He didn't miss a beat.

There was something special about every room in Luke's cabin that made me feel safe and protected. I welcomed this more than ever. Who would have thought leaving the hospital would be so taxing on my body? I was *beat*. I immediately fell into a fitful sleep, where the nightmares once again plagued me.

Panic vibrated through me as I sat bound and gagged to a chair. I was groggy, like I had been injected with some foreign substance, and it took everything I had to keep my eyes open. Hearing a loud crash behind me, I painfully turned my head and immediately wished I hadn't.

The two stinky tattooed men were hovering over my father, taking turns beating him. His listless body was being held up by chains attached to a beam overhead. Sunbeams peeked through the grime that covered the windows and cast an eerie glow to the otherwise-dark room. A single lightbulb on a nearby lamp was straining to do its job but failing miserably, and I was thankful for small favors. I didn't want to see or hear what was going on behind me, but at the same time, I had a nagging itch to watch in hopes that somehow I could help. Knowing this was impossible did little for my mental state.

Calling out to my Dad drew their attention my way and gave my Dad a small reprieve. Blood dripped from his mouth, and both of his eyes were puffy, making it impossible for them to open. Straining to see through the shadows, I saw what looked like teeth lying in a pool of blood and vomit by his feet. I yelled to him that I loved him—just when he went up in flames.

I jumped up, gasping for air and trying to slow my racing heart. I was afraid I would start having nightmares again, since I had pretty much been a living, walking nightmare lately. Looking around gave me a sense of security, as I peered out the window toward the barn. The sun had begun to set, but I could still make out an outline of the horses in the pasture. I saw an unfamiliar car parked out in front of Luke's cabin, and I suddenly remembered we were supposed to be having a meeting with the private investigator. I looked at the clock and was surprised to see it was after seven. I had slept the afternoon away and was thankful I remembered only the one nightmare.

Splashing water on my face in a feeble attempt to make myself look presentable failed. Looking at myself in the mirror quite honestly scared me a little. I had serious, heavy-duty bags under my eyes, and my skin color was an interesting mix of blues, purples and yellows from my broken nose and gash on my cheek. I managed as best as I could to remove the dried-up, crusty blood that was caked around the corners of my mouth; I ran a hand through my hair. Sadly, my hair was the only thing on my body that still looked nice.

As I made my way down the stairs, I grimaced as I slowly took one step at a time. I could hear voices coming from the kitchen. I hadn't bothered to ask Luke much about the private investigator and was surprised when I heard a woman's voice. Oddly, all of a sudden, I was keenly aware of my ghastly appearance. I found this funny because I wasn't a vain person, but, somehow, I found myself in unfamiliar territory—wanting to make a good impression. In times like this, I was thankful I had my intelligence.

I made my way into the kitchen as the smell of fresh-brewed coffee wafted through my clogged-up nostrils. The aroma was intoxicating, as hints of citrus and rich chocolates permeated the air. Luke and two other people I had never met were standing with their backs to me as I stumbled into the kitchen. I felt like I had the worst hangover of my entire life.

"Sorry to intrude, but my name is Jonathan." All three turned at once to greet me. The look on the two strangers' faces upon seeing me was nothing short of horror. I guess Luke hadn't warned them properly. My sense of humor had always been my strong suit, so I was hoping my wit was on point tonight if I wanted to win them over. It was abundantly clear I wasn't about to make a good impression with my looks alone. I was feeling a little self-conscious because my looks had always been a positive attribute. I looked like my Mom. My memory of her had faded over the years, but I could still see her beautiful smile with the dimple in her chin and at the corner of her mouth.

I had thick sandy-blond hair that was cut in a conservative style, mostly because of my job. There was a certain stigma attached to being an attorney, and one of those things was appearance. Boy, if the partners in the firm could see me now, they'd dump me like a hot potato. I stood 6'1", so I wasn't short, but neither was I huge, like Luke. The most striking thing about me was my eyes. This wouldn't be my description, but I had been told they were as blue as the sky on a fresh spring day. I was often mistaken for Scandinavian, with my fair complexion. I could feel our two house guests sizing me up. Not like they were going to take me down, but trying to get a feel for who I was and what I'd been through. Good luck with that!

Luke could tell I was starting to get a tad uncomfortable, as I nervously stepped side to side, so he jumped in and made introductions. "Lux, Quinn, this is the man of the hour, Jonathan. Jonathan, this is Lux Carpenter, the private investigator I've hired, and his lovely assistant Quinn Bishop." If Luke had known about there being an assistant, I was certain that he had left that part out. I was also a million percent certain that he had failed to mention how breathtakingly stunning she was. She had strawberry-blond hair that cascaded over her shoulders, illuminating the room with its shine. Her eyes were the color of emeralds, and, as she smiled, the cutest dimples formed in her cheeks. I was instantly mesmerized and suddenly all the more aware of my horrible state. I couldn't help but feel straight out of *Beauty and the Beast*, with me playing the part of the Beast, of course, and Quinn as Belle.

We shook hands, and I felt a jolt all the way down my spine and butterflies having a picnic in my stomach. I hadn't felt this way about a girl since I'd been in high school, and then I had only been interested in a few. As we locked eyes, I couldn't help but notice a familiarity about her I couldn't place. I got lost for a moment in her eyes, and time seemed to stand still as I nonchalantly let go of her hand. I cleared my throat, and, as I looked away, I noticed both Luke and Lux giving each other sly smiles and a thumbs-up from Luke. Were my actions that obvious, and was the attraction mutual?

After my awkward moment had passed, we settled around the kitchen table to talk strategy. I couldn't get the nagging thought out of my mind that I knew Quinn from somewhere, but, just like everything else in my life lately, I had no clue. First on the agenda for our brainstorming session was to list what we knew to be fact.

1. Whoever was the brains behind the attacks weren't interested in seeing me dead. Not yet, anyway. They had been given the chance and had allowed me to escape.

114

CHAPTER TWENTY-THREE

2. They were not afraid to kill others, maim me, or scare the crap out of me.
3. They wanted my attention.
4. They were seriously pissed and meant business.
5. They had thugs working for them with greasy long hair and tattoos covering their arms.
6. They had eyes and ears everywhere, watching my every move.
7. My Dad and Brie had both suffered an untimely death because of me (or so it seemed).
8. I didn't have a clue in hell who was behind it.
9. Anyone I had contact with was in potential danger.

I didn't like the looks of this list in the least. As I sat among these three, I became increasingly uncomfortable. Mostly due to the fact that it was blatantly obvious that I was responsible for two innocent people's death. Not just any two people, either, but my Dad, who meant the world to me, and Brie, my trusty right hand. I was a good person. I knew I was, and I had lived a clean life. As far as I knew, I had no enemies. Even though I was quiet, people always gravitated toward me, so who in the world could be so irate that they would resort to murder?

Feeling like my world was about to cave in on me, I got up and began pacing, running my hands through my hair and nervously picking at some dry skin in the corner of my thumbnail. I was disappointed and pissed at myself for not using my brain. It had always been one of my strongest traits, but it was failing me now. I was hoping that this was temporary, caused by trauma and lasting effects of the medication. Though, to be on the safe side, Luke and I would be lying low for the time being.

Quinn was the next to speak, and, when she did, I got goosebumps. Is this what my Dad had felt for my Mom all those years ago? Love at first sight was always something I thought happened only in the movies, not in real life, but I was second-guessing that now. She started explaining about the ballistics report they had run on the bullet taken out of my Dad's arm and was becoming quite animated. There was something about her mannerisms and the waving of her hands that struck me as familiar, and then, it hit me.

"Oh, my God. From the first second I saw you, Quinn, you had a very familiar vibe about you that I couldn't place, but I think I just figured it out. Are you related to Ann Bishop by any chance?" I questioned. I hadn't thought about Ann Bishop in two decades. She was the district attorney who'd tried the case against the Mount Sierra killer back in 2000. Luke and I had been given keys to the city and deemed hometown heros; that had been one of my finest hours. Now that I looked closely at Quinn, I was beginning to see the resemblance.

Quinn, caught off guard, stopped in mid-sentence and looked at me for a second before she responded. "Why, yes—that's my Mom! How do you know her?" I proceeded to tell

Quinn the circumstances when our paths had crossed—and how fond I was of her mother for helping me during one of the most difficult times of my life. We all agreed that it was a small world we lived in.

CHAPTER TWENTY-FOUR

Luke joined in on the conversation and agreed that Quinn, indeed, looked like her Mom and shared many of the same mannerisms. There was something about the twinkle in their eyes—and that slightly crooked smile—that was undeniable. I was starting to think that forces were intervening, somehow, and that Quinn and I were destined to meet. As much as I wanted the evening to continue, it had gotten late, and I was exhausted. Even though there weren't enough hours in the day for me to get enough beauty sleep, I needed to rest. We made plans to meet up in a couple of days to discuss the next plans and go over what else they had discovered through their various investigations.

Not wanting to discuss my feelings for Quinn with Luke just yet, I bid him goodnight and disappeared into the loft.

It's not that I didn't want him to know, but *I* needed to know first. This feeling was foreign to me, and I wanted to take time to figure it out and revel in its greatness. As I lay down, snuggling with Autumn nestled between my legs, I once again inhaled the lavender essential oils Luke had sprayed on the down pillow. I ached for the loss of my Dad but had a warm glow in my gut for what possibly could be. As I drifted off to sleep, I had Quinn on my mind.

Standing, turning my gaze toward the green crafts-man-style home I had grown up in, Quinn, with a baby in her arms, walked up next to me and snuggled by my side. I put my arm around her and pulled her close. At the same time, I planted a kiss on the forehead of my newborn son, Michael. We stood admiring the "Sold" sign hung on the real estate "For Sale" sign. A slight breeze was blowing her strawberry-blond locks, and I stood mesmerized by not only her beauty but the beauty of nature. Beautiful pink, purple and yellow pansies were in full bloom in the flower beds that lined the front of the house. The boxwood hedge from years ago was gone, and new landscaping and a fresh coat of paint had given the house life. We were lucky enough to be at the right place at the right time and were now the proud owners of my previous home on Ferndale Lane. My life had taken a one-eighty, and I was happy and content.

As I tried to get my bearings and wipe the sleep from my eyes, I was shocked to see I had been asleep for twelve hours straight. I was disoriented, peaceful and distraught all at the same time, which left me confused and a tad anxious. Having been away from Luke's for so long, it felt strange, in an odd way, but comforting, too. I clearly was having a hard time pinpointing my mood. Needless to say, I was still grieving for my father, and I doubted that would change anytime in the near future. One thing I was positive about was that my dream had left me hopeful.

After my Mom had been killed, I had suffered from repeated nightmares that were vivid and often left me shaken for days, but, over the years, as I learned to cope with her death, they had, thankfully, dissipated. Just recently, with my hospital stay, they had reappeared, and I was scared of what this might mean. So, to say I was relieved to have a happy dream was an understatement. I often struggled to remember my dreams, but this one was as clear as day, and I caught myself smiling from ear to ear. As of late, my life had been in shambles, so I was due some good news.

Making my way downstairs, I had a slight spring to my step, which I could attribute only to the possibility of a relationship with Quinn. My body was healing, slowly but surely, and I was happy to report it was making steps in the right direction. I ached for the time when this would be behind me, which startled me back into the reality that I still had not one clue as to why these unfathomable things were happening and what despicable person was responsible. The meeting Luke and I'd had last night with Lux and Quinn was a start. In the past, Luke and I would have tackled this together, but times had changed. He was getting up in years now, in his seventies, and I was—well, I was still physically a disaster, and, unfortunately, my mind wasn't in tip-top shape, either.

Knowing that our meeting with Lux and Quinn had been set up for a couple of days in the future, I was surprised and curious when I heard voices coming from the den. I stopped and listened before rounding the corner to make sure Luke wasn't in danger of any type. I despised that I questioned everyone and everything, but, unfortunately, we were all learning the hard way. This was something I was going to have to live with for the rest of my life, and I was more determined than ever not to have any more fatalities on my conscience.

The voices were male but didn't sound angry. They were talking in a normal tone, which put my mind immediately at ease. As I strained to listen to what they were saying, I recognized one of the voices—it was that jerk of a deputy sheriff, Osborne. What the hell did he want? I didn't like him, and, more than that, I didn't trust him. I had inherited my good judge of character from my Mom, and this guy was screaming *Bad News*.

Luke saw me lurking around the corner and pleaded with his eyes to come save him from the men he was talking to. This wasn't a good sign. "Deputy Osborne, what can I do you for?" I questioned. Hatred dripped from my words no matter how hard I was trying not to show my true feelings. I couldn't help it, though. This guy had an attitude and clearly hated me as much as I hated him, if that was even possible.

I could tell I'd caught him off guard, as he jumped in the air upon hearing me speak. No introductions were made as to who the other guy was. He didn't look familiar and was definitely not the short, semi-compassionate guy whose name was "Titus," I believe, from the other day. He had probably lost his job for caring. As Osborne spoke, I saw a glimmer in his eye that told me he was enjoying himself—a little too much, considering what had transpired lately. I braced myself for what was coming and told myself that, no matter what he told me, I wouldn't show any emotion. I was not about to give him the satisfaction.

"As I was telling your friend Luke, before you so rudely interrupted, we are investigating a murder. Or so it seems. There most definitely has been foul play involved. Tom Watson, the editor from the *Pacific Sun-Times* was found this morning in the park adjacent to the east side of the forest, with his throat slit. He bled out and was dead before anyone found him."

I audibly gasped. My knees gave out, and I hit the floor. So much for my poker face. My mind was numb, and, as I tried to formulate a response, nothing came out. I looked at him dumbfounded and in shock. Was this because of me as well? Were these predators picking off my family and friends one by one? *Wait*—did he think *I* was responsible?

CHAPTER TWENTY-FOUR

Standing with his right hand resting on his holster, his thumb gently massaging his gun handle, he smirked at me as his eyes shot daggers through my heart. "Preliminary reports show the time of death between nine and midnight. I'd like to know where you were last night between those times."

I struggled to gain composure as I managed to utter "Are you serious? You really think I am capable of murder? And a friend at that? You must be out of your mind!" I was enraged and on the verge of losing my temper when Luke jumped to my defense.

"Jonathan doesn't have to answer your ludicrous insinuations. I can vouch for him because he was right here with me and our two private investigators for a good portion of the night. Now unless you have anything constructive to tell us regarding Michael Elliott's death, you need to go. You are no longer welcome in my home!" Luke was pissed and trying to keep a level head, but I, once again, saw the telltale stressful twitch in the corner of his mouth. I took a step toward Osborne with my arms hanging loosely by my side, my hands clenched into tight fists, trying to calm myself. I started to speak, but Luke quickly intervened and told me I didn't owe them an explanation. I listened; being an attorney, I knew this was solid advice.

Osborne and his cohort turned to leave but not before he pointed a finger in my direction, telling me to not leave town. "You haven't seen the end of me, loser!" he obnoxiously proclaimed. And then he boldly looked us up and down before he spat on the floor by our feet. Luke made a move toward him, but I grabbed his arm to hold him back. It was better to let them go. A confrontation would get us nowhere quick and only cause the situation to escalate.

CHAPTER TWENTY-FIVE

Mystified about what had just transpired, we stood in silence for a minute, staring at the space where Osborne had stood seconds before. All kinds of scenarios were running through my head, and none of them were good. "It's apparent that I'm toxic and that everyone I come in contact with is in danger!" I blurted out. Sweat had started to run down my back, making me feel chilled, and I had the sudden urge to vomit. As I ran to the bathroom, I tripped over a corner of the rug that was spread out, covering the hardwood floor throughout the cabin. What a klutz. I managed to get onto my knees before heaving uncontrollably. Luckily, I didn't have anything in my stomach, so it was all for show, but it left me trembling and wondering what I could possibly have done to warrant these adverse reactions from others. Tom didn't deserve this. But then, again, neither had Brie or my Dad. That was still assuming there was a correlation between the three and myself. Once again, I was reminded that Luke wasn't allowed out of my sight and that Lux and Quinn needed to be warned ASAP.

Looking up, I saw a concerned Luke hovering over me, offering a hand to help me up. In the past, when times had gotten rough and we were left with questions about why, we had tried to find humor in the situation and, more times than not, laughed till tears ran down our faces. It was great stress relief, but, today I couldn't even conjure up a smile. I was destroyed. I was confused, and I was mystified. But, most of all, I was heartbroken. Three deaths in a matter of weeks was daunting, to say the least.

"What is going on, Luke? I don't think I can take much more of this, and the thought of anything happening to you is unfathomable." He took me in one of his infamous hugs I had loved for years. For a second, I forgot about everything and reveled in the comfort of his embrace, feeling loved and cared for, but, above all, untouchable. I didn't want it to end.

I took a second to look at Luke—really, really look at him. I took in every wrinkle he had so proudly earned and every scar that told a story. I looked deep into his eyes, all the way to his soul. It was as if, subconsciously, I was expecting something to happen. I wanted to remember everything about him, in case the unthinkable became a reality. His eyes were brown, like murky lake water, with gold specks that sparkled like diamonds. His hair had turned gray over the years and had thinned; tufts floated like gray clouds atop his head. His smile was so genuine and warm that you couldn't help but feel his kindness and a sensation of being the most important person in his world. He was the most wonderful of humans, and he glowed with an angelic aura. I would rather die myself than let anything happen to him.

"Penny for your thoughts?" Luke inquired, bringing me out of my trance. "You were so intently staring at me, it was like you were memorizing every little detail in case something were to happen to me."

How was he so wise and intuitive? Or was I that transparent?

"I'm sorry. I didn't mean to weird you out. You know you mean the world to me, and, oftentimes, we take others for granted and stare past them instead of *at* them. I guess I somehow was searching for answers," I explained. "After all, you are one of the most intuitive and smartest men I know. If anyone could have ideas about what's going on, it would be you." As much as I wanted Luke to have answers, I knew he didn't—he would have shared them by now.

"Jonathan, what I want for you is to concentrate on getting yourself one hundred percent better. We will get to the bottom of this. I promise you, and you know that a promise is sacred to me. I don't make them lightly. I make them only when I know I won't have to break them." Oddly, this made me feel better about things. At least the part about getting to the bottom of this fiasco. It would take way more than a promise to make me feel better about my Dad being gone. It would take a miracle for that to happen.

The rest of the afternoon remained drama-free. I was afraid to show my face outside, in case someone was lurking behind a tree, ready to end my life. I couldn't and wouldn't live like this. I was too young to become a recluse. Instead, I stood gazing toward the barn, watching the horses having the time of their lives in the spring air. Flowers were in bloom, welcoming a new season and new beginnings, but neither of these things was something I felt confident about.

Luke had whipped up some of his legendary chicken soup. He was convinced it was comfort food and good for the soul. I still couldn't chew, but the broth was amazing and was just what the doctor ordered. We tackled my Dad's burial and funeral plans, and I felt somewhat accomplished with the progress we had made. The sun made its way down behind the magnificent mountains that surrounded his property. The sky was full of stars, and, against my better judgment, I opened the door to stand on the porch to wish on one. This was something I had done for years. It started after my Mom passed, and it was something I still did on a regular basis. I found astrology interesting and was the proud owner of my very own star in the galaxy.

And that's when I heard it—a terrifying scream that made the hair on the back of my neck stand up. Hearing this brought me immediately back to twenty years ago, when a blood-curdling scream started my investigation into the

Mount Sierra serial killer. The scream was coming from the forest, piercing through the night, waking the animals from their slumber. I held my breath, waiting to hear another one, but all I heard were owls hooting in the distance and some bullfrogs croaking nearby.

I wanted in the worst way to grab Luke and our forest gear, and head out, but I listened to reason and instead walked inside to find Luke in the kitchen, stirring a pot of hot chocolate over his Wolfe stove. I contemplated not telling him, partially because I knew he would feel like dropping everything and venturing out. I hesitated because I wasn't sure he was physically capable of it. The last thing I wanted was to put him in harm's way. If I knew him like I thought I did, he wouldn't want to let me down and would hide how he was feeling, to his detriment.

Instead, I sat down and began to beat my fingers against the table out of nervousness and pent-up energy. Subconsciously, my knee joined in, and my mind started to go places that were unthinkable. As much as I liked a good adventure and always thought Luke and I would take another together, I was still haunted by what had transpired years ago in the same forest. The darkness of the forest and dense tree cover partnered with the fact that it was off the beaten path and made it a perfect backdrop for gruesome activity.

The more I sat and thought about the scream, the more my mind questioned it. Was I imagining it? Was I making it into something more terrifying than it was? Could it have been an animal and not a human? I had been off my drugs for a while, allowing me to think more clearly, but I was on edge over just recently finding out about Tom and being accused. I was so absorbed in my thoughts. Going places I shouldn't, I didn't even notice Luke standing over me with a mug of steaming hot chocolate. I wasn't sure how long he had been standing there, but his glasses were fogged up, and he had a puzzled look on his face.

"What has made you a bundle of nerves and lost in space that you didn't see me?" he asked. He delicately placed the mug in front of me as he eased himself into the chair opposite me, groaning as if he were in pain.

"Forget about me, old man," I joked. "What's with the groan? Is there something you're not telling me?" That's all I needed on my plate—worrying about Luke. Through the years, he had suffered a lot of physical pain, coupled with a great deal of emotional pain. He was a Gulf War veteran and had been injured in battle. Not that any pain was good, but I was hoping it was a flare-up of that and nothing new.

Luke began to chuckle. I loved his laugh. It shook his robust belly and, more times than not, got me to join in. "I see what you're doing. You're trying to make this conversation about me, when it's you that we both should be concerned with," Luke kidded.

Uh, oh—he was on to me. He wasn't falling for my shit and shifted the conversation back to me.

With reassurances from Luke that he was fine—just old and arthritic—eased my mind a little. I wasn't entirely sure he was telling me the truth, even though I didn't see him lying to me, either. I caved, as I knew I would, and told Luke about the creepy, scary scream and asked what he thought it might mean. When I told him, though, I was wrong about his reaction. I initially thought he would be like me and want to investigate on the spot, but, instead, he approached it with a level head. Don't get me wrong—he was plenty suspicious but knew the timing wasn't right for either one of us to throw caution to the wind and take off exploring. He made a good point that I hadn't considered, and wondered if it could have been staged. If we had taken the bait, the creeps could have been lying in wait to ambush us the second we walked into the forest.

After discussing this further, I had to agree with him. That's precisely what was happening, I hoped, in a weird way. It was better than the alternative—that someone had been tortured or even possibly killed. I caught myself hunched over, wrapping my arms around myself in a hug. Just when I had convinced myself that it was only mind games, there was a loud *bang* outside the door that shook the windows. The entire cabin became illuminated in light, and we saw brightness—like something had been set on fire. Our first impulse was to run to the windows to look out, but even that simple act had to be considered. Was it another trap?

We both knew calling the Sheriff's Department wasn't an option. I wasn't altogether convinced Deputy Osborne wasn't behind some of this shady business. I wouldn't put it past him. After all, he was the spawn of the devil himself. We tried to ignore what was going on, but as the light got brighter and our curiosity grew, we knew something had to be done. We were both sweating bullets and holding our breath, as Luke armed himself. We gave each other a thumbs-up, and, as I peeked around the curtains, I couldn't believe my eyes.

CHAPTER TWENTY-SIX

There, before my eyes, was an inferno. Luke's truck was engulfed in flames. The windshield had blown out, and intense red flames were licking the hood and sweeping across the body, leaving the tires melting and dripping into hissing puddles. I yelled at Luke to call 911, but, not hearing a response, I realized he was gone. A sudden chill washed over me as my attention was drawn to the entryway, where the door was standing wide open, and a blistering hot breeze was slapping me in the face. As I ran outside, I saw Luke frantically spraying the fire with a hose but not making a dent, as the flames increased and began to spread. I ran back inside, calling 911, hoping and praying that the fire trucks would arrive before the fire reached the cabin.

There was a sharp, acrid smell permeating the air that was beginning to burn my already-compromised lungs. My nose began to burn, and darkness began to close on me like a velvet curtain that signaled the end of a theater performance. I woke up with a start as I inhaled a strong ammonia smell. As my eyes began to focus, I realized I was lying on the couch in Luke's cabin. He was standing over me, with my hand grasped tightly in his own giant paw. He was not alone, though, as a couple of paramedics, holding smelling salts, were hovering over me, taking vitals and asking me questions. Did I know where I was? What was my name? What day was it? That one stumped me because all my days had become a blur lately, one blending into the other.

I must have passed their test, because, after what seemed like a half an hour, they announced that I was free to stay here and that there would be no need to transport me back to the hospital. That was music to my ears. If I never saw that place again, it would be too soon. With my promise that I would see my regular doctor in the morning, they were off. That worked out perfectly, because I already had an appointment set up with Dr. *GQ* at 9 a.m. the next day.

Clearing the cobwebs out of my head and hearing Luke describe what had happened, I considered myself fortunate. While Luke had been fighting a losing battle, the fire trucks had shown up to save the day. The damage had been contained mostly to his truck, which was sitting outside, a smoldering heap of melted metal. Further investigations would have to take place, but our first, initial reaction was that a Molotov cocktail had been the culprit. Shards of a glass bottle were found lying on Luke's floorboard. Molotov cocktails were also known as a "poor man's grenade," which fit their persona. They were made by filling a bottle with combustible liquid, stuffing a fuel-soaked rag into the neck of the bottle, acting as a wick, and igniting it. It wouldn't surprise me in the least if that had been the cause. The lists of crimes they had committed continued to grow, as arson got added to murder, assault, and kidnapping.

Even after my marathon twelve-hour sleep, I was bone tired. I couldn't help thinking this was my body trying to deal with all of the mess surrounding my life, demanding sleep as a coping mechanism. I promised Luke we would talk in the morning and retired to the loft with a good book and Autumn following two steps behind me. As I curled up under the covers, I opened the book but had lost the desire to read. I lay still, subconsciously petting Autumn, who was pressed tight against me, spooning me. Before I knew it, my eyelids were heavy, and sleep overtook me.

The forest was dark and damp. I loved the smell the forest offered no matter what time of the year I was here. It was a mixture of moss, pine trees and campfire soot. My mind traveled back to twenty years before, when the smell of metal had permeated the air, with a tinge of cigar smoke. Tonight I smelled something different, and I couldn't place it yet. As I strained to see, I realized I had been blindfolded. I was being prodded in the back with some kind of sharp object like the end of an umbrella, but that seemed unlikely, since it hadn't rained in days. I stopped to get my bearings but found it impossible without vision. My other senses started kicking in, and I heard owls hooting, rodents scurrying up trees and the swaying of tree limbs . . . *swish, swish, swish.* The smell from before was familiar and nauseating, but it still escaped me.

My time of reflection must have taken too long, because I was being poked and shoved. Then, I heard a loud grumble, "Move your ass NOW!!!" Hearing this made me have an *a-ha* moment, and I was able to place the voice and smell. My mind wandered back to the morgue adventure and my captors. The smell of patchouli mixed with week-old sweat assaulted my nostrils. I tried to scream, out of instinct alone, but the second I opened my mouth, I was pushed to the ground. "No funny business, asshole!" he yelled.

Sweat started rolling down my back, and I painfully stood up, brushing off pine needles and moss from my trousers. My mind was once again playing mind games with me. As much as I told myself not to panic, I felt myself start to hyperventilate as my heart thumped so loud I was sure they could hear it. When I was younger, I would calm myself by going to my happy place to escape my present situation. Conjuring up images of my time on the farm, nuzzling the horses and riding them as the wind blew away my troubles, seemed to calm me for a second.

As I made my way deeper and deeper into the forest, being poked and prodded the whole way, I soon noticed a change. I wasn't sure what was entirely different about it, but the swaying of the trees was less evident, which made me think we had arrived at a clearing of sorts. A warm sensation enveloped my body, and I started sweating again, but, this time, not from terror. The mask was ripped off my eyes, and I was standing smack dab in front of a firepit. Not the same firepit I had seen in the past, but one that was bigger, with a spit ranging at least six feet in width. Boulders had been placed around the edges. Inside, pine needles and wood had been placed and ignited. Popping and hissing could be heard as the fire caught and started to gain ground. Within a matter of minutes, the flames were licking the sky.

Wondering what the hell was going on, I stood glaring at a trio of tattooed, long-haired, smelly heathens. They were whispering among themselves, but every now and then, I caught a word here and there. I heard them mention their boss and my Dad more than once. Before I could put two and two together, they disappeared behind a tree and came back dragging something behind them. Was it some kind of animal, and what did they have planned? I was imagining them roasting a wild boar on the spit, but was I ever wrong! Because, out of nowhere, my Dad appeared, blindfolded and gagged.

I yelled to him but was immediately punched in the gut and shoved to the ground. I watched in horror as my Dad's gag and blindfold were removed, and he was maneuvered onto the spit, screaming blood-curdling screams. He was being burned alive, and I was forced to watch the horror unfold while they all laughed—like they were having a party. I must have yelled because the next thing I knew, Luke was sitting next to me with a concerned look and assurance that we would get through this. All I could think was *Thank God it was a nightmare,* but why did it seem so real? Subconsciously, my mind was conjuring images of my Dad as he met his maker.

Melting into Luke's arms, I let him comfort me. I didn't care that I was a grown man—I needed him right now, almost as much as I had ever needed him before. I sat in silence while he patted my back and promised me it would be all right. I wanted to believe him, but I didn't. I had the strongest feeling that this was just the beginning of a very long year that would change who I was. What you went through defined who you were and what you became. I didn't want to change. I liked who I was. I was just Jonathan, but I stood for so much that was good and pure in the world. I didn't want to become bitter, suspicious and callous to life. If only I knew the reason these things were happening, maybe then I could change the course of my life. But that was a tall order.

CHAPTER TWENTY-SEVEN

W hy does the middle of the night seem scarier and sinister, leaving you vulnerable? After I had calmed down and explained my nightmare to Luke, he understood completely what had left me shaken and in a puddle of sweat. I hadn't seen a therapist in years—actually since a year after my Mom's death—but the more I thought about it, the better the idea sounded. I was clearly in over my head and knew from past experiences that keeping it bottled up was more detrimental in the long run. Note to self: Ask Luke if our therapist from years ago was still practicing. She had been a Godsend and had helped me come to terms with my Mom's death. She gave me the confidence to believe in myself again.

Luke, having left earlier, begged me to get more sleep, but as I tossed and turned, trying my hardest, I was dreading another nightmare leaving me conflicted. The clock said three a.m. An ungodly hour to be awake. Something about the wee night hours always brought out negativity in me, as opposed to during the day, when I was upbeat. At least I used to be upbeat. It's as if a dark cloud hovered over the house, chucking my positive, happy thoughts out the window and replacing them with menacing, foreboding thoughts. The more I tried to sleep, the harder it became, so I gave up. Rolling out of bed was more difficult when it was dark outside, too. It was all mental but, all the same, real to me. I tried not to wake Autumn as she lay sprawled on her back with her paws straight in the air, but I failed. She bounded off the bed, eagerly licking me and begging for pets and ear scratches.

I expected to be alone, but when I entered the kitchen, there sat Luke at the kitchen table, hunched over, with his head resting on top of his folded arms. I thought he had passed out from exhaustion, but I was wrong. Dead wrong. He was weeping. I was torn over whether I should leave him in peace to cry it out alone, or console him, like he had done for me so many times in the past. I really wasn't much help these days and figured I would do more harm than good, so I turned, tiptoeing out of the room. I would have been successful if it hadn't been for Autumn. She got so excited when she saw Luke that she let out a high-pitched squeal, looking for a toy to put in her mouth.

He lifted his head, wiped the wetness from his tear-streaked face with the sleeve of his red plaid robe and blew his nose loud enough to wake the dead. He was startled to see me standing there but welcomed me with a warm smile. "Hi, son. What a lovely surprise. I'm not quite sure why you're up at this hour, but I'll make us a pot of coffee, and we can both welcome in a new day together." There was no mention of the tears, and I remained quiet until he was ready to talk about it—if ever. Knowing Luke, he wouldn't, because he wouldn't want to burden me. He had always looked out for my best interests and tried his hardest to shield me from the bad in the world. Unfortunately, he was failing miserably this time, because bad was prevailing and sucking the goodness out of us both.

Being up at this hour ended up being a blessing in disguise. We sat quietly at the kitchen table, sipping our coffee and talking about our fondest memories of my Dad. Luke lit some candles, and we both ended up shedding a tear or two, but, in the long run, it was therapeutic, and, in a weird way, it felt like we had honored him. Just Luke and I. Earlier in the day, we had planned his memorial service, which was set for three days from now. For obvious reasons, there would be no viewing, but the service we had arranged would offer closure to his friends and co-workers. We owed him that.

As we watched the sun come up, we heard the roosters welcoming a new day—a day that I hoped and prayed would be a turning point for me. We needed to tend to the farm animals, but, quite frankly, I was scared shitless to walk outside. Luke and I figured there was safety in numbers, so, mustering up all the courage we could, we ventured out, both packing heat. I wasn't very good at shooting, and my aim was awful, but I knew I could scare the crap out of them, and that's really what mattered in the long run, anyway.

As one of us collected eggs, the other stood watch. We fed the animals and watched as the sun rose over the picturesque mountains that encompassed Luke's land. There was a slight breeze in the air, and it smelled like new beginnings. I was glad we had stared danger in the face and overcome our fears to venture outside. I wasn't about to live my whole life in fear, but it was all about balance. Seeing the animals with all their unconditional love always brought joy to my heart. I stood, staring up at the sky, letting the sun warm myself and my soul. The sun had a way of making me feel good physically as well as emotionally, and it gave me a sense of power like I was a badass, ready to take on the world.

Thankfully, the morning proved uneventful, and we made it to the hospital for my exam with Dr. *GQ* without incident. I sat fidgeting, twiddling my thumbs and looking around nervously. Sitting in the waiting room proved to be insufferable. I picked up a magazine sitting on the side table, trying to lose myself in an article about dogs. There was a team of researchers that had developed a program to interpret dog barks. Even though I found this very interesting, I was still feeling agitated and jumpy.

The sunshine and positivity from earlier was gone. My suspicions about everyone had multiplied tenfold, and it was becoming near impossible for me not to think I was about to be stabbed from behind or tackled to the ground before I was injected with lethal poison. Or worse, someone would attack Luke. I was barely living with the guilt I had, thinking I was responsible for three deaths. I was afraid a fourth would push me over the edge.

Feeling like I was being watched, I jerked my head toward the entrance and saw him. One of the slimy, tattooed guys, in all his disgusting glory, was standing there, staring me down. Could I really smell him from here, or was I imagining it? He had that unkempt dirty look to him that made him look like he stank. Even though I was about to crap my pants, I wasn't about to let him see the intimidation on my face, so I stared back, not blinking. Alerting Luke to the danger, I kicked him in the shin and motioned with my hand in my lap toward the door, trying to be inconspicuous. He winked and whispered in a low tone that he had my back. Minutes continued to tick away as I shut out the world around me. It was me and the tattoo man in a stare-off that I was determined to win. I could have been in an isolated room, because I heard nothing around me except my heartbeat deep in my chest.

Time stood still, and I was not even aware that my name had been called multiple times before Luke tapped me on the shoulder to bring me out of my trance. I was bummed that I was the one who had to avert my eyes, but having the last laugh, I waved my middle finger in his direction as I followed the nurse into the hallway that led to my examining room. My life had been so unpredictable lately that it was hard to guess what was going to happen next, but one thing was for certain: I was positive this wouldn't be the last run-in I'd have with this guy.

My legs and feet dangled off the edge of the examining table, as I sat, agitated, picking a hangnail I had started in the corner of my thumb. My breathing had calmed considerably, but I wouldn't have been the least bit surprised if my blood pressure was off the charts. For the love of God! Why wouldn't these jerks give me a second to collect myself without breathing down my back? I was getting the message loud and clear that they weren't my biggest fans. Far from it—more like public enemy number one.

The second I was about to jump down to go check on Luke, Dr. *GQ* sauntered through the door, looking like he'd just walked off the runway. He was dressed to the nines in a custom-cut Tom Ford gray-pinstriped suit over a pink dress shirt and a pink and gray matching paisley tie. A pink pocket square that matched his shirt poked out of his pocket. What had I heard before . . . real men wear pink? No white lab coat for this guy. He held out his hand to shake mine while flashing his pearly whites. "Jonathan, so nice to see you looking better than the last time. I see you must be following the doctor's orders and getting lots of rest and staying out of trouble." If he only knew what had been taking place, he'd probably soil his pants. In that second, I decided to keep him in the dark. What he didn't know wouldn't hurt him, and repeating it would only serve to get my blood pressure boiling again.

CHAPTER TWENTY-SEVEN

Upon the conclusion of my exam, it turned out that my luck wasn't in the shitter after all, because I was given props for my progress. The packing was removed from my nose, and I felt like a million bucks. My chest was sounding clear, and my cuts and broken ribs were healing nicely. Now, if I could get my jaw to cooperate with the rest of my body, I was certain I would dance a little jig right there for all to see.

Making an appointment to be seen again in a week, I felt like a new man. I'm sure I still looked like death, but baby steps were all I could expect right now. Before joining Luke, I took a second to inspect the room for shady-looking characters. The room was relatively bare, which I found encouraging. We were free and clear for the time being, so I called out Luke's name. There was no response. It's like he hadn't even heard me. As I walked closer, I called out to him again. Still nothing. Panicked at this point, I ran the couple-of-feet distance between us and stood frozen.

CHAPTER TWENTY-EIGHT

ooking at Luke, I wasn't sure he was alive. He was sitting slumped over, with his chin resting against his chest. In the few seconds it took me to take this all in, a hundred million scenarios ran on a reel through my mind. I started to feel nauseous as I looked around. Everything seemed in place. There was an older gentleman in a black trench coat and brown, weathered derby hat, holding a cane, hovering in the corner; a young mother with a nose piercing was happily sitting, reading to a little girl on her lap with braids. The air in the room was stale, and, even though my packing had been removed, I had to draw a deep breath in through my mouth. I tasted something rancid. Does fear have a taste?

I kneeled in front of Luke and shook him gently while pleading and praying that he was still alive. He opened his eyes and raised his head slowly; he looked through me like he didn't recognize me or didn't know where he was. His coloring was ashen, and he looked old. Even though I had given him the once-over the other day, he looked older and confused. Somehow, he kept aging right before my eyes.

"Luke, Luke! Are you okay? What happened? Did the tattoo guy hurt you? Do you need some water?"

I was practically in tears waiting for his response, and, when he spoke, it made no sense.

"Who are you, and what have you done with my wife?" he said, slurring his words.

Clearly something was amiss. Had he suffered a stroke? Had the creepy guy injected him with something?

With fear gripping me, I mumbled, "Luke, it's me. Jonathan. Stay put while I get help."

Today was proving to be luckier than I thought when I had woken up at 3:00 this morning. Luke was apparently still alive. Not wanting to leave Luke's side, I stepped a couple feet away from him and yelled across the room to the receptionist, who was sitting behind the counter window, filing her nails and blowing the biggest bubbles I had ever seen. I couldn't help but think she must have had a minimum of five pieces of gum in her mouth to create those bubbles, half the size of her face.

"Excuse me, Ma'am. Can you please help?" She glanced up at me, irritated that I had interrupted her, as a massive bubble popped in her face, leaving residue on her eyelashes. *Serves her right.*

"My friend seems to be in some kind of distress, and I don't want to leave him. Could you please send help?" I pleaded.

I wanted to jump over the counter and bitch-slap the attitude right out of her, but, instead, I decided to kill her with kindness. With an audible sigh, she got up and disappeared into the back office. While I waited, I sat next to Luke and put his massive hand in mine. I rubbed his back and reassured him that help was on the way. The older gentleman from the corner appeared out of nowhere, holding a cup of water and offering a heartfelt smile.

Minutes later, Dr. *GQ* was standing in front of Luke, asking him question after question. I was starting to think I had made the whole thing up, because Luke's color was back to normal, and he was coherent, answering every question accurately every time. The doctor looked at me, confused, like I was the one who might need a mental evaluation. *It might not be a bad idea.*

"Doctor, I swear to you, when I came from seeing you, Luke was talking nonsense and looked like a cadaver. He didn't even know who I was and was asking where his *wife* was. Might I add that she has been dead for close to fifty years."

Now it was my turn to answer questions; as Luke looked on, concern flooded his eyes. I was positive about what I had seen and heard, so the only explanation was exhaustion. I had woken Luke from a much-needed nap and caught him off guard. He was probably dreaming about his wife, Claire, like he frequently did, and, in his dazed state, he had spoken before he was fully awake.

Thankfully, to err on the side of caution, the doctor took Luke back into the examining room, while I—not too patiently—waited, pacing back and forth. Was I the root cause of this, too? I had always prided myself on being a stand-up guy, but, with all that had happened, I was beginning to doubt my own morality at this point in time.

By the time Luke returned, I had all but worn a hole in the carpet. My mind was back to thinking negatively, and I was left wondering how I could go on if something happened to Luke. I wasn't a worst-case-scenario kinda guy, and my glass was always half full. But, I *was* human, after all, and everyone has their tipping point—the point where they call it quits and wallow in self-pity. I would fight that tooth and nail, but I knew myself well enough to know that I could never, ever forgive myself if I inadvertently caused Luke harm.

I wanted to scream for joy when the doctor reassured me that all was fine on the Luke front; he was probably suffering only from pure exhaustion. The past couple of weeks had taken their toll on him. He had barely slept a wink, between worrying about me, dealing with my Dad's relapse and trying to come to terms with my Dad's death, not to mention the firebombing of his truck. He admitted that he was putting on a brave face and that, inside, he was crumbling right before my eyes, afraid to sleep. Having these creeps watching our every move was not only frightening, but now it had also become detrimental to our health.

Refusing to let Luke drive me back to the cabin, I got behind the wheel to drive us home. I planned a pit stop to pick up shakes, and homeward bound we were, until I noticed the car was off kilter. Pulling over, I got out to inspect the car, only to find two of the tires had been slashed. I second-guessed my flipping off the guy at my doctor's appointment because this may have been his retaliation. Or maybe not. These guys were taking every opportunity to act out against us, and I was fed up with it all.

I practically had to threaten Luke within an inch of his life to get him to stay seat-belted in while I called AAA and addressed the tire situation. I was getting better at not being self-conscious of my appearance, at least with strangers, anyway. I knew I looked something short of human, but it was what it was. I visualized random people who came into contact with me, not knowing my backstory, getting together with their friends and trying to explain the monster they'd met that day. I figured, *What the heck—let them have a laugh at my expense. Or a nightmare.* I was fine with either one.

I was all but convinced the slashers were one and the same as the arsonists, murderers and lowlife scum-suckers extraordinaire. I promised myself that, as soon as I got home, I was going to pull out a journal and document this stuff. There had been so many incidents that I was afraid I'd leave something out. Then, when the time came to bring these jerks down, I wouldn't have my ducks in a row. Visions of them dying in the electric chair danced in my head as I headed back to the cabin.

As we pulled up front, there was a surprise waiting for us. Sitting on the bench on the porch was none other than Lux and Quinn, with a happy Autumn, wagging her tail and standing by their feet. I tried to contain my giddiness, but Luke caught me with a shit-eating grin on my face and chuckled.

"Go get your girl, son!" he said.

Had I been that transparent? She had been occupying a good portion of my waking moments—and dreams, too, for that matter. I had to admit: I was smitten.

She looked every bit as beautiful as I remembered from the other night. Her strawberry-blond hair hung loosely down to her shoulders, blowing slightly in the breeze. She was wearing cat's-eye sunglasses, but I knew that, under those, her beautiful green eyes twinkled. As we got out of the car, she waved. Her smile—not to mention those dimples—was so beautiful that it took my breath away. At that moment, I knew she was the one for me—the one I would fall in love with and build a life with. Years ago, I'd heard my Mom and Dad talk about love at first sight, and now I knew firsthand what they had experienced. Now, more than ever, I ached for my parents to be alive so that they could meet my future wife and watch our life together unfold.

Keenly aware of my appearance, I tried to hide behind Luke as we made our way up the walkway, but he was having no part of it. He playfully pushed me toward her and chuckled, while giving me a thumbs-up and mumbling something inaudible under his breath. As we approached, Lux and Quinn stood and walked toward us, while Autumn came barreling full steam ahead, shrieking and carrying on as if we'd been gone for a month. She couldn't contain her excitement and jumped up on Luke, catching him off guard and making him stumble. I barely caught him before he hit the ground. Another broken bone or trip to the emergency room was not something either one of us wanted. Knowing Luke was fine, my eyes focused on Quinn. I looked her up and down in complete awe and admiration. She stood about 5'7", with a thin build but not skinny. She looked athletic under her boyfriend jeans and navy-blue cardigan that she had smartly placed over a plain, white, button-up Oxford shirt. In all her simplicity, she was still breathtakingly, drop-dead gorgeous.

"What a pleasant surprise to see you two. I hope you haven't been waiting too long," I said, trying to camouflage my enthusiasm.

I really couldn't have cared less if Lux was there or not, but, since they were a package deal, I figured I might as well be cordial to him. Wanting to look debonair, I was ever so thankful that I had been to the doctor and the nose packing had been removed. As every hour went by, I was slowly but surely starting to resemble my old self, one I was hoping she would find handsome and irresistible. The dried blood that had been caked around my nose and the corners of my mouth had been cleaned up, and I looked human—in an apocalyptic kind of way, at least.

The closer I got to her, the more the butterflies started their mating dance within my stomach. I caught a whiff of her perfume, and I was immediately transported back twenty-plus years ago. Lavender with a hint of vanilla wafted through my now-freed-up nostrils, and I felt a tear form in the corner of my eye. It was the same perfume my mother used to wear. I was flooded with memories of my Mom and of our time together as a family as well as our time we had sharing special Mom-and-son moments. It was as if time was standing still as I made my way down memory lane, and it was Luke's turn to shake me and ask me if I was all right.

Coming out of my trance, I was greeted with concerned looks from Luke, Quinn and Lux. Autumn pawed at my leg while whimpering.

With a quavering voice, Luke asked, "Jonathan, are you all right? You have me worried, son."

One of the many reasons that Luke and I got along so well was because we were two peas in a pod. We were both in touch with our feminine side, not afraid to wear our heart on our sleeve—or any other cliches you could think of to explain sensitivity in a guy. For a second, I considered making up a lie as to why I had wandered off into LaLa Land, but I wanted to start off my relationship with Quinn on a positive, honest note.

"I'm sorry, you guys. I didn't mean to concern any of you, but, quite honestly, Quinn's perfume is the same one my

Mom used to wear, and it caught me off guard. I took a trip down memory lane for a second," I confessed.

Turns out honesty was the best decision, because Quinn reached out and pulled me into the most gentle, caring hug I had ever felt. If hugs could talk, this one would have said, "I'm so sorry for your loss, and I'm here for you, no matter what." I didn't want it to end, but neither did I want to seem like a creeper, so I pulled away. I was on cloud ten, because clearly cloud nine wasn't high enough for the way I was feeling. We locked eyes, and, at that moment, I knew she felt the same pull that I did. To say I was ecstatic wouldn't have been adequate to explain how I was feeling. Our pull toward each other must have been stronger than I'd thought, if she was able to see past my present state and visualize who I really was. At that moment, I wanted more than anything to be alone with her, without a care in the world. Unfortunately, I was keenly aware of Luke and Lux looming in the background, acting like we were invisible, talking between themselves.

Autumn sat impatiently by my feet, waiting for her pets, while I continued to hold Quinn's hand in mine. "Would you like to come inside so that Luke and I can catch you up on the latest?" At the mention of his name, Luke turned and hobbled toward us, with Lux in tow. There was a lot that had happened in a short time that needed to be addressed, and there was no time like the present.

Once inside, we again all settled around the kitchen table as Luke busied himself with grinding fresh coffee beans for a pot of coffee and putting together a charcuterie board that would rival anything Julia Child had ever whipped up. I guess it was time to add creativity to his long list of talents. As I longingly looked on as they all devoured olives, cheeses, crackers, salami, and such, I wiped saliva from the corner of my mouth before it landed on the table and caused me embarrassment. I would have to be satisfied with Ensure through a straw for the time being, but I was thinking, *Watch out, everyone—don't get in my way once I'm given the green light to eat again.*

I sat, mesmerized by Quinn's beauty, soaking up all her mannerisms as she munched on crackers and nonchalantly brushed a crumb off the corner of her mouth. She must have felt my gaze, because she stopped what she was doing and looked my way with an innocent smile. There was something easy about the way she carried herself and in the way she spoke. I was left wondering if I was the only one that was noticing or if she had that effect on everyone. We had so many things to discuss—my life had been a complete whirlwind lately, but all I wanted to do was sit and talk to her for hours about the little things that made her who she was. I felt an indescribable desire to know her favorite color, what she ate for breakfast and where she last went on vacation. I wanted to know every single fact in great detail that made her the woman I was already head over heels for.

To my dismay, this would have to wait. Luke got up and was pacing back and forth as he cleared his throat to get my attention. I had never known him to be an impatient man, but the stress of the past weeks, coupled with his lack of sleep, had definitely begun to take its toll on him. What nerves he had left were frayed and frazzled, at best. I understood, because I was feeling the same way, except for Quinn getting my mind and heart thinking differently. For the first time in weeks, I was hopeful that my life was taking a turn for the better. That is, until there was an extra loud *bang* at the door and a whole bunch of commotion outside drew my attention elsewhere.

We all four heard it at the same time and jumped out of our skin, looking puzzled at one another. "What in tarnation is all the racket outside?" Luke questioned as he ran toward the window to peek out. "Oh, for the love of God, there are at least ten Sheriff's cars by the barn."

He sounded pissed as he limped to the door, cursing under his breath. I was almost afraid to follow, not knowing what had happened this time, but noticing Quinn's interest was piqued, I put on a brave face and followed close behind Luke.

Luke opened the door to none other than Mr. Cranky Pants himself, Deputy Sheriff Osborne. He stood leaning all his weight against the door frame, looking smug like the cat who had just swallowed the canary. I'm not sure how many deputies were employed with the Sheriff's Department, but with him was someone whom I had not had the displeasure of meeting in the past. Osborne hovered over him while the other guy stood visibly shaking with what I could only imagine was intimidation. It was a good thing Osborne had chosen this line of work, because I kept thinking about what a horrible bedside manner he would have if he were a doctor.

"It is imperative that you two, pointing to Luke and myself, follow me to the barn because you have some serious explaining to do. And you, Elliott, no funny business. In fact, you need to come up in front where I can keep an eye on you," Osborne spat out.

Before I could object, he grabbed my arm and jerked me to his side, knocking Quinn over.

"Get your hands off of me," I angrily yelled, trying desperately to get to Quinn's side as she lay in the bush that adorned Luke's cabin.

He wasn't letting go, and I pleaded with Lux to go assist her. "Who do you think you are—coming over here and raising havoc? This is personal property, and you're not welcome!"

I didn't often get mad, but I was pissed and saw stars. Before I knew it, Luke was in Osborne's face faster than I could say boo. For such a big guy, he was surprisingly agile, which came as a complete shock to me. Screaming in Osborne's face, spit flying everywhere, Luke was bright red and angrier than I ever imagined he could get.

"Get your filthy hands off of him NOW. How dare you come on my property and manhandle my son? If you know what's good for you, you'll leave now, while you can!"

While tightening his grip on me, Osborne stood his ground, looking at Luke like he had lost his mind and gone too far.

"Old man, I don't know who you think you are talking to me that way, because I have every reason to be here. I am a man of the law, and there has been a murder on your property. I have reason to believe Elliott is responsible, and I'm not giving him the opportunity to run."

"A *what*? A . . . *murder*? On Luke's property? What are you talking about?" I managed to eek out, looking on, not believing my ears.

I must have looked as shocked as I felt because Quinn, Luke and Lux in unison all asked if I was all right. Before I could say another word, Luke punched Osborne with the best left jab I had ever seen. In all fairness, I hadn't seen a ton, but this was impressive, nonetheless. Osborne had not seen it coming and fell like a deck of cards. As I stood there dumbfounded and at a loss for what to do next, Lux pulled Luke off of Osborne before any more damage could take place. Luke had a look of hatred in his eyes, and a crazy-huge vein had popped out on his forehead.

"Luke, what have you done? Have you gone mad? I appreciate you coming to my defense, but I'm pretty sure violence is not the answer here," I said, imploring him to come to his senses.

The other deputy was bent down on the ground, trying to slap Osborne awake, when another Sheriff's car came buzzing toward us, sirens blaring, stopping abruptly, and leaving us all in a cloud of dust. Everything had happened so fast, I hadn't had a second to check on Quinn, but when I looked around, I saw her standing off to the side with a concerned look on her face. What the hell had just happened? The bigger question was *Why?*

CHAPTER THIRTY

sborne was out cold, and I was starting to get concerned about what this could mean for Luke. I knew we were all innocent of the supposed murder, but Luke could easily be charged with aggravated assault if push came to shove, and I wouldn't put anything past Osborne. He was a man on a mission to bring us down, once and for all. *For what*, I still wasn't sure, but what I did know was that people on missions were the hardest to deal with. They rarely listen to reason and most always end up causing more harm than good. We had trouble brewing, and I wasn't a bit happy about it.

As I looked at all the chaos going on, I contemplated Osborne being behind the killings and the other heinous acts that had been going on. It was a possibility worth investigating, but my gut was telling me otherwise. My gut was wise, and I had no reason to doubt it now. Which left me with the ever-present looming question . . . then, who?

Feeling something brush against my side and smelling lavender and vanilla, I turned to see Quinn standing next to me. She took my hand in hers and gave me a reassuring squeeze. At least that's the way I was interpreting it. Whatever the reason, it felt good. Warm and soft, like it belonged there. I felt goosebumps make the hair on my arms stand up, like I was a teenager again. I had missed this feeling. The warmness in the pit of your stomach, the joy in your heart, but, most of all, the wanting to be alone with just that person, shutting out the world and becoming one.

My mind had wandered, so I was surprised when Luke spoke. "So—you three, what are your thoughts?" That was a loaded question that needed a minute or two to decipher. Was he referring to Osborne, who was now sitting up, looking more pissed than ever, brushing dirt off his uniform and massaging his jaw? Was he referring to the so-called murder in the barn? Or did he really know who the mastermind was behind this craziness?

This prompted me to look toward the barn, and all I saw was a sea of khaki swarming in and out of the barn, spooking the horses. I could hear a lot of talking, but I couldn't make out any words. Whatever they were saying, I was more than positive it was not going to be good news for me—or Luke, for that matter. Today was turning out to be a shitshow—except for my hug from Quinn. I looked her way and gave her a wink before meandering toward the barn. She, Luke and Lux followed close behind.

There was no time like the present to find out once and for all what had supposedly happened and what we were up against. But finding out *why* would have to wait for another day. The wind had picked up and was swirling around, creating little tornadoes of dirt and hay. I had to laugh as I saw a couple of campaign hats getting caught up, causing the deputies to run after them, like kids chasing a ball on the playground. I guess we are all kids at heart, to a certain degree.

Having Osborne momentarily out of the picture was, hopefully, my opportunity to be treated with respect and their chance to be forthcoming with information before jumping to conclusions. I wasn't in any kind of mood to be playing mind games, and I certainly was not about to be accused of something I had no part in.

We walked up to the barn, and the horses immediately caught sight of us and began neighing and prancing around. They were agitated, running to and fro, causing dirt to collect in the air. The mood had a strange vibe to it and seemed something just short of jovial. Was it a tool of the trade that one became callous to death?

The compassionate shorter deputy from the hospital, Deputy Titus, approached us as we stood at the entrance of the barn. All I could see was yellow caution tape strung from one pole to the next and hanging down from the rafters. I saw a sea of red, splattered on a bale of hay and a body bag zipped on the ground next to the horse stables. There must have been at least 25 uniformed deputies milling around, shooting the shit with one another and having a grand old time. I couldn't help but hope there wasn't another emergency that required their assistance, because with a town the size of Mount Sierra, I was pretty sure this was the whole department.

When he spoke, he was barely audible and non-accusatory. Hearing his voice, the other gentlemen stopped talking and were *all ears*. "Have you had a conversation with Deputy Osborne yet? And by the way, where is he?" he inquired. Filling him in on the slightest of details, I let him know that Osborne would be here shortly and asked to be filled in on what had transpired in the barn. Thankfully, I was not accused of any foul play. He explained that, at about two p.m. an anonymous tip had been called in to the department, regarding a potential homicide out on the Travers property. At that time, a patrol car was alerted and made their way over to do the initial investigating. Upon their arrival, before they entered the barn, they made an attempt to make contact with anyone at the main house. No one was available.

This was about the time we were all in the kitchen, and Luke was whipping up his charcuterie board. I had to call bullshit on us "being contacted," because we had not heard a knock on the door until Osborne's rude banging on it. He started shooting daggers at all of us with his eyes minutes before we got here, but I remained quiet and listened intently.

As he continued on, he explained, upon entering the barn, a male body was spotted over by one of the horse stalls. Upon closer investigation, he was found to be unresponsive, covered in blood with what appeared to be a gunshot to the heart. I watched him intently as he spoke, but he showed no emotion. I found this very strange. If *I* had stumbled upon a murder, I would be shitting my pants, barfing in the bushes or, at the very least, showing it in my facial expressions. Nope, nothing.

The mention of murder caught Quinn off-guard; she let out a gasp and looked as if she were about to faint. Her coloring went from rosy to white within a matter of seconds. I reached for her just as her knees began to buckle, and caught her in my arms. Carrying her over to a hay bale on the opposite side of where the body bag lay, I sat her down. Taking her hands in mine, it was just us. I was aware there was a great deal of activity around us, but, to me, it was she and I caught in a moment of vulnerability. Her breathing was labored, and, despite the cool temperature, a trail of sweat ran down the side of her face before plopping down on her jeans. When she spoke, it was a whisper—breathy, and it smelled like strawberries.

"Jonathan, are we in danger by being here? Shouldn't we leave immediately and let them continue their investigation?"

This was a strange question coming from a private investigator, who, I supposed, had been in some sticky, stressful situations in the past. The only thing I could attribute it to was that this was hitting too close to home and affecting those she cared about. I didn't dare say *love*, because, even though I knew what I was feeling, I wouldn't begin to put words in her mouth or heart. With all that happening, all I could think about was taking care of her. I took that as my cue to take her back to the cabin, and the sooner, the better.

Not that I felt like I needed to give the deputies a play-by-play of my actions. I did anyway. I excused myself and let them know where I would be if further questions were to arise. Luke gave me a pat on the shoulder and assured me he would oversee the crime scene. I was thankful for him, but, at the same time, I wasn't confident I could trust him to keep a level head. Losing his temper on Osborne was way out of character for him, and I was certain he was on the verge of losing it again if someone even so much as looked sideways at him. Pleading with my eyes to Lux to keep Luke subdued, I made my way back to the cabin with Quinn nestled tightly in my grasp.

I had never been the type of man to shy away from a confrontation, but it wasn't about me this time. Well, it *was* about me, but I had more pressing matters to attend to. I knew there was no way on God's green Earth I was going to be left alone for more than a few minutes, so I needed to use my time wisely and make sure Quinn felt secure and safe.

Glancing at the spot where Luke and Osborne had had their altercation was not the smartest of moves on my part, but I couldn't help myself. It was a bustle of activity and had been joined by an ambulance and even more deputies, all milling about. It reminded me of a bunch of ants swarming on a piece of donut that had fallen from the sticky fingers of a toddler. I gave the area a wide berth but noticed Osborne was standing. I could hear bits and pieces of him answering the paramedics' questions. He didn't appear to be any worse for wear, but I was still worried about where Luke's actions might lead. Osborne saw me walk by, and our eyes met for a brief second, but, surprisingly enough, he looked away. He had bigger fish to fry at the moment, and Luke was the shark Osborne was about to spear.

Once inside, I laid Quinn down on the sofa and went to get her a glass of water, while Autumn hovered over Quinn, licking her hand. Dogs have a sixth sense and are keenly aware of danger or any type of change of behavior or dynamic. I was torn, because, as much as I wanted and needed to be by Quinn's side, the activity outside was pulling at me. I knew there was a storm brewing, and I needed to be in the know so I wouldn't be caught with my thumb up my ass.

Needing to see the body before it was hauled away was crucial. It was obviously vital to see who had perished, but, most importantly, it was essential to see with my own two eyes that there was, indeed, a dead body in the zipped-up body bag. I had my doubts. What little I saw *looked* like a crime scene, but was it really, or could it have been staged to place blame?

Really, all I knew was hearsay. If the mastermind behind all these crazy incidents wanted to set me up, it wouldn't have been difficult. Fake blood can be purchased anywhere, and, for all I knew, there was hay shoved inside the bag. Knowing it would be on my mind until seeing it with my own eyes, I decided there was no time like the present to let Quinn know.

"How are you feeling?" I asked as I stroked her arm and propped a pillow behind her head. The color had returned to her cheeks, and, once again, I was lost momentarily in her green eyes. "I don't want to leave you, but my gut is telling me that things are about to turn ugly outside. I never have been one to ignore my gut, and I don't want to start now, but, honestly, you are my number-one priority. I'll deal with the aftermath later if need be."

She sat up and smiled the most beautiful smile I had ever seen, and she grabbed my hand, leading me to the door. "I'm good. Don't worry about me. I had a weak moment, but I'm solid now. I'm in total agreement with you." And with that, we were out the door, this time with Autumn happily wagging her tail as she strolled next to us.

Walking out the front door was all that was needed to know that things had gone south, real fast. Although the barn was at least 300 yards or so away, I could hear screaming and a scuffle taking place, causing dirt to fly. The horses were all in a tizzy, letting out distressed neighs. Autumn took off in a full sprint with some kind of sixth sense all dogs seem to possess. I looked for Luke's goliath stature, but he was nowhere to be seen. It was out of my hands right now, but I was hoping with everything that I had that he wasn't the one in the scuffle. My Dad's funeral was set to take place in three days, and I didn't need the extra hassle of dealing with the aftermath of Luke's temper.

With Quinn's hand in mine, we cautiously made our way over to the barn. Standing around in a circle, the deputies were whooping it up and having a good old time, like they were watching a pig race at the county fair. I half expected them to be taking bets on the outcome that was going on before our eyes. There were no pigs racing, and, instead, I saw Luke and Osborne rolling around throwing punch after punch. Luke was not a young man anymore, and I feared for the outcome. Appalled at the audacity of the situation, I searched the crowd for Lux, needing answers immediately. All I could see were deputies acting like children, forgetting that they were men of the law.

I looked down at Quinn—she, too, was wearing a look of disgust. "Have you seen Lux?" I inquired. A shrug of her shoulders told me all I needed to know. I tapped a deputy on the shoulder, asking politely if he could please get this fight under control. The response I got angered me even more. He sneered at me and said, "Are you out of your mind? This is the most fun I've had since Uncle Bob fell off the ladder while hanging Christmas lights." This guy was a bundle of laughs, not to mention not the least bit concerned.

For some strange reason, I felt very protective of Quinn and didn't want her to be a part of this male machismo at its worst, so I walked her over to the back side of the barn, where we were somewhat out of sight. We were definitely not out of noise range, as cheers erupted, encouraging Osborne to kick Luke in the balls and put an end to him once and for all. I didn't like the sound of that in the least, and it was out of hand. I pleaded with Quinn to stay put, and I promised that I would return momentarily. She could see how distressed I was and agreed without so much as an inkling of an argument. God bless her.

As I rounded the corner, I ran smack dab into Lux. I had never been so happy to see anybody in my whole life. "Where have you been, and, more importantly, what the hell is going on?" I asked.

Not waiting for an answer, we both took off in a full sprint toward the fight. I was shocked—it was still going strong, but Luke seemed to be holding his own. Not bad for a man in his seventies. Spotting the reasonably nice Deputy Titus (let's just say *nicer than the others had been*), I begged him to put an end to the madness.

I'm not sure if it was the way I asked or if he could see the panic in my eyes, but he took pity on me. Jumping on to the horse-corral fence, he yelled at the top of his lungs.

"Okay, everyone—the show is over! Let's all remember we are men of the law and act accordingly, please!"

At first everyone looked at him like he was being a killjoy but, soon, a couple of the other deputies, out of respect for Titus, I assumed, joined in. Before I knew it, Osborne was being pulled off of Luke, and they both were being helped to their feet.

Lux and I ran to Luke's side, concerned and seeking answers. He looked exactly as I would expect him to. His left eye was swollen shut, there was a nasty cut on his lip, and blood was dripping from his nose. As bad as he looked, I hoped that Osborne looked worse, but I highly doubted it was possible. I tried to look over the crowd surrounding him, but he was being shielded from my view.

Lux and I got on either side of Luke and helped him walk over to a bench at the front of the stables within the barn. I wasn't sure if I was imagining this, but his limp seemed more pronounced. On further inspection, I could see that it wasn't only his face that was a gnarled mess. The sleeve of his red plaid flannel shirt had been ripped, showcasing a deep cut that was oozing blood and most likely would require numerous stitches. Poor guy was too old for that kind of activity. As we tended to Luke, I couldn't help but think there was some underlying sinister plot developing within the Sheriff's Department.

It had been twenty years since Luke and I had been instrumental in uncovering how corrupt the Sheriff's Department had been operating, making the idea seem far-fetched, at best, but it was a thought that wouldn't go away, like a worm making its way through an apple. I would have thought my mind was playing tricks on me and fabricating ludicrous scenarios for me if Osborne wasn't in the picture. Any offspring of the old Sheriff had to be rotten to the core and capable of anything—illegal or not. Was it possible that, after all these years, he was somehow still holding a grudge? Or could he be in cahoots with someone who wanted to cause us harm as much as he did?

Pushing these ideas to the back of my mind to address later proved to be difficult. I was aching to get to the bottom of everything bad that had been haunting me since Brie had dropped dead in my office, but I needed to deal with the situation at hand. It needed serious attention, as Luke was fired up, seeing red. He was ranting about what an asshole Osborne was (surprise, surprise—no argument from me there) and how he wanted another piece of him. Trying to convince him that was a bad idea—actually one of the worst he'd had—was like telling him not to breathe. It took everything Lux and I had to hold him down so I could talk sense into his thick skull. No matter what I said, I wasn't getting through, and, almost losing hope, so I played the Dad card.

"Luke, please settle down. If not for me, please do this for my Dad. In his memory." I pleaded. And, shock of all shocks, it's like a lightbulb went off in his head once he heard mention of my Dad, his best friend.

Shaking his head and absentmindedly scratching his beard, he finally looked *at* me and not *through* me.

He winced at the pain his scratching had caused and said, "I'm sorry, son. I don't know what came over me, but when Osborne approached me with accusations regarding you, I flipped out."

He was still livid, his face bright red and the twitch in the corner of his mouth working overtime. I was worried about his blood pressure at this point and searched for the paramedics who had been here moments ago. But, of course, with *my* luck, they had already taken off.

I sat down beside Luke and slung my arm over his shoulders, trying my best to comfort him, all the while hoping he felt my concern. I whispered for Lux to give us a moment and to please go check on Quinn. I didn't need something happening to her on top of all this other crap that had gone down. Luke let out the biggest, loudest sigh I had ever heard. It was if he had the weight of the world on his shoulders and wasn't sure how to go about dealing with it. Guilt took hold of me, and I wondered if it was because of something I had done. Was I somehow responsible for causing these feelings? In all actuality, I felt guilty for the whole mess, starting with Brie clear to the present. Now, more than ever, I was determined to protect those in my inner circle. And if that meant putting myself in harm's way to snuff out the man behind my turmoil, then so be it. But for now, all my attention was on Luke.

"Talk to me. I mean, *really* talk to me like you've never done before. Tell me your fears and what has made you so on edge?" I pleaded.

If I was asking for his honesty, I needed to be honest with myself, too. Feeling scared that something had snapped inside of Luke after my Dad was killed, knowing that everyone had their breaking point was concerning. If I was reading the situation correctly, I think Luke had met his head on. As I waited patiently for him to collect his thoughts, I tried to block out my surroundings, but, unfortunately, Osborne kept screaming obscenities with my and Luke's name mixed in.

The day was gorgeous, with a slight breeze blowing the weathervane that sat perched on the edge of the barn, but I was having trouble concentrating on the beauty of the day when my life was in turmoil. I watched Luke; his facial expressions showed a plethora of emotions, ranging from physical pain, to emotional pain, to confusion. I knew he was struggling within himself about how much he was willing to share. We had always had the most honest of relationships, but I also knew that he had intentionally shielded me throughout the years.

When I was younger and struggling so badly to come to terms with my Mom's death, my home life with my Dad was anything but pleasant. Instead, it had been filled with abuse and neglect as my Dad dealt with his own struggles after losing his one true love. With Luke's undying support and countless therapeutic talks, I had come out on the other side, none the worse for wear—the exact opposite, in fact. I learned to live and love again, and I owed it all to this man sitting in front of me. My second Dad. My *only* Dad now. He looked up at me as a lone tear ran down his cheek. My heart broke.

"Jonathan, I'm afraid I've let you down. I let my inner demons rear their ugly heads, and the old me showed itself. As you know, I've spent a lifetime overcoming my past and learning to deal with my PTSD, among the other obstacles that have been thrown my way. I pray that you'll forgive me," he pleaded.

His defeated look crushed me. He could never disappoint me.

"*Forgive* you? There's nothing to forgive. You are human, Luke, and I owe you my life. We all have breaking points when life gets tough. You just chose the wrong time and person to show your vulnerabilities to. I'm afraid of the repercussions this may have. But you must always remember that I will always be here for you. No matter what. Truth and honesty will prevail."

And, just as the words exited my mouth, Osborne was standing in front of us, screaming at Luke to stand up and face him like a man.

Osborne looked more like his deranged dad when he was pissed. His face had turned various shades of red, and spittle flew out of his mouth and ran down his chin. He was livid and, sadly, not done harassing Luke. I stood while putting my hand on Luke's shoulder to keep him seated. Another repeat from earlier would only cause more harm than good. I was thinking clearer than Luke and a reasonably level head was in order to try to defuse the current situation, so I took command.

"Can we please act and talk like gentlemen here?" I threw it out there, hoping against all odds he would bite. Well, that was the wrong thing to say because Osborne took this as an insult and lunged at me with his fists flying, trying his hardest to connect. I wasn't about to play his game. Dodging his punches, I had to think fast; in that instant, I decided to try to clear the air once and for all. With not a trace of the disgust I was feeling, I nicely asked him to cool his jets and to bring it down a notch. Or two. My performance was Oscar-worthy because what I wished I could do was pummel him into a useless piece of bleeding flesh.

He wanted no part of my offer of a truce. Even though he stopped throwing punches, he still was highly agitated.

"What's your angle, Elliott? You are nothing but a troublemaking SOB who needs to be incarcerated for the rest of your miserable life!"

He clearly thought I was somebody I wasn't, but I didn't give a shit. Knowing I'd done nothing wrong, I didn't owe him an explanation—the exact opposite, in fact. I could hear Luke stirring and breathing hard, giving me reason to believe he was about to raise hell again. Adjusting my grip on his shoulder, digging my fingertips deep into his flesh, hoping to keep him in place, I felt his body relax under my grip, so I continued.

"What is it that you think I've done, Osborne? My curiosity has been building, but now I'm at my tipping point. This nonsense has got to stop once and for all, because you're making my life a living hell!"

Staring him down and holding my ground, I was careful not to show the aggressiveness I was feeling. I knew if I was going to gain even an inch, I would have to let him think I was at his mercy. In some respects, I was, since he was the law, but that's where it stopped. I wasn't going to let him bully us for one more second.

A crowd of deputies had gathered around, encircling us, acting like we were the main attraction at the local circus. Out of the corner of my eye, I saw Lux rounding the corner of the barn, walking with his arm around Quinn, leading her toward the showdown. I wasn't sure how I felt about her seeing me in this light, but it was out of my hands now. Luke had finally come to terms with the fact that I meant business and remained seated. The quietness that had fallen upon the gathering was eerie. It was as if everyone was collectively holding their breath, waiting for the other shoe to drop. And when Osborne opened his mouth to speak, I could see why.

CHAPTER THIRTY-TWO

"**Y**ou are under arrest for the murder of Tom Watson and the body in the barn, which we have yet to identify, as well as the arson and death of Michael Elliott, your father. Come quietly with me, because I'm not afraid to use force."

I heard a gasp escape from Quinn's mouth and felt Luke trying his hardest to stand. If my jaw could have hit the ground, it would have, because this was utter nonsense. There was not one shred of truth in this accusation. Just as those thoughts swirled around in my head, Osborne yanked at my arms and slapped handcuffs on me. They instantly cut off circulation in my hands and made me fearful of what was next.

Since I was unable to hold Luke down, he shot up and started yelling obscenities. The Papa bear was out of hibernation and ready to devour whoever got in his way. This would not end well for either of us if I didn't find a way to nip it in the bud. The lawyer in me knew they could not arrest me without probable cause, but it was clear that they didn't play by the rules. Arresting me because of some bullshit, delusional vendetta would not hold up in a court of law, so I wasn't overly concerned. What did concern me, though, was that they might fabricate evidence just to make my life miserable and make me look guilty. They seemed to be masters at achieving this, and, judging by what I had seen recently, I wouldn't have been surprised if that's what they had up their sleeve.

"Come on, Osborne. Can't we knock off the bravado and discuss things in a civilized manner?" I said.

I already knew the answer, but I was buying time. I'm not sure what I was expecting to change, but I needed time to think—and to cool Luke down before all hell broke loose again. Miraculously, Lux and Quinn appeared at my side to save the day. At least that's what I was hoping. Anything to end this nonsense. I saw Lux grab Luke's arm and gently lead him away, while Quinn stayed by my side. Before she had a chance to speak, Osborne came at us with both barrels.

Sneering at Quinn, he spat out, "Are you such a pansy, Elliott, that you need your girlfriend to stand up for you?"

That was all I needed to snap. I wasn't about to stand by and let him bring innocent Quinn into this mess.

Losing control wasn't in my nature, but everyone has their breaking point, and I feared I had reached mine. I strained to remain in control, wanting more than anything to lash out and cause him physical harm. I hated how I felt, but I kept seeing visions of him laid out cold, with blood dripping from his mouth. If there was one thing I wasn't, it was mean, physically or mentally, so I chose the high road.

I threw a Hail Mary and tried the "If you can't beat them, join them" mentality. I bit my cheek and, with as much sincerity that I could muster, said, "You know what, Osborne? I don't want to put up a fight, so I'll go with you and answer your questions under one circumstance."

He almost fell over in a dead faint, he was so caught off guard. I could see the confusion in his facial expressions: he wasn't sure if he could trust me or if he was about to fall into a trap he might not be able to find his way out of.

There was no trap. Pure and simple, I knew that I was fighting a losing battle, so I was going to use my brains to throw him off. I could see it was working. I needed to know if there was a body in the barn or if this was all a ploy to set me up and take the fall for something that was pure fabrication on their end.

I looked Osborne in the eye and said, "Show me the body, and I won't put up a fight." It was showtime, and the ball was in his proverbial court.

I don't know if I was expecting a flat-out denial, a compromise or a tongue lashing, but what I didn't expect was for him to agree without so much as a moment's hesitation. He was doing an excellent job at masking his irritation, but I could tell he was irritated by the way the vein in his forehead protruded; he remained silent. His assent came in the form of a nod.

He grabbed my arm, and we started walking toward the barn; he instructed one of the deputies to step aside. Time stood still as we walked to the body, and I was keenly aware of my surroundings. The deputies had dispersed to either side of us, like Moses parting the Red Sea; they all looked on with trepidation etched on their faces. I was sure the horses felt the tension in the air, as they came to the side of the corral, hanging their heads as their silky manes blew in the breeze.

Quinn still remained by my side, holding my arm. I saw Lux hovering over Luke, as he remained seated on the bench. He mouthed to me that he had things under control. I whispered to Quinn to please join them. As she trotted off without an argument, I realized what a big relief it was not to have her there to witness what was in the body bag. I felt like I was being led to my execution, and I didn't need distractions. Why I felt this way, I wasn't sure, but I knew whatever was in the body bag was going to determine my fate—at least for the time being, because I would remain steadfast in my innocence.

The barn was big by barn standards and housed twelve stalls for the horses and a section off to the side where supplies were kept. Bales of hay were piled high, and a hay tedder sat idle close by. The aroma of fresh-harvested hay filtered through the air, and I was transported back to the many times I'd gone to the county fair throughout my childhood. I always adored the animals and would spend hours in the petting zoo among the goats, sheep and pigs. I could see my Mom and Dad looking on as they urged me to say goodbye. *Oh, God—how I missed them!*

I was startled back into the present by Osborne tugging on me. The cuffs cut into my wrists, causing sharp pains to shoot up my arms. I felt wetness that could only mean that they had cut in so deeply that I had started to bleed. As we walked by, he grabbed one of the deputies close by to do his dirty work and unzip the body bag.

I broke out in a cold sweat that proceeded to slither down my back, drenching my shirt. I took a quick glance toward Osborne, who was casually leaning against a stall with his legs crossed at the ankles and chewing on a piece of straw, taking pleasure in my uneasiness. My heartbeat was fast and loud in my ears as I looked straight into an all-too-familiar face. The man's coloring had drained from his face, and a gray pallor of death had taken over. His designer shirt was covered in blood, and I saw that it had been ripped open, exposing a bullet hole that had gone straight into his heart. Feeling as if I might faint, I took in a couple of deep breaths, slowing down my heart rate and giving me a clearer head.

I managed another look at the open body bag and couldn't believe I was staring straight into the vacant, lifeless eyes of the debonair Dr. *GQ.*

His once-handsome face was distorted. He was now wearing an infinite grimace that indicated he had been aware of what was about to happen to him or that he was confused. That's when I fainted.

CHAPTER THIRTY-THREE

I'm not sure when I had become a wuss, but it apparently had happened when I wasn't looking. I never would have classified myself as a badass, but I did take pride in standing up for myself and not being taken advantage of. But, then again, I had never been around this much violence. Death was becoming an everyday occurrence—one I could or would never get used to.

As I lay on the ground in the barn, I was aware that my head was resting on something soft and that a scratchy and heavy blanket was covering me. I heard others talking about me like I wasn't there. Snippets of accusations and some nonsense about me staging my blackout filtered in and out of my foggy mind. I tried to speak in protest, but I couldn't find my voice, so I took the time to regain my lucidity. It was actually a great plan, because, if the deputies thought I was out cold, I could gain insight into their plans.

"Did you see the look on Elliott's face when he saw the body? He must have gone to acting school, because he genuinely looked surprised," Osborne said to no one in particular. They were having a good laugh at my expense as I heard a whole bunch of guffaws in response. As I labored to sit up, I had a revelation.

It was clear that Osborne disliked me due to some misguided vision of the treatment of his father, but it was more than that. He really thought I was guilty. If I put myself in his shoes, I could vaguely see why. After all, Tom and Dr. *GQ* both had ties to me, and they'd both wound up dead shortly after spending time with me. The huge loophole in this was motive. Why would I want them dead? And what about my Dad? I most certainly did not want *that* to happen. Osborne clearly was not getting the big picture; he was concentrating on only the murders. Some *man of the law* he was.

Looking around, regaining my strength, I locked eyes with Osborne. He had a look of bewilderment etched on his callused face. One thing was for sure: he was not about to tip his hand. I wondered once again what was going through his warped mind and why he despised me so much. I had come to two revelations while I'd been lying there. First, and most importantly, I was almost positive Brie's death was of no fault of her own. Talk about some shit luck and being at the wrong place at the wrong time. She somehow had come face to face with the killer or his minions while they were plotting to grab my attention. One by one, they were picking off people who were close to me. Secondly, I was positive that the next attempt at my life would be the last. The incidents were getting more frequent, more violent and closer to home.

"Satisfied now, Elliott? A deal is a deal. You need to come peacefully down to the station to answer my questions as promised," Osborne said, behind a devious grin. I was not looking forward to spending any more time with him, but he was right: a deal is a deal, so I shook my head in agreement and slowly walked next to him, searching for Lux, Luke and Quinn. They needed to know what was going down, so they didn't think I'd vanished into thin air. Boy, don't I *wish* that was possible.

Turns out I didn't have to look far, because, twenty-five feet away or so, an agitated Luke was being cuffed despite his loud protests. They didn't give two craps that he was unhappy. But I did. I wasn't the least bit surprised to see Luke being cuffed and led away. Osborne had such a pompous, egotistical attitude about him that it wasn't in his mental capacity not to have the upper hand. He was abusing his power, and I was only going along with it for the time being, but things would start to shift in our favor soon because this shit needed to stop ASAP.

I managed a kiss on Quinn's cheek and made a promise I would be fine. I told her not to worry before I was loaded into the back of the Sheriff's cruiser. It was filthy and reeked of vomit mixed with stale cigarette breath and body odor. The seats had crusted brown spots, which I could only imagine were dried feces, from where someone had shit themselves. Stains on the windows from dried-up phlegm and grime kept me from seeing clearly out the windows. I remained stoic, not wanting to give them the satisfaction of knowing how repulsed and disgusted I was.

Small talk was not on my mind, which was just as well, because none was offered. I decided to make the best of it and quietly sat back and daydreamed about life with Quinn. Raising a family and working in my thriving law practice—all while being madly in love—left a much-needed smile on my face as we pulled up in front of the jail.

The jail was drab brown, with noticeable peeling paint and a couple of holes—I imagined some belligerent drunk trying to get revenge by kicking the wall with a pair of steel-toed work boots. There was a separate building, adjoined by a long hallway to the main part of the Sheriff's department building, where the offices were housed. It was in such dilapidated shape, I was surprised they still conducted business here. Judging by the looks of the car and this building, it was clear that they took zero pride in ownership, which often reflected on their job performance or lack thereof. I was finding that to be the case here, for sure. I would have thought that, after the fiasco twenty years ago, this place would have cleaned house and revamped their policies. I was clearly mistaken.

Walking up to the door, I had a feeling of dread. The optimism I had felt earlier as I kissed Quinn goodbye had all but packed up and departed on a long journey. My only hope at this point was to give them what they needed/wanted so I could be on my merry way. I took a quick glance around, looking for Luke, but he was nowhere to be seen. I was confronted with the steely-eyed glare of Osborne. He had a real stick up his ass, as he sneered while grabbing my arm to lead me through the open door.

I was expecting utter chaos inside to match the outside, but, I have to admit, I was pleasantly surprised. Although the furnishings were sparse, with no frills, the basics were in place and in decent shape. Rows of steel desks were lined up, all with computers and neatly stacked folders. Upon closer look at the desks, I saw many contained framed pictures of their families. Cute little girls with toothless smiles and pink ribbons tied around pigtails. Little boys and girls alike proudly holding up trophies, dressed in soccer uniforms or proudly displaying a fish on a line. I don't know why, but it struck me as odd that these men could be married, with families. It humanized them, when I thought of them only as ruthless savages. At the same time, it gave me a sliver of hope that I might be able to reason with one or two of them.

To my right, steel filing cabinets adorned the wall nearest the door. I couldn't help notice a couple of huge dents in them, making me realize disgruntled deputies resided in here. There were a couple of murder books thrown on top, but, all in all, it wasn't the disaster I would have placed bets on.

There was a decent amount of chatter taking place among the deputies while some old-school honky-tonk country music played from a radio nearby. A hint of burned grilled cheese and tomato soup filtered through the air, which made my stomach growl. I was famished, but I had a feeling nourishment wasn't coming any time soon. As Osborne entered the room, silence washed over the place, and I was immediately aware of my heartbeat in my ears. I hadn't realized how on edge I was. Or scared. I was wrestling with how I would describe my feelings exactly, but *pissed* came to mind. I was so pissed, a sea of red tainted my view. That would account for the loud, menacing heartbeat.

"What do we have here, Osborne? Is that the infamous troublemaker, Jonathan Elliott?" one of the deputies questioned.

A nervous giggle escaped my mouth before I could contain it. "Infamous?" I asked, finding this not only humorous but troublesome.

"For those of you who don't know me—which is everyone—I am anything but a troublemaker, or infamous for that matter! Let's set the record straight right now before all of you get some crazy notion in your mind that I'm someone I'm not!"

Feeling the red creep into my cheeks, I looked out at the men, who were all staring back, with looks of disgust and mistrust. I wasn't sure why I felt the need to explain myself, because I was never one to like the spotlight. Whether good or bad, I preferred to blend into the background. I am and always have been just Jonathan, a what-you-see-is what-you-get kinda guy.

Everyone began talking all at once, and I was being bombarded with questions. Osborne screamed, "All of you, shut up—immediately! This is *my* prisoner, and I will not have any one of you think otherwise!" He was under some delusions of grandeur, because I was positive he wasn't in charge, no matter how he felt.

"Hey—wait one second, Osborne," I blurted out. Let's get this clear—I'm not your personal property and most definitely not your prisoner. I came here on my own volition, not because you arrested me. Or, for that matter, had any reason to!"

A plethora of emotions and thoughts were racing through my head competing for attention. Not only was I pissed but I was perplexed at what Osborne's angle was. Did he believe these bullshit accusations to be true beyond a shadow of a doubt, or did he have just an inkling of suspicion? Or was it pure harassment for some unknown reason I still had not been able to uncover? As I looked at him, he stared back with pure hatred oozing out of every pore; other than that, his face remained free of emotion.

His response to my comment shouldn't have surprised me, but yet it did.

"Oh, I beg to differ with you, Elliott. You're on my turf now and are mine to do with whatever I see fit. And you can't stop me. I know you're guilty, and I'm going to make sure you fry for your misdeeds," snarled Osborne as he spit on my foot and yanked my arm simultaneously. I started to protest but knew it would fall on deaf ears, so, instead, I held my head high and stumbled alongside him.

He dragged me down a short hall that was lined with an assortment of framed pictures of past-to-present Sheriffs. I spotted Sheriff Osborne's picture immediately because it stuck out like a sore thumb. I couldn't help myself and let out a laugh when I saw a fake mustache and a big wart with hairs growing out of it scribbled over his face. This was a perfect example of the mentality that worked inside these walls.

"What's so damn funny, Elliott?" Osborne questioned. Without a word from me, he followed my gaze. I saw his neck turn red as he spotted the picture. With one swift move, he grabbed the picture off the wall and mumbled something along the lines of "You assholes will pay for this!" I'm sure they were all quaking in their boots. It appeared Osborne wasn't the hotshot he thought he was.

Stashing the picture under his arm, he motioned for me to enter into a small, sterile room that had one steel table with one chair on either side. A camera was mounted at the top of the wall where it met the ceiling. You didn't have to tell me twice that this was their interrogation room—or should I say *intimidation* room.

Reaching inside my pocket to retrieve my phone, I came up empty-handed. It was very unlikely that it had fallen out somehow but quite likely it had been removed while I was momentarily out like a light in the barn. This infuriated me even more because I feared the worst.

"Could you take me to a phone so I can call my attorney before you question me?" I asked, very politely, when I really felt like clawing his eyes out. Osborne let out a big belly laugh like I had just told a joke and was the next Bob Saget. I failed to see the humor. I knew my rights, and I was allowed one phone call. Who was I kidding? I didn't even have to be here. My mistake.

"Not going to happen, jerk face!" he spat at me. "Maybe you didn't hear me the first time, so I'll speak slower so your peabrain can keep up. You are on my turf. My rules apply here, and that does not include phone calls. No way, no how, so don't waste your breath!"

My fear was coming true.

I was caught between a rock and hard place. I wasn't about to answer his questions, knowing they would be tainted, just waiting to coerce me into something I hadn't done. I hadn't gone to law school for four long years and busted my butt not to know the law. Not only had I learned in school to always have an attorney present when being questioned, but my Dad had drilled it into my head on numerous occasions.

Ah, my Dad. Gosh, I missed him. So much had been happening since his death, I felt like I hadn't given myself the time to grieve properly. I felt gutted. Thinking about him now had me on the verge of tears. Tears for a life gone too soon, tears for no more father-son dates and tears for all that could have been. His funeral was in three days, and I still needed to finalize arrangements. Pleading my case to Osborne would be useless, because, knowing what little I did about him, I knew his heart was made of stone and that the meaning of love was nonexistent.

My Dad didn't deserve this. But then, again, neither did Brie, Tom, or Dr. *GQ*. The bodies were adding up quickly, and here I was sitting in some godforsaken interrogation room with my hands cuffed behind my back. A lot of good I was doing to help. Then, out of nowhere, my mind went where it shouldn't have. I wondered—just wondered—if Luke was next.

The sheer thought of it ignited a fire deep in my soul. I was not about to sit back and let them harm Luke. But what could I do to help? Strike up a deal? I knew that that was off the table, since I was living the fruits of my last deal at the moment and not faring well in the least.

Swearing wasn't in my nature and something I ordinarily didn't do, but desperate times call for desperate measures, and, unfortunately, as much as this pained me to say, I was in a fucking pickle, not knowing what my next move could be. Getting mad at myself for believing Osborne would keep up his end of our bargain wasn't going to get me anywhere, but I couldn't help but be furious, anyway.

"Enough is enough, Osborne! I'm not your prisoner any more than I'm your best friend. Take these cuffs off and let me go before I sue you for false imprisonment."

I proceeded to quote verbatim the definition of false imprisonment, outlining every detail that was applicable to me. I would have a case, and he would have to be an idiot not to understand that. Holding me against my will was a blatant disregard for the law, one he had sworn to uphold.

But instead of verbally responding, he looked at me like he hadn't heard a word I said, with his ever-present scowl but a blank stare. In all my years, I had never seen hatred in anyone's eyes like I did in his. Either he was lost in thought or having a petit mal seizure because he was in nowhere land for a good twenty seconds before he came to and slammed his fist so hard down on the table that I heard a couple of framed pictures fall off the adjoining wall.

"Shut up, now—and sit down before you make me use force. I'm tired of hearing you blab on and on about meaningless shit that makes no sense. Haven't you learned by now that there are no laws within these walls? The only thing that matters is what I say!"

Talk about an ego trip. Starting to protest, I thought better of it and remained passively seated while my blood was boiling in my veins. This seemed to pacify him for the time being, as he busied himself arranging papers and folders on the table. It was getting increasingly difficult to breathe in the room as the tension multiplied. I nervously tapped my foot to a vague rhythm that played on repeat in my brain, trying to keep my mind off my current situation and buy myself some time.

I was determined not to let Osborne know that I was uneasy and on the verge of losing my shit, so I didn't try to make small talk or even glance his way. I could feel his eyes on me, looking at me and boring into my soul, but I willed myself to keep calm.

After what seemed like an eternity, he sat and turned on a tape recorder that he had positioned in the middle of the table. It looked as old as him, and I imagined him getting it as a present as an infant, when there was still promise in the air of raising a decent human. That, sadly, wasn't to be. Trying to sound professional for once in his life, he started what he assumed would be an interrogation.

"Testing, testing. Let this be known that I, Deputy Sheriff Harold Osborne, on this day, the third of April 2039, sit here with Jonathan Elliott. This will act as an interrogation into the deaths of three gentlemen of his acquaintance as well as numerous other incidents, including arson."

Stopping, he motioned for me to talk. I had news for him. I wasn't saying a thing. Not even my name. I had a very strong suspicion that this was going to piss him off even further and make for a very long night, but I didn't give two shits.

Lo and behold, I was right. What started out with Osborne asking me to state my name for the record, turned into him screaming at me to cooperate. I might as well have had a lock on my mouth with no key, because I didn't so much as utter a peep. He grew increasingly irritated, as I grew increasingly wary and exhausted. I was parched, hungry and defeated—none of which I saw changing anytime in the near future.

For all Osborne cared, I could have dropped dead on the spot, and he would have rejoiced and made up some cockamamie bullshit story about how he beat me down, getting me to confess, leading me to end my own life out of shame. Little did he know that I was stronger and more determined than ever not to let him get his way.

One hour turned into two, followed by three, and I held my ground. Osborne stood and let out a loud burp as he scratched his crotch. I wasn't the least bit surprised to hear him burp—because he certainly was full of enough hot air. He shot me a glare and announced "No funny business" while he took a break, leaving me to stew with my own thoughts. I was overjoyed to have some time alone without his constant, meaningless babble. His accusations weren't questions. Not one. He had it in his mind that I was guilty, and he wasn't there to listen to anything other than a confession—one I would never make.

Time had been ticking by slowly and monotonously. I had no clue if it was nighttime or morning. It felt like it had been an eternity. I missed my watch, but that had been removed from me the minute I'd set foot in the building. Add that to another violation of my rights. When this was all said and done, they had better watch their backs. They were messing with the wrong guy. Just as I was wondering if Osborne would return, I heard a huge commotion outside the door.

"Get your filthy hands off of me and let me see my son now, or there'll be hell to pay!" I heard Luke screaming at whomever was in his path. I stood and made an attempt to open the door, which proved fruitless, with my hands still painfully cuffed behind my back. But I still had my voice and yelled, "Luke, I'm in here. Please come quickly!"

All hell had erupted, and I heard chairs being thrown as well as what sounded like punches connecting. Osborne burst through the door looking like a crazed maniac. His eyes were bloodshot and glazed over, and his uniform was torn on the sleeve. It wasn't clear to me if these were fresh abrasions or the ones he had received earlier from his tussle with Luke, but he looked like death warmed over. One thing was for certain: he was pissed and panicked. His breath was coming in ragged gasps while he shielded the door so no one could enter.

I wanted to ask what had happened, but that would mean breaking my silence, which I had vowed not to do. So, I sat quietly, leaning my head against the wall with a passive smirk across my face. Patience wasn't what I would call one of my virtues, but I could conjure it up when need be, and this was, indeed, one of those times. Osborne stole a glance my way as he used all his weight against a door that was partially opening. For lack of a better description, I would say he was pleading with me to reason with Luke, the gentle giant, who was gaining the upper hand.

I was enjoying the ride. Two things had become abundantly clear with this outburst happening right before my eyes. Number one, nothing could stand in Luke's way when it came to protecting me, and, number two, Osborne did not have the backing of his fellow deputies. Or at least not all of them. He was putting up a fake façade, acting like a hotshot who ran the show. Clearly, this was not the case.

Fearing Osborne would blow a gasket and shoot Luke, I intervened—only for Luke's sake, because I obviously didn't want to see him hurt. Watching Osborne blow a gasket, on the other hand, was something I would pay big money for, so I could get a front-row seat.

"Luke, it's okay. I'm okay. Please get control of yourself and stop—he has a gun. I'm afraid you're putting yourself in harm's way, again." I shouted with frantic urgency. "No more hurt, God. Please—no more hurt," I pleaded, noticing that the sound of my voice and my reassurances caused Luke to use less force, which resulted in Osborne losing his footing and falling flat on his ass. The door opened, and in walked Luke, red as a crab. He was not alone. A couple of deputies meandered into the room, looking amused, as they caught sight of Osborne sprawled on the floor.

Laughter filled the room. It was music to my ears and a perfect segue to me getting out of here. Or so I thought. What I wasn't expecting was how much this angered Osborne. It was as if someone had poked a bear and it was coming at you on all fours, with blood and a thirst for killing in its eyes. He was up faster than I would have ever given him credit for, and, in one quick, faster-than-lightning movement, released his taser gun and fired it straight at Luke.

Luke instantly folded like a deck of cards but with so much force the vibration knocked a significant number of pictures off the wall outside the room. I wasn't entirely sure what had angered Osborne more—the deputies poking fun at him and having a laugh at his expense or Luke having the upper hand. Or maybe a combination of the two? All I really knew for certain was that his blood was beyond the boiling point and that he was not afraid to use force to regain control.

Mortified at what I was witnessing, my head dropped, heavy with the weight of the burden, as I looked at Luke, who had just received a significant electric shock and was messed up. He was lying on the floor, unable to gain control of his muscles as they involuntarily twitched. He appeared to be in tremendous pain. He let out a yelp that could have woken the dead as he made numerous feeble attempts to stand, only to fall in a heap of useless flesh. I clenched my eyes shut, hoping that, when I opened them, this nightmare would be over, as I tried in vain to talk to him, unable to offer any other assistance. Osborne was standing, leaning against the door frame with a look of contentment spread across his face.

"Don't get any ideas, Elliott, or you will end up the same way as your useless friend here," he gloated.

How someone could be proud of inflicting pain on another person was a foreign concept to me, but he was downright euphoric watching Luke struggle. All this proved to me was that he was just as ruthless and evil as his Dad. Some people weren't meant to reproduce.

Time ticked by as I silently begged Luke to be okay; all the while, Osborne busied himself clipping his nails and whistling, "Happy Days Are Here Again." After about fifteen minutes, Luke was up on all fours, shaking his head and trying to clear the cobwebs that remained. He looked as if he had been woken out of a deep sleep. He had a couple of small burn marks where the barbed darts had made contact, but, aside from that, he looked no worse for wear from this latest assault.

Awkwardly making my way out of my chair, I knelt next to Luke, who was struggling to speak. "Take your time, and get your bearings," I suggested. He looked at me with a blank stare. I could tell he was still feeling the effects and having issues recognizing where he was. I needed to choose my words wisely, because Osborne was on the verge of losing his shit again. After the taser incident, the other deputies had made themselves scarce. It was Luke and I against Osborne, and I didn't like our odds.

F earing Osborne was on the verge of another tirade, I tested the waters by glancing his way. He stood with hatred dripping from every pore in his body. In his right hand, he was clenching his taser gun so tightly that I feared it might snap in two. His left hand was massaging his jaw as if he were deep in thought, planning his next move—a crucial one, if I was reading him correctly.

Luke was coming around. I could hear him talking gibberish while his tongue caught up with his brain. I was pretty positive he would be fine if we could somehow, someway get released. The longer we stayed here, the more chance we had of not seeing the light of day anytime soon. Not unless a miracle happened, and I wasn't big on expecting the unexpected.

Sitting on the floor next to Luke, I wanted to hug him, or, at the least, rub his back and reassure him that I was here by his side, but I was painfully reminded that my hands were numb behind my back. My earlier request for removal of the handcuffs had been denied with a, "Are you fucking out of your mind, loser?!" I didn't dare ask again. Instead, I homed in on the sounds outside of the walls I was trapped in.

Faint country music still played in the background. An old classic that I found very appropriate for our current situation, "Achy Breaky Heart," was belting out of speakers. *". . . And if you tell my heart/my achy breaky heart/He might blow up and kill this man . . ."*

It was difficult to know how many deputies were still out there because I heard only hushed tones with an occasional snippet of conversation. I could have sworn I heard someone mention how Osborne had lost his shit and was a loose cannon. I was hoping I was wrong, but I knew in my heart I wasn't. He wasn't thinking clearly, letting his ego take over, and that was a recipe for disaster.

"Hey—Earth to Osborne," I bravely called out. "If it's not clear to you yet, I'm not about to talk without an attorney, and, since you refuse to grant me my rights, I would like to be released now, please. Or, at the very least, remove these cuffs that have made me bloody and numb." I wasn't dumb. I knew his answer would be "No," but I thought if I was polite, he might decide he had bigger fish to fry and focus on Luke only. I could definitely get things rolling in the right direction if I was "on the outside." In here, I was as useless as tits on a bull.

Whether he was lost in space, having another petit mal seizure, or ignoring me altogether, remained to be seen, because all I got for a response was a blank stare. Nothing. By this time, Luke was fully coherent and spitting fire. Knowing Luke like I did, I knew there wasn't a word I could say to make him stay calm. He had lost all sense of decency and was out for blood. I was scared where this might lead. *Nowhere good*, I thought, imagining the worst.

Just as Luke stood up, Osborne came out of his trance, shook his head a couple of times and then holstered his taser. I was unsure if it was the commotion outside or the movement inside, but he was now ready to fight, with his hands balled into fists, protecting his jaw. The sight of him made me burst out in laughter. I couldn't help it. I knew this would only anger him further, but I was hoping it would diffuse a bad situation before it went off the rails. I didn't succeed. My track record had been pitiful lately.

"Stop in your tracks, Travers. And you, Elliott, what's so damn funny?" Osborne yelled. He was livid. He had one of those personalities that thought everyone was against him. Again—or more like *still*—I was beginning to wonder if this guy lived in a perpetual state of grumpiness. Was one of those desks out front his, with pictures of smiling happy kids? It seemed highly unlikely, and I took a moment of silence to mourn for the poor spouse and kids he may have.

With Osborne's latest outburst, a bunch of deputies came running down the hall to see what was about to go down.

They were a nosy bunch. I swear I could see the difference in Osborne's physical demeanor change right before my eyes when his cohorts were around. He puffed out his chest, taking on an air of toxic masculinity I hadn't noticed before. It was clear he wanted approval and cared what others thought. This wasn't going to work in our favor.

The deputies barreled into the room, pushing each other out of the way to gain access. The room was small to start with, but now it had been reduced in size, making it difficult to turn around. The mood in the room shifted immediately, causing the air to turn to evil, making it hard to breathe. I could feel Luke tense up, feeling what I was feeling. How could he not? He would have to be deaf, dumb and blind not to feel the eerieness in the room.

"Come on, Osborne, Mr. Tough Guy, show us what you're made of," the deputies cheered in unison. They were egging him on, pushing him to take the next step. This only increased our chances of something bad happening. He wasn't about to be fair—or even *human*, for that matter—when his fellow deputies were there to witness his next move.

"You want to see what's in store for these two losers?" he replied, while swiftly moving beside us and yanking me up by my hair. At the same time, he used some wild karate sweep with his leg that brought Luke down flat on his back. With that, he proceeded to stomp on top of his torso with his steel-toed boot, to keep him in place. I had to admit I was impressed by his agility but pissed for the treatment we were receiving.

"No more games for you two. The time has come for you to think about what you've done and spend a little time in our local facilities, otherwise known as our *special jailhouse*," he excitedly yelled, unable to contain his excitement. I had a hunch that this was where our night was headed. Or was it night? I longed to know what time it was, even though it wouldn't change anything. We both were at his mercy, and he was so full of himself at the moment that I was petrified of the outcome.

Now that I was standing, I glanced at Luke, who was still on the floor, lying in a supine position, nursing a sore back. Osborne grabbed my arm, practically yanking it out of its socket, as I was pulled down a different hall, barely able to keep up, stumbling over my own two feet. This hall was dark, with a couple of flickering, dim fluorescent lights overhead. It had a dampness about it, and it reminded me of the forest with the earthy, pungent smell the ground gave off, covered by a canopy of trees and rarely receiving any direct sunlight. I got an uneasy feeling that I was being pulled down below the buildings, struggling to stay vertical. We weaved through a labyrinth of tunnels as we neared a brighter light.

Once we arrived at our destination, I was sweating profusely. I struggled to wipe the sweat out of my eyes by twisting around, connecting my shoulder to my face. My eyes stung with the saltiness of my sweat and were clearly seeing things that weren't there. Or were they?

CHAPTER THIRTY-SIX

Before me were two makeshift cells with a couple of Edison bulbs burning over each. They were empty and bare except for a feeble-looking excuse for a cot and a threadbare, crusty blanket. They were rudimentary at best, making the room look more like a dungeon than a civilized jail cell. My heart sank as I envisioned myself rotting away, while people looked for me to no avail. This is where people went to die, and I could smell the death seeping out of the walls, screaming for help falling on deaf ears.

"Oh, come on, Osborne—you can't be serious! I have been nothing but respectful to you, so I expect the same in return. Putting me down here will only cause more harm than good."

It was just he and I, so while I had a captive audience, I was planning on taking advantage of it. My life depended on it, and he knew it. He looked at me with the most sinister of smirks, leaning against the bars, with his legs crossed at the ankles. He was taking immense enjoyment out of my plight, begging for my life. He seemed to like watching me squirm.

I pleaded my case. "People will come looking for me, and, when they don't find me, you'll have hell to pay. You have to remember that I was last seen with you, which will bring you to the forefront of the investigation into my disappearance. Is that the attention you want?" I hoped to at least give him something to think about. As I watched closely, I could see the rusty wheels in his head turning while he contemplated the bad publicity for him that this would result in.

Rambling on, pleading my case even further, I half expected to be thrown in the cell and left for dead, but, to my surprise, he started laughing. It was a slight giggle at first that turned into a guffaw. I wasn't sure what to make of this latest outburst, so I remained silent, watching him entertain himself. I wasn't sure if it was an inside joke or something I'd said, but, to be quite honest, as long as it eased the tension, I was on-board with it.

Wiping the tears from his eyes, he spoke. "You're dumber than you look. I'm just messin' with you. Do you honestly think I would be that stupid to put you down here? Not to say I won't in the future, but that depends on you! I guess you could call it a reprieve of sorts, so use it wisely."

Considering this, I chose to play his game for a while and thanked him, though I didn't *want* to thank him. In fact, I felt the exact opposite. I had visions of bodily harm running through my head—severe and debilitating—but I put my best foot forward and plastered the fakest smile on my face. If he saw through it, he didn't act as if he did. He was beaming with pride and proud of himself for putting the fear of God in me. Damn loser.

Now that I had seen what hell looked like, he yanked my arm even harder this time, if possible, and we started weaving our way back to civilization. I couldn't help notice the spring in his step, as I managed to trip over my own feet time and time again. I'd never realized how much one used their arms for balance, or was it the dark, uneven ground that was causing my clumsiness?

All I really cared about was getting out of this air-sucking hellhole and being able to breathe some air that wasn't laden with undertones of damp, earthy moss, intertwined with death and torture. Not a great combination by even the worst of standards.

Before we crossed into civilization, Osborne stopped and whispered into my ear. His breath was rancid—just like his personality. It smelled like sour milk, mixed with liver and onions, with a trace of whiskey.

"Don't think for a second I won't hesitate to throw your pathetic ass in that godforsaken hellhole to rot if you make one false move. I'll be watching you like a hawk, so if you value your life, you had better toe the line!" he hissed while giving me a sucker punch in the gut. I was caught off guard, and I hunched over, gasping for air and dry-heaving simultaneously. That was a low blow, even by his standards.

Tears had collected in my eyes from the punch as well as from the bright lights as we emerged from the tunnels. I was mortified and quickly tried to wipe them, to no avail. This "no-hands" thing was really cramping my style. One lone tear ran down my cheek, and that's all Osborne needed to see to erupt into fits of laughter, calling me a pussy and a mama's boy. I would have gladly been a mama's boy and worn that badge proudly.

Although it had nothing to do with that, I let him think I was weak. I didn't care what he thought, as long as I got the hell out of this place—and the sooner the better. It was reasonably quiet, with not a deputy in sight. Or Luke. I had a feeling in the pit of my stomach that I couldn't shake. My intuition was working overtime, and I knew Luke was locked up somewhere. On a positive note, I knew it wasn't the dreaded dungeon, or I would have seen him or, at the very least, felt his presence.

Osborne seemed perplexed, scratching his head as he scanned the offices and hallway. *If only I could be privy to his thoughts.* Was it odd that there wasn't anyone around? Did this signal trouble? Were they planning something behind my back? I wasn't about to ask him or show the least bit of the concern that was gnawing away at me. Time would tell, for better or worse.

"Seems as if we're alone for the time being, so, there's no time like the present to get you booked and settled into your new 'home away from home.' I'm hoping you hate it as much as I want you to," he said with the biggest smile, like a Cheshire Cat.

"Booking me is not an option. Are you forgetting that I'm an attorney and know my rights? You're in for a world of hurt if you proceed down that path." I was fuming but kept my temper in check. I doubted that he was using logic; he was probably convinced that I had committed heinous crimes. They warranted this type of punishment, making it justified. Or not. Who knew? He marched to the beat of a different drum, so he might think it was kosher. I had a news flash for him. It was anything but, and I would slap him with a lawsuit if he even tried it. And I told him so.

Turns out he didn't take too kindly to the spunky side of me and jerked my arm so hard that I lost my footing. My feet flew out from underneath me like I had been walking on ice, and I landed smack dab on my ass. It hurt like hell. Once again, Osborne roared with laughter. I was getting sick and tired of being the brunt of his jokes. I was keeping mental notes of all the abuse and laws that were being broken and looking forward to the time I would get my day in court as well as the last laugh. It was coming, and I was more determined than ever to wait it out.

Not waiting for me to stand, Osborne dragged me down the hall until we came to an abrupt stop in front of a row of jail cells—the type of cells I associated with police dramas on TV. There were ten cells in total, all looking as if they'd seen better days. The metal was rusty and giving off a strong metallic smell. I was hoping that truly was the bars I was smelling, instead of blood. Within each sat a pallet covered in a dingy, drab white sheet with a navy-blue blanket haphazardly folded at the end of the "bed." There was a latrine and a filthy sink along the back wall, and the same type of Edison bulb light I had seen in the dungeon dangling from the ceiling.

The whole image in front of me was enough to bring thoughts of doom and gloom. I searched for Luke. I knew he was in here somewhere. I felt his presence, although I wasn't allowed to look in the cells before I was uncuffed and thrown in. I heard the slam of the automatic deadlock *click* behind me.

Hearing the most sinister evil laugh I had ever had the displeasure of hearing caused me to look up into the snarling face of Osborne before he growled, "Rot in hell, you loser!" He had flipped out, and I was suffering the brunt of it. All I could do now was collect my thoughts and pray like I'd never prayed before that Lux was working behind the scenes.

CHAPTER THIRTY-SEVEN

Rubbing my numb wrists, I tried to get some feeling back into them. As I assessed the damage, I saw a couple of raw spots that were the source of the bleeding I had felt. It was nothing that wouldn't heal and, quite honestly, the least of my problems on an ever-growing list of issues. First and foremost, I needed water. I was parched, but when I turned on the grimy faucet, a trickle of water dripped out, causing a rust spot to form in the sink. This was inhuman treatment, and I sympathized with animals in shelters who suffered this kind of treatment on a daily basis. I love animals, and thinking about this made me madder than a hornet whose nest had been poked.

"Hello. Hello. Is there anybody out there?" I called out, feeling desperation seep in. I was not about to let it get the upper hand. Nothing. No response. I tried again—louder this time. I was rewarded by an appearance by Deputy Titus, the semi-nice man I had seen in the hospital last month. I let out a chuckle, realizing, *That wasn't last month—it was just days ago.*

"Can I please have some water? It seems as if the water has been shut off in my cell," I pleaded, trying to keep the pessimism out of my voice. He looked at me like I was some deranged animal and disappeared without a word. *What the hell—are they all heartless SOBs?* I wondered. But before I was allowed to wallow in my despair, Titus reappeared with bottles of water. Still voiceless, he put them through the slot in my door. We made eye contact for a brief moment before he vanished, and I was left wondering if what I saw was a mirage. Was I imagining the hint of compassion and pity in his eyes? This gave me some hope to hang on to as I sat on my pallet guzzling water.

Hydration is a wonderful thing; I was already thinking more clearly, but I was still bone-tired. The events of the day had left me exhausted physically as well as mentally, and, before I could stop it, I was overcome and so fatigued that I had no choice but to give in. Lying down, I fell into a fitful sleep, which, of course, brought along a new batch of nightmares.

Darkness surrounded me. As far as I could tell, I was alone, but I heard voices, and—*ewww*—the smell that filtered through my nostrils was putrid. If death had a specific smell, this would be it. My eyes watered, and I leaned over to heave.

But where was it going? It was an abyss of darkness as I tried to take a step, with the toe of my Doc Martens feeling the way. I caught myself as I was on the verge of tumbling to my death. The air was cold, and I wrapped my jacket around me, wishing I had a beanie to warm my head. The cold wasn't a normal cold but a bitter, bone-aching cold—the kind that caused your teeth to chatter uncontrollably. As I reached out with my arms, I felt a presence I couldn't explain. The sensation descended—not as a possibility, but an absolute certainty, the way you know it's raining because you are suddenly wet. I could feel my my Mom and Dad standing there, with outstretched arms. My eyes scoured the contours of the darkness for shapes, silhouettes. Petrified and alone, I called out to them, needing the warmth of their embrace. But, just as I did, a lightning storm lit up the sky, and I was rudely woken, with Osborne standing over me with a flashlight in my face.

"Wake up, loser. I was just informed you've been causing problems, demanding water. You are in no position to make demands. Let's make that abundantly clear right now."

I started to respond but thought better of it; I kept my thoughts of hatred and death to myself. My fifth- and four-teenth-amendments rights had already been violated, and I was curious how many other violations they were going to chalk up before it was all said and done. The time would come when he'd be the one shaking in his boots. I could hardly wait.

As quick as he came, he was gone. Thankfully. I would rather spend my days alone than with the likes of him. Now that I had been so rudely interrupted, I caught a second wind, allowing me to contemplate the horrible predicament I was in. I scanned the room; my furnishings were sparse, at best. Walking the perimeter of the room, I saw carvings on the wall where someone had used it as a calendar, counting down their dark days of incarceration. As sad as this was, it made me smile because I had seen this same thing in every TV show or movie I'd ever watched that had a jail cell in it. Why I found comfort in that was beyond me, but I was grasping at any signs of normalcy at this point.

The floor was cold cement and filthy, with caked-on grossness that would require a chisel and a power washer to break it free. My pallet was made out of some sort of thin mattress. As I slid my hand under it, looking for clues about its last inhabitants, I felt what I imagined was a book or some type of box. I grasped it as a shiver ran down my spine, more from the cold breeze that blew through, rather than from my discovery, but it got me thinking the book might hold secrets worth hiding. Random belongings, no running water, no cot, no food, and cold conditions left me wondering what else I had to look forward to. This was proving to be barbaric, at best.

Sitting in front of me was, indeed, a book titled *The Sword of Death and Hunger*, by Eva Alton. It was an intriguing title, but I hoped it was not a foreshadowing of what was to come. As I opened it to take a glance inside, I was immediately transported back to medieval times. I felt a presence in the room. Startled, I looked around, but I was alone and starving. I was pretty sure my request for some hot soup would be denied, so I busied myself with a chapter or two, wondering if the book had any significance or had been left by some other poor soul to help pass the time.

Not being much of a fantasy reader, I wasn't familiar with this author. Although in all fairness, I usually gravitated toward suspense or courtroom drama—besides law journals and case studies, of course—but I was feeling antsy and needed to relax my mind. Reading had always had that effect on me and put me to sleep half the time. I remembered getting some of my best rest while studying for the bar. My internal clock told me it had to be the middle of the night, and, no matter how hard I tried to stay awake, fitful sleep once again took hold.

Looking down at myself, I saw I was dressed from head to toe in a suit of armor, with a crossbow slung over my shoulder, sitting atop a majestic chestnut-brown horse. Surrounded by others dressed just like me, I looked around and saw in the near distance a castle that sat atop a hill, surrounded by a moat with a functioning drawbridge. I half expected to see Rapunzel appear in an open window, dropping her hair down over the ledge. It was so authentic in the way it appeared, I felt like it was a scene straight out of Camelot.

Just as I was wondering about what was going on, two of the tattooed men galloped up next to me, shouting at me in some foreign tongue I couldn't begin to decipher. What I did know was that they were pissed and meant business, as they grabbed the reins of my horse while loading their crossbows. I scanned the group for someone to help me, but everywhere I looked, everyone was faceless. I was on my own. I tried to reason with them as I was being led deep into a forest, but the more I talked, the madder they got. The forest smelled just as it did in real life, earthy, with undertones of moldy, mildewing pine. I had always found immense pleasure in the forest, but this was not the case tonight. I was apprehensive and uneasy as the two talked in hushed tones to each other. I looked around trying to find an escape route when I heard someone calling my name. I made a mad dash, trying to escape, when I felt a piercing pain in my chest.

I jolted awake, swinging my arms as if I were in a fistfight with an invisible opponent, only to see Osborne standing over me, shouting my name and poking me in the ribs with his finger.

"What the hell, Elliott? You were screaming so loud you could have been heard all the way in Portland. I strongly suggest you take it down a notch—or I won't be held responsible for what will happen!"

I wasn't big on idle threats, and I boldly told him so, only to piss him off further.

"Trust me, this is not an idle threat, but a promise," he replied as he slammed the cell door behind him.

I was once again left alone, cold, hungry and miserable. The book had only elicited nightmares, so I chose not to read anymore and instead replayed in my mind what had transpired since Brie's untimely death. Almost three weeks had passed since she'd met her maker, but a lifetime of events had taken place. Except for meeting Quinn, none of it had been good.

Not knowing what was in store for me tomorrow, I started counting sheep so I could conserve my energy and sleep. I had never had luck with this before, but, then again, I had never had injuries like I did, on top of being kept against my will. I was starting to feel the aftermath of the last month, and it felt like I had taken two steps back in my recovery.

Lo and behold, it must have worked, because I woke up groggy, like I had a major hangover. Every muscle in my body was hurting and stiff, but my senses were stimulated by the smell of coffee. It was intoxicating. I assumed that it was the next morning, and I felt encouraged. I had managed to get a couple of hours of sleep—without any more crazy nightmares or incidents—so I declared today a blue-ribbon day already. I was bound and determined to get out of here and leave this nightmare behind. Now to figure out a way.

It was like someone had been reading my mind, dissecting my thoughts. I heard a commotion somewhere in the building. There was yelling, and I heard my name and "release" in the same sentence. I was up in a shot, trying desperately to hear more.

"Hello, hello! Whoever is out there—it's me, Jonathan Elliott, and I'm being held against my will in the jail cells in the back!" I screamed, trying to keep the panic out of my voice. If I could hear them, I was positive they could hear me. I held my breath, straining to hear more, but I was greeted with unwelcome silence. I began to pace, my mind racing as my thoughts went to a dark place. Not only was I concerned with the silence from the deputies, but I was also concerned with the lack of response from Luke. If he was being held in one of these ten cells, I would have expected a response from him. All I got was crickets.

Not knowing what was happening gave me a severe case of paranoia. The feelings I was experiencing of late were uncharacteristic of my personality. I was anything but gloom and doom with a huge dash of paranoia. Instead, I was happy to say I took after my Mom and Dad—in the best of ways. I was a lover of animals and full of life and optimism like my Mom; I was also a bit of an introvert, with a quick wit, like my Dad—but smart like them both. I knew I was smart enough to figure a way out before I was left for dead.

I wasn't a fan of the new me—at least the falsely incarcerated me. I sat back down to try to calm my nerves as I picked at a hangnail that had appeared in the corner of my left thumb. As I subconsciously rubbed my face, I realized I was in dire need of a shave and an attitude adjustment, not necessarily in that order. My patience was all but worn thin, and I started second-guessing the ruckus I'd heard moments before. The silence pierced through me, and I was starting to spiral out of control when Osborne appeared, with Lux and Charlie Turner, one my fellow attorneys at the firm I worked for in Portland, trailing close behind.

CHAPTER THIRTY-EIGHT

osing myself and forgetting I was a thirty-three-year-old grown-up, I felt excitement coursing through my veins. The feeling exploded inside of me as I jumped up and down like a kid who'd just won first place at the local spelling bee. The cavalry had arrived, and there was no way in hell Osborne could keep me detained. He didn't have a leg to stand on, and I knew *he* knew it by the look in his eyes. He had been caught with his pants down, so to speak, and he looked nervous. Assuming he had even half a brain in his warped noggin, he had to know that the shit was about to hit the fan. The best part was that he hadn't begun to see what I was capable of. A shitstorm was brewing on the horizon, blowing its way into Mount Sierra.

"What a sight for sore eyes you two are!" I rejoiced as Osborne looked on with disgust. He looked as if he were on the verge of losing his breakfast, and I couldn't help hoping he would fall violently ill. He was taking his damn sweet time, as he pretended he had misplaced the key to my cell. He wasn't fooling me or Lux, who grabbed the keys out of Osborne's hands—the *click* of the door was instantaneous. Ah, the feel of freedom was exhilarating, and I let out a cheer and danced a little jig.

Much to Osborne's dismay, we were walking out the front door, with not so much as a glance backwards. My watch and phone were secure in my pocket. I felt his hatred burrowing through me, but I was out of his grasp and feeling on top of the world. The air seemed sweeter, as honey bees buzzed around, searching for flowers to pollinate. The sun had made a miraculous appearance, and a slight breeze had joined in the celebration of my freedom. The Pacific Northwest was notorious for its copious amounts of rainfall and dreary, overcast skies, so the sunshine was not lost on me. It felt like a rebirth of sorts, and I couldn't help but feel the tides turn in my favor.

"Not to dampen this day, but do you two know where Luke is? I haven't seen him since last night." I cautiously questioned just as I caught sight of Quinn standing next to Charlie's car. The sight of her took my breath away and made me forget about the harrowing experience I had just endured. She was wearing a brightly colored floral sundress with a mustard-yellow cardigan tied around her shoulders. The color complemented her hair as wisps blew in the breeze.

Her cheeks dimpled, and the corners of her eyes wrinkled as her smile beamed, radiating happiness and relief.

My question was forgotten. I ran into her anxiously awaiting arms and shared a kiss that made my arm hair stand at attention while butterflies rejoiced in my release. I felt it all the way to my toes. The joy I felt in her arms was like no other I had experienced, and I knew deep in my heart and soul we were meant to be together, for better or worse, from this day forward. And best of all, I could tell she felt the same way.

"Okay, you two lovebirds. As much as I cherish love and think the world of you two, we need to discuss what's happening right in front of us—we need to discuss Luke," Lux interrupted.

As much as I didn't want my blissful moment to end, he was right. I knew in my heart Quinn and I would be able to share a lifetime of magic moments, but, for now, it had to be business as usual.

"Unfortunately, what Charlie and I have found out isn't all great news. Luke is, indeed, in custody and being held at the jail, but, unlike you, Jonathan, he has been officially charged and fingerprinted. Osborne has charged him with aggravated assault. He is set to be arraigned tomorrow, so he'll have to chill in jail for the day. I have checked on him, though, and he seems to be nursing his ego more than anything. He was more concerned with you than himself, Jonathan. Although it pains me to say this, I think this is the best place for him to get his temper in check and reflect on his past transgressions."

Hearing what Lux had to say made me want to go check on Luke and give him a little pep talk, but I listened to reason and decided it was best not to tempt fate. Instead, I jumped into Charlie's car, allowing Lux to ride shotgun so I could nestle with Quinn in the back seat. There was nowhere I'd rather be.

I was feeling anything but fresh and clean, but Quinn didn't seem to notice. Or if she did, she was being polite by not dwelling on the obvious. We held hands while I gawked out the window, admiring the simplicity of what nature had to offer. There's nothing like seeing beauty through the eyes of a person who—just a measly twelve hours ago—was being shown a dungeon and wasn't sure what fate had in store for him.

Pulling up in front of Luke's, reality slapped me in the face as I saw the remnants from where his truck had burned to the ground—as well as bloodstains on the front step, where my Dad had stood, bleeding, after being shot. My life was anything but rainbows and unicorns, and I made a silent vow that, if it was the last thing I did, I would get revenge for my Dad's death as well as the others'. First things first: Luke needed out, so we could give my Dad a proper burial before we loaded up both barrels to hunt down whoever was responsible for my life being in total disarray.

Autumn was ecstatic, whining and jumping for joy when I walked through the front door. I bent down and buried my face in her fur, and I was overcome with sadness. Everything that had happened in the past three weeks—or, possibly, a month (I'd lost all track of time)—hit me all at once. I was overcome with emotion, and the tears opened a floodgate that was overflowing. I didn't care that they saw me cry, but I was thankful they knew I needed time to grieve. I was left alone while the others busied themselves in the kitchen. I had always been in touch with my emotions, something Luke and I shared, but I had never felt so vulnerable and at someone's mercy who had a hidden agenda. An agenda that was filled with everything bad. Everything I wasn't.

For what seemed like an eternity, I sat clutching Autumn in a firm embrace, crying into her fur for the loss of my innocence. I no longer saw life through the same lens I had before. I wasn't naive—I knew bad people existed—but I hadn't had to deal with any of them since my teens. It made them seem invisible in a world with billions of people in it. At least not to this extent, I hadn't dealt with scum like this. Whoever was behind this travesty had given new meaning to the word "evil." I guess you would say it was an eye-opener into the underworld of corruption and death—one that I had no desire to be a part of.

Needing that cry for no other reason than the loss of my Dad, I felt rejuvenated and ready to bring this corrupt sucker to his knees. Making my way into the bathroom for a much-needed shower, I walked by the library, where, through the years, Luke had collected books upon books. I loved the way this room smelled. One of my fondest memories as a child was going to the library with my Mom and walking aimlessly down the aisles, taking in the sights and smells surrounding me. Books take you to another realm, another dimension. Books allow you to get lost in your own reality, as you live vicariously through someone else's. As a thirteen-year-old, I hadn't felt the attraction to this room as I did now. I found solace in here and could spend hours perusing the shelves.

Walking in, I noticed things seemed to be a bit discombobulated. Luke took great pains with his cabin to keep everything in an orderly fashion, but especially this room. It was his sanctuary of sorts, and I knew he would have never left it in this condition. To the naked eye, it appeared orderly, but I knew better. Someone had been rifling through his desk and moving the books around. Knowing that it had been sometime last night, when we were both being held against our will, gave me the willies. What were they looking for—and had they found it? Were they still lurking behind the shadows, hidden away in a closet or under a bed?

Doing my best to straighten things up, back to the way they were and how Luke would have done it, I knew my shower would have to wait. As I ran into the kitchen, the aroma of coffee was heavenly. Charlie, Lux and Quinn were sitting around the knotty-pine table, with steaming hot mugs, having a meeting. Papers, journals and law books littered the table as well as the floor next to the chair where Charlie was sitting. They were deep in conversation when I blurted out that we may not be alone.

Without going into great detail, I explained my thoughts that there was potentially an intruder hiding close to us at this very minute. Before my frantic message had even sunk in, there was a loud *bang* in the great room, and the front door slammed. We all ran in to find the lamp that usually sat atop the entryway table had been knocked over. It was now lying on the floor in a slew of broken shards of glass.

Throwing open the front door, we all witnessed two men running like their life depended on it, toward the forest. They were dressed from head to toe in black, just like the tattooed guys that had been haunting me lately. In a strange way, this comforted me. Now I realized that there weren't multiple sets of people after me—only the crazed, stinky ones.

Knowing there was no way we could catch them and realizing it wasn't wise to confront them, we closed the door behind us and made our way back into the kitchen. Were they getting careless, or did they *want* to get caught? Somehow, the wires between them and their boss had gotten crossed, and it could have been disastrous for us all. Breaking and entering was one more crime they had broken. The way they were at it, once they were caught—and I was positive they would be—they would be locked away for years, never to see the light of day again.

We felt violated—especially me, since I considered this my second home. We were reasonably sure there weren't any intruders left behind, but we split up and did a thorough sweep of the place, including the barn. I still wasn't sure what they were after. It could have all been an attempt at intimidating us. I'm sorry to say that it had worked, and we were now all on edge, feeling eyes watching our every move. And then it hit me . . . maybe they weren't after anything, after all.

CHAPTER THIRTY-NINE

"I wonder if the intruders were here with the intent not to steal but eavesdrop instead, by planting listening devices?" I questioned, looking over my shoulder. It would make sense, and the more thought I gave it, I was sure I was on to something. Lux, Quinn and Charlie all shook their heads in unison and agreed that it made perfect sense. Splitting up once again, we went in search of surveillance devices.

I took off to the loft, Autumn trailing closely behind. I wasn't entirely sure what I was looking for, but I was confident I'd know it if I saw it. Getting down on my hands and knees, searching, I was rewarded. Upon combing the baseboards, I came upon a very small, round, black button-looking contraption. I had an eerie feeling it had friends scattered throughout the cabin, which made me extremely uncomfortable. My search yielded one more device before I was confident I had thoroughly turned everything inside out.

Meeting in the family room, we dumped out our discoveries on the distressed oaken coffee table, counting a total of twelve. Twelve too many. We all took a moment to let this sink in. As we looked at the table with twelve intruders staring us in the face, we couldn't deny the fact that we were in danger. We needed to destroy these bugs ASAP, but the question was *How?* By now, the ninjas who'd planted them would know we were on to them, so the only question that remained was how we wanted to send a message, letting them know that we were not to be screwed with.

Not wanting to tip our hand, I ran to the library to find paper and pens, so all of us could come up with ideas to dispose of them. If anyone had seen us then, they would have had quite a chuckle as we all huddled over our papers, dreaming up ideas. The final consensus was to dig a big hole out back and bury them, but not until we blew them to smithereens in hopes we would burst someone's eardrums.

I was having a hard time coming to grips with my upside-down, running-for-my-life, looking-over-my-shoulder existence. I felt like I couldn't catch a break, and I was wondering what was in store for me next—all of it was wearing me down. The thought of burying my Dad in two days was a crippling feeling. I needed to talk to Luke. Not just to reaffirm that he was strong and holding his own, but to put me in the headspace I needed to think clearly.

"Jonathan, do you need a moment?" Lux asked, apprehensively. I must have looked like I had lost my best friend—which was an accurate observation, since I felt exactly that way. Luke, thank God, was still part of the living, but Dr. Jacobs, aka Dr. *GQ*, my friend from high school Tom, Brie, my right hand, and my Dad had not fared so well. *My Dad*—I couldn't even say the words, let alone allow myself to believe them. How was I to forgive myself when I knew that I was inadvertently responsible for his untimely, gruesome death?

Waving Lux off with what I hoped appeared to be an affirmation that I was fine, I excused myself with the promise that I would return in a moment. Giving Quinn a thumbs-up, I hurried into the bathroom, where I collapsed on the floor. The mosaic tile floor was cold beneath my body as goosebumps formed on my arms and shivers ran down my spine. I once again found myself sobbing, mourning what had happened, what was and what might have been. Not wanting the others to hear what a sorry state I was in, I managed to heave myself up to turn on the faucet in hopes of drowning out my sobs. I was even getting tired of the tears that kept taking over my life lately. The only excuse I could find was the trauma that I had endured, coupled with my losses. I made a promise to myself that it was time to man up as soon as I got this out of my system.

Wanting to scream, I put a cloth to my mouth and silenced my desperate howls of pain. Feeling alone and defeated, I curled into a fetal position on the fluffy taupe rugs that were spread across the floor, giving the floor a walking-on-a-cloud sensation. The distress I found myself in was like a kick in the stomach. I ran my hands through my hair, searching for answers I couldn't find.

Flashbacks of my life ran on a reel, on repeat, tormenting me but comforting me all the same. Saturdays spent with my Dad on our special "Daddy and me" days when I was a kid, flying kites or watching the LA Dodgers win the World Series. Afternoons spent curled in my Mom's lap, feeling intoxicated breathing in her signature scent of lavender and vanilla as she read me my favorite Winnie the Pooh books or when she valiantly tried to teach me how to make her award-winning sugar cookies I loved so much. The camping trips to the mountains where we became one with nature and laughed until tears ran down our faces. I cried for an innocence gone and for the two most wonderful parents a child could ever have been blessed with.

I was alone in the world. No parents, no siblings, no grandparents. Just me, in a never-ending nightmare I never would have dreamed imaginable. Here I was, lying on the floor in the middle of the bathroom, feeling sorry for myself, watching a trail of ants line up like little soldiers bravely making their way along the baseboard, up the wall and out a tiny crack next to the window. I wanted to join them to escape my reality. But instead, I lay wondering how I was going to find the strength I needed to just get through the next few days. Suddenly, a warmth washed over me—like a spirit had entered the room and given me the strength to carry on.

I was not a spiritual person by nature, but, over the last twenty years, I'd embraced spirituality more. Probably the most-asked question about spiritual matters concerned whether there was an afterlife. I believed my Mom had come to see me many times in the past, giving me encouragement when I had been at my lowest, with one foot firmly planted in the rabbit hole. I had been to a psychic once, and the spirits of my grandparents and my Mom, with a plate of fresh-baked cookies, had come down from the heavens, showering me with love and instilling the fortitude I needed to carry on and excel at life. I was more than positive this was one of those moments.

Even though I wasn't normally much of a crier as an adult, I was not ashamed of giving into my vulnerable state. Positive the tears I had cried after my Mom passed over twenty-one years ago would have lasted a lifetime, I found myself mistaken and at the mercy of my emotions. Gingerly sitting up, I wiped the tears from my eyes and blew my nose, feeling pain shoot through my sinuses that reminded me that I was a wreck not only mentally, but my physical being was still in a very fragile state as well. It was official: I was a disaster.

After giving myself the time I needed to regroup, I sat in the shower as the rainfall shower head beat down on me, enveloping me in warmth, breathing life back into me. Slowly, I began to regain my sanity bit by bit, and the tears were replaced with anger—an anger so fierce that it scared even me. And by the time I emerged from the bathroom to rejoin the others, my meltdown was tucked safely away in my memory.

"Wow, it's amazing how a hot shower can make a new man out of you," I exclaimed while raiding the fridge in search of fruits for my smoothie. Throwing in a banana, blueberries, a dollop of peanut butter and a tablespoon of protein powder, I added oat milk to the Vitamix, watching it churn to the perfect consistency before throwing in a straw to drink my breakfast. I was famished, exhausted and surprisingly rejuvenated. A good cry or two was good for mental clarity and for cleansing my soul.

If I said the three of them didn't look shocked at my physical and mental transformation, I would have been lying, and my nose would have grown right before their eyes, giving me away. Their mouths gaped open as I turned to face them with some newfound energy I wasn't entirely feeling but was adamant about exuding. There was work to do, and I was done wallowing in self-pity. For the time being, anyway. I wasn't foolish enough to believe I wouldn't find myself on the other side of happiness in the future, but, for now, I felt encouraged.

We packed up the bugs and headed out back. "Who's ready to have some fun?" I asked, beaming from ear to ear. I was taking great pleasure out of destroying what they thought had been a rock-solid plan. They obviously didn't give us any credit for intelligence. Lux dug the hole and gave me the pleasure of dumping them in and lighting the firecracker Luke had left over from who knows what. The boom gave me more pleasure than I could have imagined. Lux threw the dirt on top as we all bid them a farewell while flipping them off.

Gathering around the table once again, this time with my head clear, we began discussing the next plan of action. I was eternally grateful for Lux, for using his noggin. Contacting my law firm had been the perfect solution. Having Charlie here was a godsend in its own right, but when he pulled out Brie's daily planner and her phone records, I had to contain myself from jumping across the table and hugging him. This is the information we needed to start our dive into the underbelly of Brie's life before her untimely demise.

"Do you guys mind if I take a walk out to the stables to check on the horses before we dive in? I know myself all too well, and I'm a gazillion percent positive I will be all consumed to so much as even take a breath if I don't go now. And if it's all the same to you, can I steal Quinn away with me?" I sheepishly asked while standing and holding my hand out to her. She eagerly agreed while the other two smiled their consent.

Truth be told, as much as I loved the animals, I was craving time with Quinn. I briefly wondered if they saw through my façade, but the heart wants what it wants, and all I cared about was how Quinn was holding up. I know this had been more than she bargained for lately, and I needed to know if it had taken its toll.

"If we're not back in two hours, send the troops to rescue us," I said jokingly, but half serious. I was taking a leap of faith and hoping it didn't backfire on me.

I grabbed a shotgun as we headed out the door, just to be on the safe side. If I were a betting man, there were two things I would have wagered my life savings on. One was that whoever was ultimately responsible for these horrendous misdeeds had not packed up and left town. And the other was that I was head over heels in love with Quinn. And I could tell she felt the same way.

Tucking the shotgun under my left arm, I eagerly entwined my fingers in Quinn's as I held her hand. It was as soft as a baby's butt and instantly woke up the butterflies that lived in my stomach. I had brought Autumn along for companionship as well as protection. She was fiercely loyal and wouldn't tolerate anyone coming between us. The morning held the promise of a beautiful day. The sun was out in all its warm glory as a slight breeze licked across our faces, causing Quinn's hair to swirl like a halo above her head. At that moment, all was right with the world.

Nature's backdrop of wildflowers, in every color imaginable, was blooming all around us, telling us in all their beauty that spring was in full swing and that the heat of summer was just around the corner. With the vast amounts of rain the PNW received, this was one of its perks. You could always count on breathtaking scenery, no matter which way you looked. From sprawling mountains to greenery the color of envy, I couldn't imagine myself living anywhere else. Now what I needed to focus on was *living*. I was more optimistic now than I had been knowing we had four intelligent, driven people who would work on this non-stop until we put an end to this once and for all. *Watch out assholes—I'm coming for you.*

Grabbing a blanket Luke kept hidden in the rafters of the stables, Quinn and I found a perfect spot under a massive oak tree. Sitting there reminded me of story after story I'd heard from my parents about a tree just like this one. They spent hours under it every summer as they vacationed by the lake. I caught myself reliving my memory, with no tears this time—only happy thoughts knowing my parents were reunited, spending the rest of eternity together once again. I was in a reflective but optimistic mood and had a backlog of things I needed to address before we could tackle the planner and phone records.

Finding myself at a loss for words caught me off guard. As a teen, I had always been awkward around girls, but, as I matured through the years and *found* myself, I prided myself on my proficient and quick wit. But this was different because these words were coming from the heart. I was nervously picking at a loose thread on the corner of the blanket, and my mind went blank.

Sensing my reluctance to start, she dove right in and saved the day. "I can't tell you how happy it makes my heart to have you here and out of that miserable existence of a jail. Lux and I were frantic for a while, until I had the idea of calling your work in Portland."

I looked startled. "You called them? I just assumed Lux had the idea—not that it really makes a difference, I guess—but thank you," I beamed. She was a quick thinker, which I found very appealing—on top of the physical attraction I had for her.

"There's something else that's been on my mind that I would like you to be aware of. I didn't say anything at the time because I didn't want to make an already stressful situation more tense, but I'm not a damsel in distress. When the fight was taking place between Luke and Osborne, and the dead body was unveiled, you whisked me away like I was fragile and I would break. Trust me, Jonathan—I'm kind of a badass and have seen more than you have, I'm sure, and never once shied away from it. It comes with the territory. I chose this job because I crave adventure."

I sat mesmerized by her confession. She was a dream come true in every sense of the word.

As she continued on about how she appreciated my efforts to shield her, she snickered telling me she thought it was chivalrous of me. That's me all right—a knight in shining armor. I laughed with her, telling her I would have found her attractive either way, but to know she was a badass and adventurous was everything I could ask for.

Minutes turned into hours as she became animated, telling me stories about her childhood and reliving the time she came face to face with death. I knew that feeling all too well, and it wasn't a pleasant one. We laughed until our cheeks hurt and lost all track of time. The next thing we knew, Lux and Charlie were upon us, checking to make sure we were all right. We were more than all right—we were on top of the world. A major triumph, considering the circumstances.

Making our way back to the cabin, I was filled with an abundance of thoughts and feelings. I was more than excited to get started on our research, but I wanted my special time with Quinn to continue. Knowing we would have a lifetime to share stories, we all took our places at the table, all of them with gigantic club sandwiches, while I settled on homemade chicken broth, which Luke had lovingly made from scratch. Lux and Charlie had started without us, but to no avail. It looked like the answers were not in plain sight, which meant some digging and a fair share of good luck were needed.

Hours flew by as I combed through the planner, taking notes when anything remotely suspicious caught my eye. Before I knew it, the sun had set behind the mountains, and God had painted the most magnificent of sunsets turning the sky pinks and oranges. No matter how absorbed I was, my eyes crossed, and I started seeing double. My sleep last night in the musty old jail cell had not been restful, and, today, I was just plain tired.

Saying goodnight to Quinn proved much harder than I imagined. I was smitten in the best of ways, and her presence consumed me. We shared a passionate kiss as I bid her goodnight, with promises to resume our search after Luke's arraignment in the morning.

Selfishly, I convinced Charlie to stay at the cabin. I was still more than a little on edge not knowing what was in store for me and felt more comfortable having a buddy sleep over. It was like I was in high school again, when friends spent the night in my rainbow room, staying up all night, telling ghost stories and gossiping about girls. Except we were grown-ups now with responsibilities. I missed the innocence of my youth but loved the grown-up I had become. With a pat on the back for Charlie, I locked up and made my way up to the loft with Autumn.

Carelessly forgetting to set the alarm clock, I laid my head on the pillow. Overwhelmed by tiredness, sleep took over immediately, and the nightmares began. I was on the balcony of an unknown condominium as a gust of wind blew the cocktail napkin from my hand. A slight drizzle was beginning to fall, and a chill overcame me as I wrapped my coat tightly around myself. As I looked inside through the sheer curtains that hung from ceiling to floor, they fluttered in the wind, giving the illusion of clouds floating. Lots of people were milling around, laughing and hugging like they were long-lost friends, yet nobody looked familiar. Bits of conversation filtered through the air.

"Have you seen Serene since she got the nose job? She looks like a beast," some mean woman cackled to her friend. Another voice boomed over others, "Hey, Ben, old pal—how's that new job treating you? Our tee time is at 7 tomorrow, *capiche*?"

I knew I should go inside and mingle. After all, the soirée was in my honor. I had just made partner at my prestigious law firm by putting in eighty-hour work weeks and billing my clients a thousand dollars an hour. I had been on the short list of nominees and had just been given the fantastic news yesterday. Or *was* it fantastic news? The firm's expectations of me increased tenfold, and I could already see burnout looming on the horizon.

Making my way inside with a fake smile plastered on my face, I was not in a celebratory mood. Something I couldn't explain was occupying my thoughts, gnawing away at my brain. I was the man of the hour, so I brushed it aside and circulated around the room, accepting congratulations from well-wishers I didn't recognize. Were they here for me? I was searching the crowd for a familiar face when I felt a light tug on my sleeve at the same time a familiar Jo Malone scent permeated my nostrils. I turned and came face to face with Brie, who stood before me frazzled and unkempt. Her coloring was that of a corpse, and a huge red spot, which I imagined could only be blood, had soaked through her blouse. As she opened her mouth to speak, beetles crawled out of it, and blood began gushing from her nose right before she collapsed at my feet.

My attempts to resuscitate her were in vain, and I screamed for help. No one came. The party around me continued, giving me the illusion that I was invisible. I placed her in a chair as I frantically searched for help. All of a sudden, right before my eyes, the room turned into a sea of black. Everyone around me was dressed from head to toe in black, all yelling in unison, "You can't run from us, Jonathan!"

Needing air, I ran to the balcony only to find the charred remains of my Dad begging me to save him. I grabbed at him and lost my footing, tumbling over the side and falling four stories into the swimming pool below.

I woke up drenched in sweat, lying entangled in sheets on the floor, with Autumn moaning and licking my face. My medications, which I had placed on the bedside table, as well as a glass of water, had both been knocked over, causing the water to spill and pool on the hardwood. Pills littered the floor as I scrambled to regain my bearings, only to slip and fall again. Making my way into the bathroom, I wasn't sure what the reflection in the mirror would be. Was I soaking wet from sweat from my nightmare, or was I suffering a relapse of sorts, spiking a fever?

Closing my eyes and bracing for the worst, I was pleasantly surprised. My coloring was good, the gash on my cheek was improving, and there was not a trace of blood anywhere. My hair was standing at attention, causing me to stifle a giggle, but, all in all, I was feeling optimistic. Jumping into the shower to wash away the nightmare, I made a promise to myself that I would go talk to a professional to get these nightmares under control. They had the potential to become all-consuming, and I needed my sleep to regain my stamina and heal properly.

Settling into bed again, with Autumn curled between my legs, I glanced at the clock, which read 3:00 a.m. Why hadn't I noticed before that it was my Super Mario clock from my childhood? Leave it to Luke to save this. A smile spread across my face, thinking of all that Luke meant to me.

The next thing I knew, birds were chirping, the sun was peeking through the shutters, promising another glorious day, as I stretched. The rest of my night had been filled with happy dreams of my life with Quinn, lifting my spirits until I looked at Super Mario. The clock said 10 a.m., and I had missed Luke's arraignment. I was pissed at myself for oversleeping. Not the start of my day I was hoping for, but I still remained optimistic that things were taking a turn in my favor. It was about time.

Racing through traffic, I made it there in record time. Eschewing my normal courtroom attire, I had opted for a pair of khakis and a blue plaid button-down shirt. The courthouse was bustling with activity. As I walked up the steps, a multitude of memories flooded my mind. Twenty years gone in a breath and twenty years wiser. As I stood at the top step, I remembered the judicial snowman with the old-time curly Parliament wig and judge's robe begging for justice. I had come a long way. I silently said thanks to the lessons I'd learned here and the justice that was handed down.

Passing through security, I glanced at the docket and found Luke's courtroom assignment. I quickly walked toward Courtroom Two. I was hoping I wasn't too late, but, as I went to pull the handle on the big wooden door, Luke, Charlie, Quinn, and Lux were coming out.

"Well?" I asked, anxiously scanning their faces for answers. It was clear that Luke was free, for the time being, but what I didn't know is what had gone down inside the courtroom. I knew that he had been released on his own recognizance, or he would have been escorted back to jail to wait for bail to be posted. If bail had been denied, he would have been thrown back in jail, too. I was pretty sure this would be the outcome, but there was always uncertainty and doubt if you didn't know anything about the judge. They could be persnickety at times.

"Well, I'm so glad you could fit me into your busy schedule, sleepyhead," Luke joked as he gave me a big, hearty pat on my back. I blushed and offered my heartfelt apologies as everyone continued to give me a hard time. It was good to have us all back together again and in good spirits. The only fear I had now was the repercussions we might face from these hoodlums now that Luke and I were out of jail. It was abundantly clear that the persons responsible for the heinous acts over the past three or so weeks would stop at nothing. I put that out of my head for the time being and started the celebration with the others.

Luke looked no the worse for wear. Charlie must have brought him a suit from the cabin, because Luke was dressed to the nines—he would have given Dr. *GQ* a run for his money. His smile was his best accessory, though, and it warmed my heart to see him this way. We decided on a local pub to continue our celebration at, and, as we parted ways on the courthouse steps, Osborne walked up, sporting a clean-shaven look. He was a spitting image of his crazy Dad, and it gave me shivers to look at him.

"I wouldn't get too happy if I were you two, because this celebration will be short lived." He spat our way before he turned on his heel and stormed down the steps, tripping on the last two and falling on his ass. It was probably in bad taste to laugh at his misfortune, but I couldn't help it. I roared as he got up and brushed himself off, turning twenty shades of red.

"Enjoy your trip, Osborne?" I yelled after him as he flipped me off and vanished around the corner. What a childish thing for me to do! But I needed to lighten the mood, and it did the trick. Sometimes being an adult was overrated.

Our celebration was one for the books. They all ate the most delicious-looking burgers while I salivated and drank a shake. Watching Quinn down a couple of beers and loosen up to where her true personality emerged was the highlight of the celebration. I loved her giggle, her quick wit and the way her dimples were on full display when she laughed at her own jokes.

We laughed until we almost peed our pants and played a game of "Truth or Dare," like we were in middle school again, for old times' sake. Luke and I hadn't played this in years, but it held a special place in our hearts, especially since this is how we passed the time on our stakeout in the forest, waiting for the Mount Sierra killer to show up. The highlight of the game was when Quinn chose "Truth" over

"Dare" and had to answer the question, "Are you head over heels for Jonathan?" I held my breath for what seemed like an hour while she blushed before saying, "Yes!" I was glad my instincts hadn't failed me.

Luke and Charlie gave me a *Cliff's Notes* synopsis of the arraignment, explaining exactly what I suspected had happened. Luke would have a court date later, but, for now, he was free. I had a very strong suspicion that Osborne wasn't the Mister Fancy Pants he thought he was. I had seen clandestine eye-rolls behind his back on numerous occasions. Having the genes he had could account for some of his arrogance and hot-headedness, but his bullying tactics were bound to land him in the hot seat one day. I secretly was hoping that day had come and that it was time to pay the piper.

Allowing ourselves to have fun for once was a welcome change. It had been an intense three weeks, always looking over our shoulders, but the tide was about to change. I had a very strong feeling that we hadn't seen the end of these hoodlums. I'd recently had a vision, and it was anything but pretty. I had tried to erase it from my memory, but it wasn't about to go anywhere, no matter how much I tried. I couldn't put my finger on its meaning, but, all the same, it sent a shiver down my spine.

When Luke walked into the cabin, Autumn almost knocked him over. She was ecstatic to see him, and, the way she carried on, you would think he had been gone for a year. I loved the bond they had. As soon as this whole mess was behind us, I was planning on rescuing another golden of my own. I missed the love and companionship of a dog, but, after Canela, the golden I got when I was thirteen, I hadn't been in a position to get another. That was about to change.

Charlie, Lux and Quinn gathered around the kitchen table once again to start their digging into the phone records, while Luke and I tended to some last-minute details for my Dad's funeral tomorrow. "I'm not going to lie—I'm a little worried about tomorrow," I told Luke as I unconsciously picked at the scab on my arm. "I took the liberty of hiring a couple of bouncers to stand guard tomorrow, so there's no funny business. Is that okay with you?" I asked Luke.

"I think that's a brilliant idea. Tomorrow, above all other days, is not the time to be dealing with anything except giving your Dad a proper send-off," Luke replied while staring off into space. I knew he was finding the idea of putting my Dad into the ground difficult, just as I was. I was trying to cover every aspect of the details, so that no surprises would bite us in the butt tomorrow. Hearing he was more than okay with it eased my mind. We very rarely were at odds with our thoughts, but, out of respect, I liked to run things by him.

Walking into the kitchen, I was hoping there was some good news to be heard. A pattern in the phone records? Multiple calls to the same number? Random incoming calls with no names? I would have welcomed anything that we could grasp on to and dig deeper into, but I was met with blank stares and disappointing news.

"Unfortunately, nothing is obvious at this point, but maybe we're barking up the wrong tree. Hear me out," Lux said while rubbing his chin deep in thought. "I wonder if Brie had contact on a burner phone or through a courier memo. Is it possible she didn't know the people at all and had an unfortunate run-in?"

As I paced, I had a constant nagging in the back of my head. It was as if I held the key to some information, but it was buried under the past three weeks of trauma.

"Wait—I just remembered something! I was in my office when Brie stumbled in. She was trying desperately to tell me something, and, before she took her last breath, she uttered something that sounded like *hard kiss*," I excitedly exclaimed. "This has to mean something. Is there a name anywhere that sounds like that? 'Marcus,' perhaps?" I knew I was grasping at straws, but straws were all I had. I had a feeling in the pit of my stomach that we were running out of time. Something bad was in the works, and time wasn't in our favor.

Why had I not remembered to tell them this before? I was pissed at myself, and it was proof positive that the head trauma I had suffered was still messing with me. Coupled with the simple fact that I had a case of *Too-Much-Going-on-at-Once Syndrome*, I was finding it difficult to compartmentalize everything. But then again, was it really that important, and had I even heard her right?

As the hours ticked by, we all became more frustrated but made a promise to each other that we would prevail—somehow, someway. As much as I knew the importance of this task, my mind kept wandering to tomorrow. I was fortunate enough not to have been to a funeral since my Mom's, twenty years earlier, and I was concerned with how this was going to affect me. I was a grown man and wanted to put on a brave face, but I also knew myself. I was crumbling inside at the thought of burying my Dad—my last remaining relative.

Quinn and I were able to steal some time away from the others. "I can't tell you how much I appreciate you helping out with this case as well as being here for me. I wish with all my heart you could have met my parents. They would have adored you as much as I do," I gushed as I brushed my thumb against her soft hand in mine. She looked into my eyes, and, at that moment, our souls connected, and we shared a kiss that spoke of desire. For another time—hopefully, in the near future.

Bidding everyone goodnight, knowing we would meet up tomorrow at the gravesite, Luke and I retired into the family room to say our private goodbyes to my Dad. Although we had shared stories and memories right after he was killed, we wanted to light candles in his honor and share our favorite memories in private.

Sifting through my memory, I had so many events that made me smile and laugh out loud. Our relationship hadn't always been a "Hallmark Moment," but I had never given up on him, even when he was at his worst. Our time as a family was etched into my heart, giving me insight into the pain and suffering he endured after my Mom was taken from us. It was a horrible time for us, but we found our way back to each other and gained respect along the way.

Luke reflected back on the night we had gone out for ice cream to celebrate my Dad's one-year-sober mark. Although I was only fourteen, I remember it like it was yesterday. We gorged on hot fudge and marshmallow sundaes until my stomach hurt so bad I almost barfed. We laughed till our cheeks hurt and had the best time. Those were the days when life seemed simpler—the days as a child, when your biggest decision of the day was deciding what you wanted for breakfast, and essentials magically appeared when you ran out. Adulting took more effort than a child could ever know. Why kids always wanted to grow up was beyond me.

My good memories were so plentiful that I found it impossible to choose one, so, instead, I told Luke about all the times we camped as a family and our trips to the lake every summer. I was sure I had told him before, but he showed no signs of being bored and became animated as he listened, reliving my special times with me.

Retiring to the loft for the night wasn't something I was looking forward to. I was afraid of the nightmares that might rear their ugly heads, and knowing when I would wake up, it would be the day I had been dreading. The final goodbye was weighing heavily on my mind. I tossed and turned for the better part of the night, fighting sleep, until it overcame me, and I fell into a peaceful sleep, dreaming of my child-hood, with both of my parents embracing me in warm, security-blanket hugs. I will never understand dreams—my whole wonderful childhood was replayed in a span of an hour. Right before I woke, my parents, holding hands, came as a vision to reassure me that I would never be alone and that their love for me was unwavering.

Waking up not knowing what the day had in store for me left me at odds with my feelings. The dream had put a smile on my face, and my heart was filled with love, but I knew it wouldn't last. Super Mario told me it was 7:30 a.m., and the smell of coffee in the air was intoxicating. I could make out a sliver of sunlight filtering through the shutters, making dust particles dance in the air, but, as I looked out-side, I witnessed a big, gray rain cloud swallow up the sun in one big gulp. The weather looked like I was starting to feel. The gloomy sky would do nothing to brighten the mood of the day, as raindrops the size of saucers emerged from the ominous gray clouds overhead.

Cloudy, rainy weather puts a damper on most things, but it always made funerals sadder and more depressing—like the clouds were sharing in your grief and crying tears of despair. As I showered and dressed in my finest black suit, I knew in my heart that my parents would be proud of me. At the end of the day, what more could you ask for? Hoping this would be enough to get me through the day, I tucked the thought away to retrieve when it was needed the most.

Luke, dressed in his Sunday's finest black suit, was sitting at the kitchen table, hovering over a steaming cup of coffee, as I made my way downstairs. Autumn greeted me with a big sloppy kiss, as Luke went to the fridge to pour me a glass of freshly squeezed orange juice. He had a pot of steel-cut oats simmering on the stove, filling the room with cinnamon and vanilla undertones. Everything about the picture painted in front of me was filled with love. It was just the start to my morning that I needed.

CHAPTER FORTY-TWO

y Dad was a no-frills kinda guy. Even though he was a very successful attorney, he lived within his means and never was one to compete with the Joneses. For that reason alone, we had opted for a simple funeral, without all the bells and whistles. That's what my Dad would have wanted. Luke and I pulled up to the gravesite in his new pickup truck just as the grounds crew was finishing setting up black tarp-like tents to shield the guests from the elements. The rain had miraculously slowed to a drizzle. I thanked my good sense for thinking about this in advance.

In the distance, I could see my Dad's casket with a mountain of white and red roses covering it, arranged under a tent next to one with rows of folding chairs set up. Next to the casket was a large blown-up picture on an easel of my Dad that had been taken recently, when he was honored at a bar association meeting. He was all smiles and proud of his accomplishments but not half as proud as I was. He didn't deserve this. Nobody did, but having worked so hard to overcome his demons just to end up like this seemed unfair, to say the least.

Purposely arriving early, we wanted the opportunity to gather our thoughts. When I was younger, Luke had often put his big hand on my knee to ground me and give me support. So, today, when he reached over and placed his hand on my knee, I couldn't help but feel comforted. His hand had aged through the years, like the rest of him. It was now covered in age spots and wrinkled skin, reflecting the road map to his life. Even with that, it was the most beautiful hand connected to the most beautiful soul I had ever met. I hated the fact that he was getting old. The realization that he wasn't long for this Earth sent daggers straight through my heart.

Luke had always been intuitive to my moods and thoughts, so when he blurted out, "You know, Jonathan, I have no inclination to leave this Earth anytime soon," it didn't surprise me. I laughed. "Old man, get outta my head!" It was just what we needed to lighten the mood, as much as it could. The day would still prove challenging, but I was determined to power through with him by my side every step of the way.

Drawing in a deep breath, I could feel the butterflies and apprehension start a fight within my stomach. The sky had turned an ugly shade of gray, and the clouds were threatening to unleash the tears that were welling up behind my eyes. I jumped out of the truck, with Luke by my side. My body was shaking with distress, anger and, even though I had Luke, a level of abandonment. I wanted to jump back into the truck and escape my reality. My hands went to my head. It was sore and foggy, like I was carrying the dark sky of the Earth in it.

The grass was damp beneath our feet from morning dew, along with fresh raindrops. Looking around, I saw dandelions peeking through the grass, reminding me that not everything is what it seems. I mustered up the courage to make it through the eulogy, knowing that my parents were together once again, where they belonged.

By the time we made it to the tent, we were soaked up to our knees, and the wind was picking up, causing leaves to swirl in the air, chilling us to the bone. I noticed a man standing next to the casket for the first time, and this realization caught me off guard. I thought we were alone for the time being. Then I realized that it was the pastor, and I was relieved. Before greeting him, I took a quick glance around and saw the bodyguards I had hired, stationed strategically around the cemetery. They looked like innocent mourners coming to show their respects to loved ones, but these mourners were anything but innocent. They were packing heat and ready to take you down if you so much as looked sideways at Luke or me. I was hoping it wouldn't come to that, but I was glad we had our own Rambos at the ready, in case it did.

The pastor was a round, portly, older gentleman with horn-rimmed glasses perched on the tip of his bulbous nose. He was bald except for an unruly gray fringe around the edge of his skull, causing him to appear as if he were wearing a wig. He extended his hand as we made eye contact. His eyes were the color of the sky, but friendly, with a twinkle that made me feel at ease. His smile was warm and genuine, and I envied his grandchildren if he were lucky enough to have any.

"Please accept my sincerest condolences for your loss, Jonathan. I'm Reverend Sinclair. Joseph Sinclair, but please call me 'Joe.'" I immediately liked him. He oozed trust and so much spirituality that I had to look twice to make sure he hadn't sprouted wings.

We had opted for a closed casket, as if we had been given a choice. My Dad was near unrecognizable, so there was no point in the funeral mortician trying to patch him together only to make him look like a mere grotesque image of who he had been. The flowers that sat hugging the casket were a nice touch and the only beautiful thing about this event.

Taking a moment alone to say a silent prayer, I scanned the grounds as guests started filing in, taking their seats under the tent. The moment I had been dreading was here, and there was nothing I could do to change it. Being helpless was not something I was familiar with, and I didn't like it. By no means was I a control freak, but, in life, there were always decisions to make—but not this time. The decision had been made for me.

Lost in my own reality, I hadn't heard the pastor talking to me. He placed his gentle hand on my back and whispered in my ear, "Are you ready to start the service now, son?" *Was I ready?* How could I answer that? Would I ever be ready to bury my Dad?

Shaking my head "yes" without thinking, I went through the motions and managed to utter, "Yes, of course, Mr. Sinclair. My apologies for being lost in space for a minute. By all means, please feel free to start." I made my way to my front-row seat, keeping my head down to avoid eye contact. I wasn't in the right mindset at this moment to look people in the eye. I was too fragile and afraid my tears would start, and when they stopped would be anyone's guess. As I sat down, Luke wrapped his arm around my shoulders and gave me a reassuring grin while mouthing, "You've got this, son." Simultaneously, Quinn put her hand in mine. I felt the support and was eternally grateful that they were there to wrap me in love.

Taking a pause, Reverend Sinclair scratched his head, cleared his throat and began.

"On behalf of Jonathan, I want to thank you all for taking the time out of your busy lives to pay your respects to his beloved father, Michael Brian Elliott. It is with a heavy heart that we lay to rest a gentleman who was not only a father but also a widower, friend to many, and an all-around stand-up guy. His death has shattered many lives and left many questions unanswered. Jonathan has vowed to get to the bottom of this senseless act of violence, so that we can all get the closure we need."

I was keenly aware of sniffles and a couple of people blowing their noses. As Mr. Sinclair pulled out his well-worn bible, the clouds miraculously blew away, and the perfectly blue sky presented the most vibrant rainbow I had ever witnessed. Unbeknownst to me, Luke had hired a string quartet to play "Amazing Grace." As they played, I sat in awe of the beauty that surrounded me. The whole scene was out of a Hollywood movie, and I was positive that this was the sign from up above that I needed to carry on my Dad's legacy.

Wrapping everything up, Mr. Sinclair once again thanked everyone for giving my Dad a proper send-off. The sun had continued to shine, encouraging the birds to happily chirp in the nearby trees. Looking around for the first time, I was shocked to see every seat taken and many more friends standing. My Dad had been a pillar of the community for many years, and the respect people had for him showed. Not only had Mount Sierra friends shown up, but I was caught off guard by a handful from the law firm I worked at in Portland, coming up to me and offering their condolences. I had to laugh at their reaction to my present physical state, since the last time they saw me, I was in one piece and handsome, or so I've been told.

"You're never allowed to leave Portland again if this is the way the 'burbs treat you!" They laughed at my expense, but I joined right along. I knew I looked a fright, and they hadn't even seen me at my worst. I was astonished at how much I had missed seeing them. My life had most definitely taken a turn for the worst since Brie's untimely demise. It had served to light a fire under me to catch the maniac causing my unrest, so I could get back to my life—one that I was hoping Quinn would love. Giving Quinn a squeeze and holding her close, I was thrilled to introduce her to my friends. Watching her interact with them was even better. She had a friendly vibe about her that drew people in. We were going to make the power couple to beat all.

Luke was working the crowd, walking up to different groups, shooting the shit as they mingled, making small talk before they made their way off to the local Mexican restaurant, Tequila Mockingbird, where we were holding a luncheon. My Dad had been a diehard Mexican-food connoisseur, and this was his favorite restaurant to dine at. I was pretty positive they had a picture of him on their infamous "*Señores y Señoras Estupendo Amigos*" wall.

Everyone made their way to their cars as I stayed behind for a final goodbye. It was a poignant moment as I sat down next to my Dad's casket, not wanting to walk away. Walking away would mean saying goodbye *forever*, and that sent shock waves through me. Even though I knew in my heart he was gone, he was still here, lying wrapped in pillowy comfort inside his coffin.

I bit my lip; I was on the brink of tears—tears of sadness mixed with tears of mounting anger. Why had it come to this? I looked to the sky, waiting for an answer that never came. The ground was wet and cold beneath me, but all I could think about was how unfair this was.

With hands balled into fists, I looked around one last time. Seeing that I was alone, I punched the ground with everything I had, and then I poured my heart out to my Dad.

"Dad, I love you more than I can begin to put into words. You were my rock, my friend and my confidant. You were my everything, and I'm sorry that you got caught in the middle of this craziness." Tears began to roll down my face as I thought about the injustice in all of this. "I solemnly swear to you that I will get to the bottom of this and see justice served. I owe you this. Please accept my apologies, and rest well with Mom by your side. Until we meet again, I will hold you in my heart forever."

Standing up, I hugged the casket, giving him one last squeeze. I would miss his hugs. I would miss his guidance. I would miss his wit. I would miss his advice. I would miss our talks. But most of all, I would miss not having a Dad.

Luke was waiting patiently in the truck with a surprise guest, Quinn. Guessing I was going to need the people I loved the most after my final goodbye was said, he had invited her to ride with us. God, how I loved that man for always knowing the right thing to do! As I got in, she sidled up next to me, and I took comfort in her, smelling her perfume and remembering my Mom, who was now wrapped firmly in my Dad's embrace. I was proud of myself for holding it together at a time when I could have been an inconsolable mess. But as proud as I was, I knew my parents were prouder of the man I was, giving me comfort.

As we drove off, we passed the bodyguards, who flashed us a thumbs-up.

Then, to my utter shock, I saw Osborne standing behind a tree, watching us leave.

"Luke, should we go back? I saw Osborne hovering behind that tree," I questioned as I craned my neck to get a better view. He was just standing there, staring at us.

"Nope," Luke said, "there's not a reason in God's green Earth that would make me want to give that man the satisfaction of knowing he got to me."

He was right. Again. As we pulled out of the cemetery, I took one last glance back as Osborne tipped his hat in my direction. And then I put him out of my mind.

CHAPTER FORTY-THREE

The wake was a huge success. Everyone seemed to enjoy themselves, and I was able to let my hair down and look to the future instead of dwelling in the past, with a little help from the margaritas, which flowed non-stop. It was great catching up with my and my Dad's friends, some I had known since I was old enough to walk.

As we departed the restaurant, the sun was starting to sink behind the mountains, and a stiff wind was blowing debris every which way. Quinn's hair was a swirl of cotton candy as we made our way to the truck. I was a little tipsy but still this side of sober, so, when Luke jumped behind the wheel, I was thankful. Drinking and driving was a major no-no in my book, and, since Luke was as sober as they come, it was a no-brainer. Quinn was also feeling no pain. She had left her car at the cemetery, but it was clear that she was in no position to drive, so we made plans to retrieve it tomorrow.

"Seeing you enjoying yourself at the wake was the highlight of my month, son. You could use more of that behavior, if I do say so myself," Luke cheerfully said as he maneuvered through some road construction.

That wasn't saying much, since the last month or so had been dismal, at best, but I gladly took the compliment anyway. Truthfully, I had never been much of a drinker, mainly because I saw the effects it could have on your life, watching my Dad struggle with his addiction for years. Quinn was giggly, finding humor in everything. It was a side of her that I hadn't seen before, but she could do no wrong in my eyes.

"If it's all the same to you, Jonathan, I'll just Uber to the cemetery tomorrow to get my car and come to the cabin, so we can resume our research. It's painstakingly obvious that no work is getting done tonight." She laughed like she was performing stand-up at the Apollo. I helped her to her door and thanked her for lending me her support for the day, as I kissed her goodnight. I was already feeling melancholy upon her departure but knowing we'd be joined at the hip in about twelve short hours gave me something to look forward to.

If I was being brutally honest with myself, I wasn't looking forward to going back to the cemetery quite that soon, anyway, so I welcomed the idea of the Uber. The reality of my Dad being gone would slap me in my face soon enough.

I knew the next time I went to visit my Dad, he would be tucked in his final resting place, six feet under, beside my Mom, for me never to see again.

As always, Autumn went ballistic as I stumbled through the door—cries of joy followed by never-ending kisses. It never got old. Luke made a beeline to the kitchen, mumbling something under his breath about making a strong pot of coffee to sober my ass up. I rather liked the euphoric feeling that was allowing me to momentarily escape reality. I was positive that tomorrow would be a different story if the hangover from hell were to present itself in all its glory. I surely would be singing a different tune.

Coffee with Luke was the perfect ending to a challenging day. We both agreed the day had gone off without a hitch and decided we would keep the bodyguards on staff. It gave us a sense of security, and, if my intuition was spot on, as usual, things were fixing to get ugly as we dug deeper and deeper into the underbelly of the criminal world engulfing us right now.

Luckily, caffeine had never had a jolt-of-energy effect on me, so, when I retired to the loft with Autumn a couple of hours later, I immediately fell asleep, dreaming of my parents reuniting in heaven. My Mom had waited twenty-one years to see her one true love. It was as if time had stood still for them, as she welcomed him with open arms, her dimpled angelic smile spread across her beautiful face. I could honestly and literally say now that it was a match made in heaven.

Not wanting the irritating alarm clock to awaken me, I opted to sleep until I woke on my own. I was hoping this would alleviate the severity of the headache I was guaranteed to have. As I rolled over, the first thing I noticed was a ray of sunshine peeking through the shutters. It was 8 a.m., and I was only slightly worse for wear. My head was pounding, and my mouth was dry and scratchy. It was as if I had just feasted on a platter full of sandpaper sandwiches. I was second-guessing my decision to drown my sorrows the day before. I popped a couple of Advil and made my way downstairs.

Immediately, I was greeted with the aroma of fresh-baked cinnamon rolls—cinnamon and vanilla swirled through the air, doing a culinary happy dance. I could hear Luke, Lux and Charlie having a heated discussion about whether the LA Dodgers or the Atlanta Braves were going to make it to the World Series this year. What I didn't hear was Quinn, so when I breezed into the kitchen, I wasn't totally surprised to see her chair at the table empty. Looking forward to starting my day seeing her beautiful face, I was hoping her hangover wasn't keeping her in bed.

"Where's Quinn? Is she out back? Has anyone heard from her this morning? Is she running late?" I fired off a barrage of questions, not waiting for answers, as a sinking pit of doom landed in my stomach. I was trying not to listen to my intuition, but it was yelling at me that something wasn't right. It was more than sleeping in and more than a hangover. I usually loved my intuition, but, at this very moment, I was hating it with everything I had.

I frantically dialed her number while Luke tried to reassure me that my imagination was working overtime. "Son, relax. It's only 8:15 in the morning. Give the poor girl a chance to shower and make herself pretty for her man." I was hoping he was right but when the call went straight to voicemail, I knew with every fiber of my being that he wasn't. My heart started to pound in my ears as I made a conscious effort to keep the barf down that was accumulating in my mouth. *Shit, shit, shit!* What was happening, and why had she been caught up in the middle of this?

Running out of the house, sans shoes, I grabbed Luke's keys to his truck. It was imperative I get to her house immediately, and I wasn't in any mood to reason with anyone. Luke, Lux and Charlie were out the door right behind me with lightning speed. Luke was surprisingly spry for an old man with a limp—he threw himself into the truck as I was peeling out of the driveway.

"Please drive carefully, Jonathan. You are running on pure adrenaline at this point, and you don't know if anything you're thinking is true," Luke pleaded.

"With all respect, Luke, can you please just let me be? I know what I know. You are aware of my sixth sense and intuition, so why would you even try to reason with me? Enough, old man!" I screamed, barreling down the street adjacent to the forest, going eighty miles an hour, running red lights and leaving Lux and Charlie in my dust. I immediately regretted snapping at him, but time was of the essence, and I was in no mood for a lecture.

Making it to Quinn's house in record time, I jumped out of the truck, leaving it running, while Luke looked perplexed in the front seat. Quinn lived on a quiet, tree-lined street, with old-fashioned streetlight lanterns, reminiscent of those that lined the cobblestone streets of England in a distant yesteryear. Her house was a bungalow style with a sloped roof and a wide veranda. Finding the front door locked, I pounded on it but was greeted with silence. Panic coursed through my veins as I jumped the fence in one fell swoop. Knocking over the trash cans that were stored on the side of her house, I frantically ran to her back door. And that's when my heart sank and crumbled into a million pieces.

The door was a farmhouse Dutch-door, and the glass on the top had been shattered, giving easy access to open the bottom half. I was quickly reminded I had run out of Luke's in such a state that I hadn't taken the time to put shoes on. I stepped on glass, cutting the bottom of my feet. I yelped out in pain, but I didn't let it slow me down. My adrenaline was running at full throttle, camouflaging the cuts that were leaving trails of blood. I must have sounded like a maniac as I called out to Quinn while running through her house. Nothing looked out of place until I reached her bedroom.

Her drapes were partially closed, allowing the sunshine to come through the cracks, casting an eerie shadow on her belongings. Her bedroom was in total disarray. It was clear that a scuffle had taken place and that Quinn had come out on the losing end, as she was nowhere in sight.

Her bed was a rumpled-up mess of sheets intertwined with her duvet.

Having fallen or gotten knocked down from the night side table, a glass of water lay on the floor, causing water to pool under more broken glass. As I ran toward the bathroom, I tripped over her phone, which was lying under the dress she had on the day before. That's when I noticed a very faint but distinct odor of chloroform still lingering in the air.

Dresser drawers were left open, with all her clothes littering the floor as if someone had raided her drawers in search of an imaginary something. What were they looking for? The whole scene reeked of trouble. I was in a panic, but a voice in my head told me to slow down and methodically look for clues. Running around like a chicken with my head cut off would benefit no one right now.

Trying to collect my thoughts, I turned to see Luke, Lux and Charlie standing in the doorway, white as ghosts, with their mouths hanging open.

"Holy shit—what has happened here?" Luke questioned as he made his way around a tipped-over chair. It was mayhem, and I was at a loss for where to even begin. Sitting on the edge of the bed, with my face in my hands, I leaned over with my elbows digging into my knees as tears fought against my eyelids to escape. I didn't have time for tears and needed to find her before it was too late—too late for her *and* too late for me, because if she were to die, a part of me would die with her.

Taking control of the situation, Lux spoke calmly, "Luke, you need to get the hell outta here now. We need to call the authorities, and it's no secret they have it out for you. We don't need to give them any more ammunition against you, and we all know they will try to twist this into something it's not." I could tell he was hurting. This was his business partner and friend.

Luke objected, saying he needed to help and stay here for me. It pained me to admit it, but I agreed with Lux. Wanting Luke here for moral support could easily backfire. That was a chance I wasn't willing to take. "I'm a big boy, Luke. Please do as Lux says." It wasn't until I made him a solemn promise that I'd keep him in the loop that he agreed and left, begrudgingly. I watched him walk to the truck with his head down, beaten with hurt feelings.

Being a private investigator, Lux had an assortment of gloves, and we donned them immediately. We started sifting through the house, looking for any clue as to Quinn's whereabouts or to who was responsible for her abduction. We all had a strong suspicion, but it wasn't until we found a note left on her pillow that our suspicions were confirmed.

Like the many notes I'd seen before, this one was written in blood and said . . .

CHAPTER FORTY-FOUR

YOU WERE WARNED TO BACK OFF, COUNSELOR. MAYBE NOW, YOU'LL LISTEN!!!

Listen to what? I didn't know what I was supposed to listen to—unless it was the voices in my head that were causing quite a scene right now. I was going through an internal struggle, wanting to punch whoever crossed my path as opposed to thinking logically. I heard Lux calling the Sheriff's Department, and I cringed. They were the last people I wanted to deal with. I doubted they would be of any help. I had a great deal more trust in the three of us than in that whole dysfunctional bunch.

"Oh, man, Lux! Did you have to? You know they are all a bunch of bumbling idiots who are only going to make unfounded accusations and get in the way." He agreed but made me see that it was imperative we play by the rules to avoid issues further down the road.

An hour later, two deputies showed up. As luck would have it, Osborne wasn't one of them, and I said a silent thanks to the gods. Ordinarily, I would have been pissed that they had taken their sweet-ass time and were lollygagging, but it worked out perfectly, giving us the chance to thoroughly comb Quinn's place for evidence. No surprise to me, we found nothing else. The assholes who'd taken her were professionals and knew what they were doing. The opposite could be said for me, because, now, I was out of my element, grasping at the smallest of threads, unraveling with each passing second.

We had done all we could at Quinn's house, so we reluctantly let the deputies take over. I hated leaving her house to a bunch of strangers. I felt her lingering presence everywhere I stepped; I refused to believe she had been a victim of the crazed maniacs who were making my life a living hell. But I couldn't argue with the reality that she was gone; God willing, she was still alive.

Distraught didn't begin to describe my current state of mind. I was in the lowest of lows as I piled into the back seat of Charlie's car. What had started out as a promising day, with the sun shining brightly and visions of spending the day with Quinn, had gone south in a matter of a couple of hours. My mind was on the edge of the rabbit hole, about to tumble in. I couldn't help but feel that Quinn's fate was resting—very precariously—in my hands.

Looking out the window, I saw people out and about, laughing and having a grand time, without a care in the world. It always amazed me how the world carried on while someone else's life hung in the balance. Lux was trying to make small talk. I appreciated the effort, but I was in no mood to humor him or anyone else. Needless to say, the ride back to Luke's was strained.

Luke and Autumn were waiting on the bench out in front as we pulled up. He looked like the cat that had swallowed the canary—he had the biggest shit-eating grin on his face, from ear to ear. Wondering what had happened since he'd left us at the house, I jumped out, barely waiting for the car to come to a complete stop. "What, what, what, Luke? What did you find out? Did they find her? Is she inside? Is she okay?" I was starting to make this question-drilling a habit—the worst form of word vomit anyone could ask for.

Not waiting for answers, I ran through the door, expecting to see her, making my last couple of hours just a bad nightmare. She wasn't there. All I saw was a Dutch oven with simmering beef stew on the stovetop and papers strewn all over the place. I was hoping there was some method to this madness, because it looked as if a Xerox machine had blown up and spit papers everywhere. Luke burst through the door, with the others hot on his heels.

"Son, you're not going to believe this, but I think I found a paper trail that could lead us to something big!" Luke blurted out, too excited to stand still, as he paced back and forth. He was practically jumping out of his skin with anticipation of sharing. I could tell how excited he was, and I wanted to help in any way I could, but I had nothing. It was just how I had been feeling since the afternoon with Brie in my office. Who could have guessed this would have taken the turn that it had, sending my life spiraling out of control and leaving a handful of deaths in its wake?

Feeling Luke's excitement, I eagerly awaited what he had to say. I grabbed Autumn to soothe my nerves. She was a therapy dog, after all. Luke was bursting at the seams, hardly able to catch his breath as he gathered a handful of papers and took a seat. The energy in the room was palpable as we all three watched Luke in anxious anticipation.

CHAPTER FORTY-FIVE

Taking a deep breath, I sat, mortified at what I was hearing. I wanted to believe we were one step closer to possibly finding Quinn and catching these lunatics. My emotions and the anticipation had me feeling like I was having an out-of-body experience. Were we on the right track—or was this going to take us on a wild goose chase and end up with more heartache?

Feeling sorry for himself and helpless, with his feelings hurt, when he got back from Quinn's, Luke was more determined than ever to help in some way. So he chose to focus on the law firm phone records, starting with a week prior to Brie's death. The records had been combed over, but Luke dug down deep, dealing with only the calls that were transferred to my office.

"I was so damn frustrated, because every time I saw a call that had come in multiple times, it was always connected to something legitimate like the restaurant down the street or the dry cleaners. They seemed harmless, so I moved on. The records showed that, four days before Brie's death, there had been a series of calls, four in particular, five minutes apart, with different numbers but just one digit off. Every single time. The first call came from (971) 555-1234, the second one (971) 555-1235, and so on. Each call lasted no more than two minutes, which piqued my curiosity." Luke stopped to catch his breath, letting the excitement grow as he got up and nervously tapped his foot. It was so quiet in the cabin that we could hear each other's stomachs growl as we waited for the next tidbit of information.

"I called the numbers, only to find that they had all been disconnected. Finding this strange, I fast-forwarded to the day Brie died, only to find a call had come in at 9:30 a.m. registering the number as (971) 555-1238. Disconnected as well."

Luke wasn't done with his synopsis, but I interrupted for a second to have Lux call in a favor at the phone company to see who these numbers had been registered to. As we waited for his contact to get back to us, we all ran different scenarios over in our minds. Time was of the essence, so when Lux's contact got back to him moments later, we all breathed a sigh of relief.

"Well, it looks like they were burner phones. Nothing registered and no record of them whatsoever," Lux told us all as we sat on the edge of our seats, waiting for the information. "Am I the only one who finds that super fishy?" I asked, and they all shook their heads "no" in unison. I was starting to get my hopes up that Luke had, indeed, stumbled on some very valuable information. I urged him to continue; he leaned over and grabbed Brie's day planner off the table.

"Looking at the days of the phone calls, I first looked at the day when the phone calls started. She had no appointments penciled in for that day, but she had doodled in her planner. I found it very disturbing. She drew pictures of a grim reaper, along with an "OMG," with daggers and knives shooting out of it. I quickly leafed through her previous pages and saw that she was a regular doodler but soon discovered she was all about flowers, hearts and rainbows. That only made me more suspicious, since it was abundantly clear that she had been highly disturbed by the caller," Luke explained with a puzzled, perplexed look on his face.

"Well, it doesn't take a brain surgeon to figure out that those calls spooked the heebie-jeebies out of her. Do you all agree?" I asked. Not waiting for an answer, I took the planner from Luke's hands. I had seen this planner numerous times before, as it had been a staple on Brie's desk. But seeing it now gave me chills all the way down my back, making my arm hair stand straight up. It had a creepy vibe to it now. Thumbing to the page Luke had referenced, I looked into the terrifying eyes of a grim reaper, with black flowing robes and a sickle in its grasp. It spooked me just looking at it. I couldn't begin to imagine how Brie had felt as she drew it, knowing she must have been highly disturbed. I wanted desperately to know what had transpired in the conversations, but Brie had taken that to her grave, never sharing an inkling of what was happening.

Luke took back the planner, turning it to the day Brie had met her maker. My Dad had always said that everyone has an expiration date. It was such a damn shame both of them expired years before their time was up. My mind started wondering why Brie had kept these calls to herself. Did she think they were a joke? Was she trying to protect me? Clearly, she had misread the hate behind them—or *had* she?

When my mind made its way back to the present, Luke was explaining what he discovered next. "After turning to the page in her planner on the day of her death, she hadn't doodled yet, but there was a weird sentence written at the top of the page. She had written it in red and circled it multiple times, which made me think it was important to her. It read "M S *Sparkly Purple Real Unicorns Can't Escape.*" We looked at each other like we had misheard the sentence, but we knew we hadn't.

I got up and walked outside. I needed some fresh air and, hopefully, some insight. Quinn was counting on me. I took a quick glimpse to make sure our Rambo guys were at their stations on the outskirts of the forest and one by the barn. The security I felt with them protecting us was worth its weight in gold. Sitting down on the bench, I was more confused than ever as I ran my fingers through my hair. I felt like I had the world on my shoulders. An audible sigh escaped from within as Luke came and plunked himself down next to me. His face was etched with wrinkles that seemed deeper than normal; worry crossed his face.

"I'm sorry, son. I wish I had been more helpful, but I feel it's a start. Why don't you come inside so we can all spitball some ideas?" he begged. I needed time to myself. I was craving some therapeutic time with the horses, and I excused myself to go feed them. Luckily, Luke understood how therapeutic the horses had been to me and didn't press the issue to come inside. Spending time with them not only eased my nerves but also helped me to think better when I was one with nature. Numerous times, I had found the clarity I was seeking just by being in their presence, soaking up their nonjudgmental attention.

Exchanging pleasantries I wasn't feeling with the body-guard, I collected a fresh bale of hay out of the barn. If anyone had stumbled upon me at this moment, they would be convinced I had lost all my marbles, because I was having a full-on conversation with the horses as they nuzzled my neck. For some strange reason I couldn't explain, I knew they held the secret—the secret I needed to unlock before it was too late for Quinn.

I let my mind wander through different scenarios, repeat-ing her nonsensical sentence as I took in the breathtaking scenery that surrounded Luke's ten acres. This always had been where I'd done my best thinking through the years. And then it hit me. It made perfect sense that Brie had been trying to send us a code. Thanking the horses for helping me once again, I ran back to the cabin like my pants were on fire. I burst through the door, and the three of them looked shocked as I yelled, "I've got it! I know what Brie meant!"

t's a mnemonic. *Sparkly Purple Real Unicorns Can't Escape* stands for 'Spruce,' and the *MS* stands for 'Mount Sierra.' When I was out with the horses, gazing at the forest, it hit me."

Before I could even ask for a map, Lux had pulled up Spruce St. or Spruce Ave. on his computer. I wasn't sure there was a street by that name within the town limits, but I knew it was possible, since so many of the streets in Mount Sierra were named after types of trees. Sure enough—there it was: a "Spruce St." on the outskirts of town, south of the forest. We all held our breaths as we looked at an aerial shot showing a series of steel-type industrial storage sheds in basically the middle of nowhere.

Not waiting to call the deputies for backup, we shot out of there like a bat out of hell. I wasn't convinced Osborne wasn't behind all of this shit, causing problems because of some misguided desire for revenge. I wouldn't put it past him to be behind this deadly vendetta, seeking justice for his corrupt father. He was just as looney as his Dad and every bit as warped.

I let Luke drive so that I could get my wits about me. We had dashed out of the cabin so fast that we hadn't even formulated a plan. We couldn't go there half-cocked and not knowing what was in store for us. That was a recipe for disaster. I called Charlie, and we agreed to meet at a truck stop about a mile from our destination. I couldn't get there fast enough.

Twenty minutes later, we pulled in next to Charlie and Lux at the truck stop, which was bursting with activity. There were more unsuspecting people than I would have liked, but we picked a shady spot, off the beaten path, under a big oak tree, and sat at a picnic table to formulate a plan. The table was weathered, with various etchings carved in the top, documenting lovers who had come and gone. I unconsciously traced the hearts and initials with my finger while listening to Lux speak.

"We don't know what we're going to find when we get there. In fact, we don't even know specifically where *there* is, since we don't have an address. Just because the aerial view showed a desolate area does not mean it still looks like that now. I think we should send one car in to case out the joint before we pull in, guns blazing. The last thing we need to do is tip our hand and get Quinn killed, assuming she's there."

As much as I thought the idea made sense, I wanted all of us together. You know—safety in numbers, and all that. But after much discussion, I agreed that Lux's idea was the best course of action, and I begrudgingly agreed to stay back with Luke. I was too close to the situation, and everyone was afraid I would lose my cool. If I was being brutally honest, I would have to agree with them.

Watching them drive off with the promise that it was purely a scouting mission was too much for me. I was losing my shit. I could feel her. I knew she was close and was banking on me being her knight in shining armor. Luke tried to calm me, but I was having no part of it. I was inconsolable, acting like a crazed animal, pacing back and forth, silently praying that she was not harmed.

It was the longest ten minutes of my life, but when I saw Charlie and Lux pull back into the parking lot, I ran toward them. Holding his hand up, Lux motioned for me to come back and sit at the table, where Luke was sitting, apprehensively, picking at a scab on his elbow.

"Well, we have good news and bad news," Lux started out. "Good or bad news first?"

"Good news!" I shouted, unable to contain myself. "Did you see her? Is she there?"

"Hold on, Jonathan—one thing at a time. No, we didn't see her—or anyone, for that matter. That's the good news. It's all but deserted around there, so when we do go in, we won't be noticed. Now for the bad news. There are six different buildings. None have addresses or any distinct markings, so we will have to check each one out individually. I feel it's best that we go back to the cabin and collect some guns and ammunition before we proceed. I also think that, when we go in, it's best that we go in one car. We can leave it behind a tree somewhere and walk in. One of us should stay behind as a lookout. The last thing we need is to get caught breaking and entering," Lux continued, in a very calm, levelheaded manner.

Wishing I could be as levelheaded as him, I dismissed the idea immediately. My head was telling me it made sense, but my heart had overruled it and was yelling to proceed full steam ahead. I grabbed Luke's keys that he had set on the table and took off in a full sprint toward the truck before anyone could stop me. So much for having my wits about me, but all I could see was a vision of Quinn bound and gagged, hanging from the rafters, barely surviving, within an inch of her life.

I wasn't thinking clearly and realized this as I started the engine. *What was I pulling out to do, exactly? Was I crazy?* I could easily get her killed if we didn't approach this the right way. So, I reluctantly turned the engine back off and joined the other three. As luck would have it, they didn't judge me, and we proceeded with the plan Lux had proposed.

Arriving back at the cabin, Luke compiled his arsenal of guns, ammo and knives on the kitchen table. It was an impressive pile, and it would be more than sufficient, which was a good thing, since I didn't have any, and Charlie would never in his right mind have thought to bring any. Little did he know when he left Portland that he would potentially be caught smack dab in the middle of a gunfight.

The clock was straight up twelve o'clock as we made our way back to the industrial buildings. We had all decided Luke would be our lookout. He wasn't the fastest of our bunch, and, if things got ugly, a quick escape might be necessary.

As we pulled up, it was eerily quiet. The sun was shining high in the sky; there was a stiff breeze, causing the trees to make a swishing noise, which made the scene even more tense. Owls hooted in the trees, and leaves rustled, all while our nerves were on the verge of snapping like a twig. We were putting all our eggs in one basket, so to speak, hoping that we weren't being led down the wrong path only to end up empty-handed and wasting precious time.

We left Luke behind and instructed him to make a duck call if he spotted any activity coming our way. Wishing each other luck, we chose to start at the far-left building and work our way down. Hoping the door was unlocked, we slowly turned the knob. It was locked. So we did what any cat burglar would do and picked the lock. Slowly opening the door with our guns drawn, we entered into a dark, cavernous building housing farm equipment. After making the determination everything was kosher, we moved on to the next one, only to be greeted with the same situation.

We encountered the same thing over and over again. The storage units housed various types of equipment, but they were only storage units. We were dejected and frustrated, to say the least. We had been moving slowly and methodically, so as not to arouse any attention. We had all but given up hope and were wasting time we couldn't afford to waste.

It was now one o'clock, and the final building was in front of us. The second we approached it, we noticed something different. Not only did it have a door handle that was locked, but it also had a padlock. Picking both locks, Lux opened the door as Charlie and I followed close behind, ready to strike at a moment's notice. We switched on the light; the contents of the unit were illuminated in fluorescent overhead lights that cast evil shadows. My eyes popped out of my head, and I heard an audible gasp escape from Charlie's mouth simultaneously with Lux whispering, "Holy fucking shit!"

We had stumbled into the devil's lair.

It seemed like the interior had been transformed into a command center of sorts. My eyes were automatically drawn to the wall facing the west side. It was hard not to miss JONATHAN MUST DIE!!!!! spray painted in red, taking up the whole wall. I felt a shudder run up and down my spine as I broke out in a cold sweat. I felt faint and had to brace myself on the corner of a table that stood to my left. Charlie was by my side in a flash, as Lux checked the perimeter for activity.

"It's clear that we're alone for the time being, but it's just a matter of time before they return to their base." Lux matter-of-factly stated. His voice shook as he spoke, and I tried my hardest to get my shit together. The air smelled stale, with an overpowering mixture of body odor and corruption—with a twinge of patchouli drifting about. I couldn't hide my disappointment that Quinn was nowhere to be seen. Time had never been more important, and we all dispersed, weapons in one hand and our phones snapping pictures with the other.

On the table, which was a collapsible white plastic portable table I had seen at numerous potluck suppers through the years, sat a computer and printer. It also housed multiple baskets, with papers overflowing in each. Donning some gloves, I approached the first basket with apprehension and shaking hands. Inside was a stack of manila folders each with a different name on them. Grabbing the top one that had "Jonathan" written in block letters on the front, I wrestled with the toggle, as a loud *bang* thudded on the roof and vibrated through the walls. We all stood in horror, not knowing who was about to walk through the door. Lux made a mad dash to the wall, hitting the light switch, as we all stood poised, with our guns pointed toward the door, holding our breath, knowing our fate was in our hands.

For what seemed like an hour but in reality was only minutes, we stood, shaking, sweating and on the verge of regurgitating anything that remained in our stomachs—but nothing happened. We remained alone and scared shitless. Finally dismissing it as the wind playing mind tricks on us, we resumed taking in all the secrets the room held.

Once I got the toggle open on the manila folder, I found glossy color and black-and-white photos of myself staring back at me. The photos depicted my life in Portland at The Side Bar, a local lawyer pub hangout, the front of my house (homing in on the address), my Range Rover, with a blow up of the license plate and various other shots of me around town and in Mount Sierra. One photo was of me coming out of the hospital, and one was of me at Luke's cabin. You name it, it was in there. I felt violated and stupid for being naive. I had been tailed for months as I lived in my own cocoon of safety, none the wiser. Carefully putting them back in their "home," I sifted through the other folders. There were six in total, including mine. It seemed as if they, whoever *they* were, had done their homework and tailed those closest to me. Opening up each one separately, I saw some of the same for Luke, my Dad, Brie, Quinn and Lux staring back at me, totally unaware, living their daily life in total bliss.

Moving on, I tackled the next basket, which contained an assortment of burner phones, tracking devices and walk-ie-talkies. There were five baskets in all holding personal information, in total violation of our rights. I was sickened at what great lengths they had gone to, to intrude in our lives, lying in wait to make their move. It disgusted me, but it also gave me the strength I needed to power through the rest of the information in hopes that I could find evidence of who was the corrupt, warped soul behind the mask.

I took a quick glance to see what Lux and Charlie were up to. Lux was standing in front of a whiteboard, snapping picture after picture. I had only glanced at it when we came in, but upon further investigation, I noticed all our names with information written after each person. A body-count tally sheet had been added, with a big happy face at the top. The sick bastards were proud of the deaths they were causing.

Charlie was in the corner, going through what looked like hampers lined up like little school kids waiting for their turn at hopscotch. All I could see were piles of black next to each, so I assumed this was their black attire I always saw them in. I was hoping Charlie would find some evidence hidden in a pocket. I contemplated yelling to him to put a glove in his pocket to hopefully get some DNA off of, but it was risky stealing something. With all the evidence we were finding here, I doubted if DNA was even mandatory at this point.

As we all worked at lightning speed, the computer was calling my name. I hit the space bar, and, lo and behold, it came to life! I immediately pulled up the Google search; the history had not been erased. It had a list a mile long and spoke volumes to who they were. "Kidnapping" and "chloroform" were the latest searches, but, as I scrolled down, I saw "fire-bombs," "death by throat slashing," "sniper rifles" and such. At the very bottom, I found a very interesting search. It read "plea by insanity," followed by a search for a local sanitarium. *Hmmm, I wonder what that's about?*

Feeling a presence next to me, I looked up and was surprised to see Charlie and Lux staring over my shoulder. "Well, isn't *that* an interesting search," Lux said, repeating "Shady Oaks Mental Facility." "Wish I was a fly on this wall when they did their searches." I made a mental note to do further research on that later. If it was important enough for them to Google it, it was important enough to give it my undivided attention.

We had come close to exhausting our search, and we were already on borrowed time, so we quickly tackled the other baskets on the makeshift desk. There were detailed maps of all of our homes, workplaces and most popular hangouts, along with printed-out Google searches of each of us, complete with every aspect of our lives in full display. Knowing that someone had gone to great lengths to dive into my life and discover the most minute details gave me the creeps. It also reaffirmed they had accurately done their research, leaving no stone unturned. It made them a formidable opponent.

Just as we were about to walk out the door, something caught my eye. Wedged under the trash can, a corner of an envelope was sticking out. Reaching down to pick it up, I instantly knew this was a piece of the puzzle we had been missing. On the front it was addressed to . . .

Marcus Osborne
Care of Shady Oaks Mental Facility
4256 Pinehurst Way
Mount Sierra, OR

And in the corner where a return address would be was a single name . . .

Dylan Osborne

Who were these people, and what, if anything, did they have to do with the kidnapping and other crimes? I had known in my gut that Deputy Osborne was somehow connected, but to what extent remained to be seen. If there was one thing I was sure of, I was about to find that out!

Adrenaline was pumping through our veins like hot lava flowing from a recently erupted volcano. We were on a high like no other when we collected Luke and jumped into the car to get outta Dodge. Our day had proven to be very fruitful, and the next plan was to head back to the cabin to fill each other in on the newfound information.

I knew that the information we had gotten pictures of and seen firsthand was going to be instrumental in catching the killer—or I wouldn't have left. I felt it in my mind, soul and heart that Quinn was going to show up there, and the gentleman in me wanted to be here to save the day. But I also knew we needed to regroup, do some research and formulate a rock-solid plan.

Pulling onto the road, Luke blurted out, "For the love of God, spill the goods, guys!" We all started talking at once, over each other, making it impossible to comprehend anything. We laughed, cutting the tension and enjoying a welcome reprieve from the stress we'd just endured. Getting out of there unscathed was a feat all in itself that we deserved a pat on the back for.

Pulling out on the road, I sat silent, lost in my thoughts. I looked up and noticed a black late-model van turning onto the road we had just departed from—the road that led straight to the middle of nowhere except for the buildings and the lair.

"Luke, turn around now. Did you see the van that just made a right on Spruce as we were pulling onto the main road? I have a hunch—that's them," I yelled as panic rose in my throat. My hunches were not often wrong. I wasn't sure how I was feeling about this one, as my fear rose to a level I had never experienced before.

CHAPTER FORTY-EIGHT

rying not to be too conspicuous, Luke pulled a U-turn, keeping a safe distance behind the van. "What are your instincts telling you about this, Jonathan?" Luke inquired as he gripped the steering wheel so hard his knuckles turned white.

"I'll tell you what my instincts are telling me, Luke. They are flashing red warning signs yelling 'Danger Up Ahead,' but I don't have the time or the will to listen!"

Pulling over to the spot we had hidden in before, we piled out of the car in stealth-like fashion. We left Luke behind as we tiptoed to a viewing area shielded by trees. Acting quietly was of the utmost importance. Drawing attention to ourselves could prove deadly not only to us, but Quinn's life was hanging in the balance, too. Holding our breath as they opened their doors, we watched in horror as four men emerged. Two I recognized immediately as the dirty, stinky ninjas that were clothed in black. I unfortunately did not know the other two and wondered if they were the brains behind the operation. One was tall and heavy set with brown, scraggly, long hair that hung in his eyes. He was clean shaven except for the soul patch under his lip. The other appeared to be older, shorter in stature, balding and so skinny he was gaunt-looking.

"Hurry up, Marcus—we don't have all day. What's taking you so long?" the older man hissed through rotten teeth. Marcus had disappeared inside the van and re-emerged with what I could only assume was Quinn and a big black duffel bag; which he immediately passed off to one of the ninjas. My breath caught in my lungs as I tried desperately to remain calm. Whoever it was had their hands bound behind their back. They were wearing a nondescript gray sweatshirt and boxer shorts, with a black hood over their head. It was definitely a woman the size and shape of Quinn, but I couldn't be one hundred percent sure without seeing her face, even though I felt it in my soul. Marcus yanked on her, which caused her to lose her footing. She fell to the ground, releasing a string of obscenities.

Pissed, she managed to right herself as blood dripped from her skinned knees. Walking toward the door, Marcus grabbed her arm, which seemed to rile her up even more. "Get your filthy, disgusting hands off of me, you fucking animal!" she screamed as hatred dripped off every word.

"*Atta girl*," I whispered under my breath, immediately recognizing her voice. Unable to contain the rage coursing through my veins, I instinctively made a move toward her, causing a twig to snap under my foot. I froze, keenly aware of Charlie and Lux both holding their breath, as the men stopped in their tracks, looking our way. We hit the ground and prayed they would dismiss it as a varmint in the woods.

"What was that? Is there somebody spying on us, or am I being paranoid again?" questioned the tall, heavy-set man who had just been identified as "Marcus." The activity stopped, and I heard footsteps crunching on the leaves as he approached us. A loud sneeze followed by one of the men using a horseman's hankie sounded as if they were inches away. Our next move was crucial to everyone's safety as we froze, glued to the ground. "Come on, Marcus. We have a schedule, remember? We don't want Jonathan, otherwise known as the snotty-nosed kid, thinking we forgot about him. We've got plans to make his worst nightmare come true! And I can hardly wait!"

The color drained from my face, and I felt bile rise in my throat. The last and only time I had been referred to as a "snotty-nose kid" was when the Sheriff had called me that twenty years ago, back when he was pissed at Luke and me and lashed out. This was alarming, to say the least, not only for the sheer fact that a minuscule amount of people knew about it but also that they were planning another gruesome attack.

As the footsteps retreated, we were all able to breathe a sigh of relief as my mind immediately made its way back to the note that had been addressed to Luke and me from the Sheriff. I was a far cry from a kid any longer and took offense to him referring to me in such a manner. In the letter, the Sheriff made reference to him having help, but we had been so overjoyed with the outcome of our ordeal that we hadn't given it a great deal of thought. But now the puzzle pieces were perfectly fitting together, making the picture come full circle.

Coming out of my thoughts, to be revisited later, we watched as they made their way into the building, tugging and pulling at Quinn every step of the way. She wasn't making it easy for them, and I couldn't have been prouder of her for putting up a fight. With all of them inside, the door slammed behind them, only to immediately reopen.

The man called "Marcus" appeared again. He looked agitated as he ran his hands through his long hair and rubbed his chin. His hands turned to fists as he punched the wall, screaming, "I know you're out there. You can't hide from me. I won't let you come take me away again. No way am I ever going back, so leave me alone!" He was clearly being paranoid and becoming belligerent when the older man appeared. He protectively put his arm around Marcus's shoulders and whispered into his ear, trying to calm him.

"Did you forget to take your meds again, Marcus?" he inquired. This was all making perfect sense to me now as I visualized the envelope we had found hidden under the trash can. Marcus was suffering from some type of mental disorder causing paranoia and bursts of violence. Had he been released from Shady Oaks Mental Facility, or had he busted out?

Calming him down, they once again made their way in and slammed the door behind them, causing the metal sheet walls to tremble in protest. I was dying to know what was going on in there, and, as my rage peaked, it took everything in my power for me not to storm the place. Knowing this could potentially get Quinn killed, I took my anger out on the ground as I balled up my fists and punched the earth. It did little to calm me down, as I was seeing red at this point. Charlie and Lux felt helpless as they watched me struggle to contain my anger.

We had dodged a bullet and knew we'd better not press our luck anymore. Agreeing that we would return to the cabin to compare notes and formulate a plan seemed like the most logical plan of action, after we watched them leave and rescued Quinn, of course. There was no way in hell I was leaving her behind at the hands of mentally unstable hoodlums.

Having her this close and not knowing what was happening inside the lair was driving me to the point of hysteria. Lux and Charlie had their hands full trying to talk sense into me, because if it had been up to me, I would have gone in guns blazing, and asked questions later. Even when I *knew* that wasn't the best plan of action, the heart wants what the heart wants. And mine wanted and needed Quinn unharmed and safe, back in my arms again.

CHAPTER FORTY-EIGHT

"Jonathan, calm yourself, and for the love of God, use your head and not your heart! You want the least amount of bloodshed, right? Let's handle this the right way so we can see justice served and nobody gets killed due to irrational behavior," Charlie pleaded. I knew he was right, so I reluctantly retreated.

After close to an hour had passed, all four of them emerged in great spirits, laughing and carrying on as if they were inebriated and having the time of their lives. Getting into the van, they sped off, leaving a trail of gravel spewing in their wake.

My mind was mush. I was caught in the middle of an internal struggle between saving my girl and keeping us out of harm's way. I knew the next step we took would be a pivotal moment, and I didn't want to do the wrong thing. But, that being said, I knew I would never forgive myself if we left Quinn behind and something happened to her. As luck would have it, Charlie and Lux agreed with me, knowing we might not get the opportunity to save her again.

We cautiously came out of our hiding spot, still shaking and scared shitless. It was as if the forest could feel the tension in the air as the trees swayed and owls hooted. Charlie took off running like a bat out of hell to let Luke know what was going on, while Lux busied himself with picking the locks again. "Are you sure this is the right move to make, Jonathan? I agree we should save Quinn, but what if they come back before we're ready for them? Truthfully, I'm terrified of more bloodshed. We need to call in some authorities and go through the proper channels."

His voice shook as he spoke, confirming his fears. As I replied, I confirmed my fears as well and admitted it was risky, but I just didn't see another way within the time restraints we were facing. So, we plowed straight ahead with our plan to rescue the damsel in distress, knowing this could backfire in the worst of ways. Once inside again, the air smelled worse than death, and there were the weirdest screeching noises. Something was different from the last time we had been in here, and, as soon as the lights illuminated the room, we saw it!

CHAPTER FORTY-NINE

Sitting smack dab in the middle of the floor was a wire-box enclosure. With her hands bound and tied above her head to the top of the enclosure, still wearing the black bag over her head, Quinn sat hunched over in a grotesque position as raccoons and rats the size of small dogs feasted on her flesh. I leaned over the trash can and retched uncontrollably while Lux steadied himself against the table, mumbling "What the holy fuck" over and over. They had smelled her blood and were taking full advantage of her defenseless position.

The air was stale with undertones of death mixed with body odor. I yelled her name but got nothing in return. I was pretty sure she was unconscious by the way her body was contorted; I couldn't get to her fast enough. Screaming for her to please hold on, I was in a frenzy, beside myself, working on the lock to the cage. Feelings of dread ran through my blood. Losing her was not an option. Thank God we had gotten here when we did, or there would have been nothing but bones left of her.

Lux and I were more than keenly aware of the danger we were in, but he was by my side, with steady hands freeing Quinn and closing the door of the enclosure, allowing the varmints to turn on each other, crazed and bloodthirsty. The whole scene was one out of a horror movie, and to think those assholes were laughing when they departed just an hour ago made the scenario even more troublesome.

Removing the hood, I looked into the lifeless eyes of Quinn. Her eyes were rolled back in her head, and the color had drained from her face, causing her to appear gray. I kissed her cheeks, begging her to hold on as I stroked her hair, hoping she felt my touch and heard my words.

My mind was trapped in a nebulous cloud of confusion, hatred and anger as I carefully held her tight, wrapping her in my sweatshirt and ran out of the horror chamber as fast as I'd ever run in my life. Both of our lives depended on it. I was pretty sure she was in shock. Her pulse was weak and rapid as sweat poured off of her, soaking her shirt. I was afraid we might lose her any minute, as her breathing became more irregular by the second. She was so cold to the touch and needed medical assistance ASAP. There wasn't time to concern myself about how I was feeling, but I was enraged to the point that I was afraid of flying off the rails and killing someone. The audacity of those pigs to subject another human to such torture was beyond my comprehension.

Reaching the car, Luke and Charlie's eyes bulged out of their heads as they caught sight of Quinn's gnawed-up legs. Lux was right behind me as we peeled out of there, not looking back. I held Quinn gingerly on my lap, loosely wrapping her limbs in a blanket that was kept in the trunk. I blocked out my surroundings, concentrating only on her as I pleaded with her to stay with me. "Please hang on, Quinn. We are getting you help very soon. We have our whole life ahead of us. Don't let them win. I love you with my whole heart." As a tear ran down my cheek, I rocked her back and forth, promising her justice would be served.

Luke made record time, and, just as we pulled up in front of the emergency room, Quinn opened her eyes and gave me the sweetest smile, as to say *Thank you* before she blacked out again. Before I knew it, two doctors were taking her from me and whisking her away on a gurney. Her life was in their hands now, and I said a silent prayer for her recovery.

Distraught, helpless and *enraged* couldn't even begin to describe how I was feeling. I was inconsolable and refused to leave the hospital, so the other three stayed by my side, not willing to leave me alone. None of us were in the mood for small talk, as we all ran through the horrors of the day on repeat in our minds like a nightmare we couldn't wake from. There were no words for what we had witnessed, so when the doctor emerged with an update, I braced myself for the worst. He had gone to the same school as Dr. *GQ* and remained stoic, not giving hints as to her physical state.

"I'm Dr. Hawthorne, Jason Hawthorne, the attending physician to your friend. Quinn is very fortunate you two saved her when you did, or she may not have fared as well as she has. She is awake and asking to see all of you, in particular, someone named 'Jonathan.' She has suffered multiple bites, but, luckily, her muscles have been spared. We've stitched her as best we can, but in the near future, she will more than likely need some skin grafting. We've also started her on a rabies protocol to be on the safe side, along with some intravenous antibiotics. She has also lost a considerable amount of blood, so she has been given a transfusion." We all looked on apprehensively and in total dismay. Dismay that one human could do this to another and dismay that she was caught in the middle of this disaster I called "my life."

"When can we see her? What is her long-term prognosis? When will she be allowed to come home? Is she totally coherent?" I bombarded the poor doctor with questions, not allowing him a chance to answer before the next one came tumbling out of my mouth. I needed and wanted answers, but, at the same time, I was petrified at what I might hear. He exuded patience and knowledge, giving me a feeling of ease knowing she was getting the best care. I could only imagine his bedside manner was calming. Since Dr. *GQ* had met his untimely death, I needed a new doctor, and I was positive I'd found the one I wanted. A silver lining to our very clouded day.

Assuring us Quinn was looking forward to seeing us, we made a mad dash to her room to find her sitting up in bed, sipping on a straw attached to a carton of apple juice. There was the last bit of sunlight making its way in through the crack in her drapes, causing freakish shadows to dance on the wall. Her coloring was better than I expected, and she looked beautiful. A blanket was tucked in around her waist, but her legs were exposed. They were heavily bandaged with multiple layers of gauze, causing them to look twice their size and giving a mummy-like appearance.

"Hey, Queen Tut. It's so damn good to see you looking so well," I joked. I was greeted with a roomful of "ahs" and "boos," but a bright smile and hearty laugh from Quinn. "What, too soon for the jokes?" I laughed. For my own sanity, I needed to lighten the mood.

The next hour we sat around her bed, engrossed as Quinn gave us a play-by-play from when her nightmare began to her present state. I held her hand, mesmerized by her strength and fortitude. I was one lucky man. Although luck had not been on our side in the respect that she hadn't seen any of her captors' faces, the conversations and voices were forever ingrained in her mind. That should be enough to put these losers away for a very long time, if not forever. Now that they had kidnapping and intentional infliction of emotional distress added on to their long list of committed crimes, their future looked grim.

"These guys are sick in the head and seriously warped. A guy by the name of 'Dylan' is the ringleader, with another lunatic by the name of 'Marcus' as his right hand. I heard two other voices that belonged to two different guys they called 'Harry' and 'Paul.' As far as I could tell, they were the grunts and only did what they were told. I sensed a feeling of resentment amongst them," Quinn explained, growing more tired by the second. Her adrenaline high was wearing off, and her eyes were having trouble staying open.

Her recollection of the names she heard was just as we expected. Now, we had to do some digging to find out who and what we were dealing with—and *fast*—before they went back to their lair and found Quinn gone. Luke called one of the bodyguards we had hired to stand guard at her door, and we all bid her farewell for the afternoon.

It was a bittersweet moment for me as I stayed behind so that I could have a minute of alone time with Quinn. "You know, you gave me quite a scare. I'm over the moon on how you held your ground and kept your wits about you through this harrowing ordeal." I stroked her hair and kissed her on the cheek as she drifted off to sleep—but not before she whispered, "I love you" under her breath.

CHAPTER FIFTY

Time was ticking away, and if there was ever a time I wanted it to stand still, this was it. Rushing back to Luke's cabin, we needed a plan to best utilize what little time we had left, if any at all. The most pressing issue besides doing research on Dylan and Marcus was finding some authorities we could trust. My and Luke's history with the Mount Sierra Sheriff's Department was on shaky ground. Quite bluntly, we both felt they had it out for us. Or at least Osborne did. That left us in a predicament. Knowing we needed them to help, we bit the bullet and sent Charlie to diplomatically speak to them. With any luck, it would be Osborne's day off.

Armed with our computers, Lux began researching Dylan Osborne while I took on the task of finding out all I could about Marcus Osborne. We sent Luke and another bodyguard to keep an eye out at the lair. We couldn't afford for them to come back until we had all the ammunition we needed to guarantee they would be put away forever.

Hoping it wouldn't come to this, we had devised a plan that was anything but foolproof if the unthinkable were to become a reality. Everything needed to work in our favor, or it would have "Disaster" written all over it. I was finding the whole situation we were in ironic. Who could have imagined we would be seeking help from the same people who had made my life and Luke's life a living hell as of late. As much as I was still on the fence that Osborne wasn't somehow tangled up in the mess, I was starting to lean toward the idea that he was just a major league asshole with a vendetta. A deadly vendetta, if he had his way. But to be in cahoots with the other four? I didn't feel it in my gut. Plus, we hadn't seen any evidence that he was involved. One can't be judged guilty only because they share a surname.

Getting into the proper mindset was proving near impossible for me. My mind kept going to places that were dark and disturbing, picturing in great detail what had transpired in four short weeks. The adrenaline high I had been riding for weeks had crashed and burned, leaving me lost and confused. This was a foreign concept to me, since my job required me to have my shit together. I was a lot of things right now, but *having my shit together* was not something anyone would use to describe me at this moment.

Scratching my head, I got up to stretch. I was antsy, waiting for the other shoe to drop, so I told Lux I needed a moment and made my way outdoors. Clearing my head was first on the agenda. Hearing the seconds tick off in my head, I needed this to happen fast, or time would run out, and I would have no one to blame but myself. The sun was slowly making its way down over the majestic mountains that surrounded Mount Sierra. The Pacific Northwest and all it had to offer was deeply embedded in my heart. Wandering aimlessly, I found my way in the forest adjacent to Luke's property. I had always found solace amongst the tall pine trees that offered a canopy of darkness and solitude. My best thinking was often done here, while the trees swayed and whispered hidden secrets.

Making myself a pallet of pine needles, dried leaves and moss, I sat down at the base of a massive ponderosa pine. Using the tree as my backrest, I leaned up against it and thought about what I knew so far. My suspicions ran deep for Deputy Osborne. Always had. With one hundred percent certainty, I was sure the three Osbornes were related, although proof had not yet been found. It would be way too coincidental otherwise. The mere fact that they shared a surname didn't make them all guilty, though. Certain that Marcus and Dylan were as guilty as the day was long, Deputy Osborne was still iffy at best for me, at least for these crimes. He was guilty of many other things, but had he been in cahoots with the other two? Time would tell, but I was plumb out of it. The only other thing I was equally sure of was that they were evil, with a moral compass that was negatively off the charts.

As I pulled out my computer to surf the internet, I was more than thankful for the new cell towers that allowed access anywhere these days. It wouldn't be surprising if I got full coverage inside of a cave. Modern technology always amazed me in the best of ways. The internet put a plethora of information at your fingertips. The only issue was knowing where to start in order to dig up what was pertinent. Typing in "Marcus Osborne" into the Google search engine brought up information on multiple people who shared the same name.

All I really had to go on was an image I had seen from a distance, not altogether clear in my mind, and the fact that he had been receiving mail at Shady Oaks Mental Facility. My heart was beating overtime, and my palms started to sweat, which made holding my computer a challenge. I knew this was an elusive piece of the puzzle that would make it come full circle, if I could only find it. Frantically scrolling through two pages of "Marcus Osbornes" that weren't him, I breathed a sigh of relief when a headline grabbed my attention.

WARNING . . . ARMED AND DANGEROUS was the headline. I knew this had to be him, so I eagerly clicked on it, pulling up an article from *The Pacific Sun-Times* dated from six weeks earlier.

"Alarms sounded, and lockdown protocols were implemented at Shady Oaks Mental Facility, this morning at 8:14 a.m., when it was discovered a patient had escaped. Marcus Osborne, age twenty-five, has been a residential patient for numerous years, suffering from schizophrenia. He is considered armed and dangerous, so please use caution when approaching him. At this time, he is wanted for questioning in the deaths of two nurses who had been employed at the facility. Please call local authorities if you spot him at (458) 555-1212. This is an extremely urgent matter."

There was a thumbnail picture attached that looked like the same person I had seen at the lair, but I couldn't swear on it. It wasn't necessary, though, because, without any reservations, I was a million percent positive that my "Marcus Osborne" and this "Marcus Osborne" were one and the same. My breathing had become ragged while my heartbeat was elevated to concerning levels. I jumped up and ran back to the cabin as if my pants were on fire. I vaguely remember learning about schizophrenia in an undergrad psychology class I had taken at Washington University.

What I did recall was scary as shit. I knew people unfortunate enough to be suffering from this debilitating disorder interpret reality abnormally, resulting in a combination of hallucinations, delusions and extremely disordered thinking. Oftentimes, their behavior became impaired, causing daily functions to be a challenge. It wasn't something you would recover from and needed long-term treatment. The earlier it was diagnosed, the better the prognosis, although symptoms may always be present with periods of worsening and possible remission. What I really found fascinating was the cause. Researchers believe that a combination of genetics, brain chemistry and environment contributed to the development of the disorder. *Duh*, he was an Osborne, after all, and they were bad seeds through and through. I was reminded once again that not everyone was meant to reproduce, and this was a clear indicator of what can happen.

Bursting through the door totally out of breath, I came face to face with Deputy Titus and the shorter guy I'd seen in the past. Stopping dead in my tracks, I almost turned back around, thinking I, too, was suffering from hallucinations. Before I had the chance to bolt, he spoke. "Jonathan, please wait. I know you will find this hard to believe, but I want to help."

H e wasn't kidding: I *did* find it hard to believe. The Sheriff's Department had been anything but helpful in the past and recently. I was finding it hard to believe that he could be on our side and even harder to believe that there were sides. He proceeded to explain that Charlie had made some compelling thoughts and arguments about who we knew to be behind the recent attacks and vicious acts of violence. "Honestly, between us, we've had our eye on Deputy Osborne recently. He's changed and constantly has a chip on his shoulder, looking for trouble and making a big deal out of the smallest of situations. Do I think he's guilty? No, but I do have a suspicion that he might be covering for his relatives."

"Relatives?" I questioned, as my eyes grew wide in anticipation of the news I was about to become privy to. Lux piped in and said, "As I was researching Dylan Osborne, I stumbled upon some very interesting bits of information. Not only is he related to Deputy Osborne and Marcus Osborne, but he's their uncle and a brother to Sheriff Dan Osborne. That could possibly account for him knowing about the sheriff calling you a 'snotty-nosed kid.' It looks like he could have been instrumental in helping the Sheriff. He has been residing in the nearby town of Mountain View for the past twenty years, where he raised his two twin nephews."

"What? Wait. Did I hear you correctly? Did you say *twin nephews*? Nephews, as in Marcus and the Deputy are twin brothers?" The air in the room felt like it had been sucked out as I had to compose myself. If my mouth could have opened, I would have had to pick my jaw off the ground. It was all making sense to me now. They were all in cahoots, but what part, if any, did Deputy Osborne play?

My head was swimming with this newly acquired information. Holy shit, were they all a crazy bunch of lunatics holding a grudge for the past twenty years? I could think of no other reason for what had been taking place. They must be advocates of *an eye for an eye* and felt their name had been tarnished and dragged through the mud. The misfortune of the Sheriff had been of his own doing. Luke and I had just brought it to light. And now we were caught in a shitstorm. Innocent people had gotten killed and lives changed forever due to some misguided revenge.

Finding my voice again, I asked, "Did Charlie tell you that they are planning another attack of some sort tonight? I'm not sure what time it's scheduled to take place, but since the sun has begun to set, I feel like we're on borrowed time right now!"

"Yes, Jonathan. I have been fully briefed, and I agree with you that time's a-wastin'. It sounds to me like the industrial site is their command center, and, from what I hear about your private investigator Quinn, I'm sure they'll be back to regroup and dispose of her body. I have alerted some other deputies, and they have already positioned themselves in the forest surrounding what you refer to as 'the lair.' I know you have a stake in this, but you're going to have to let us handle this from here on out."

"Oh, *hell* no!" I shouted. "I don't feel comfortable with that in the slightest." I looked at Lux and Charlie, expecting them to stand up for me and agree. But they both shrugged their shoulders and admitted defeat. I was not on-board. It wasn't that I felt the need to control the situation, but more like I needed to see it through to fruition. After all, I had a huge stake in the outcome.

"I don't think I need to remind anyone that I lost my father, and my girlfriend was kidnapped and almost eaten alive. I NEED to see this through. I'll be happy to take a back seat to the authorities, but I want to see them squirm. I need to see them with fear in their eyes, knowing their reign of terror has come to an end. Please, I beg you. Let me get justice for my Dad."

Still looking anything but in tip-top shape, I used this to my advantage as I pleaded with them to let me tag along, as long as I remained quiet and out of the way. My lawyering skills paid off, and they took pity on my beat-up soul, begrudgingly.

Donning a bulletproof vest, I jumped into the back of the Sheriff's cruiser. This one was just as crusty as the last one, but, having more pressing matters weighing on my mind, it didn't seem to bother me this time around. I looked out the window as we were driving away and saw the worried looks on Lux's and Charlie's faces, even though they both offered me a thumbs-up. I prayed that I was making the right decision and I wouldn't be caught in the crossfire, and we sped away.

The sun was behind the mountains now, and darkness was creeping up on us as we drove in silence to the lair. I couldn't help but reflect on my life and how much I had grown as a person lately. When this whole fiasco started, I thought I had my shit together and my priorities in order, but I was wrong. I was an adult—but more what I would call a "man child." My life in Portland had been easy and cushy, leaving me in a rut, running in neutral. I didn't even realize how good I had it until I didn't. I was proud of how much I had overcome lately, but, even more importantly, I knew my Dad and Mom would be proud of the man I had become. I could feel their love beaming down on me, embracing me in a much-needed hug, giving me the strength and encouragement I needed to see this through to the end and get justice for the poor, defenseless people who had lost their lives.

The arrangements had been made in advance. Deputies would be stationed at various locations surrounding the lair in case the four of them tried to escape. We were banking on all four to be present. We had no indication to think otherwise, since they seemed to be joined at the hip. Titus, his partner, and I would wait inside and attack from there. Once we were inside, more deputies would come in to aid in the arrest. The plan was to arrest them without bloodshed, and I was aware of the danger to a certain extent. Either I was too excited or too stupid to fully comprehend the danger I was putting myself in, because I was downright giddy with excitement.

Charlie and Lux were going to the designated spot where Luke was positioned, to wait it out. If everything went as planned, we would meet up in the lair or in Quinn's room for a celebration. I had already instructed the champagne to be chillin' on ice.

As we pulled up, we hid the car far enough away not to be spotted. It was as quiet as a church mouse, without a soul in sight. I knew people were there, but they had done a fantastic job at making themselves incognito. Darkness was upon us, and the air was still as Titus picked the lock and entered the lair. It smelled metallic from the bloodshed. We flicked the lights on, and, inside the cage, two raccoons sat cowering in a corner, covered in blood, feasting on the remnants of the other varmints. It was a disgusting sight that I was sure would stay with me for months, if not years to come.

We wanted to retain the upper hand, so we turned the lights back off and hid in darkness and silence. The waiting was unbearable. I was fidgety and uneasy as I took a glance at my watch. It read 9:02 p.m. Just as I was about to say something, we heard a car approach. Footsteps were heard outside as four doors slammed. It was showtime, as the keys jingled in the lock. They were laughing and having the time of their life. Their behavior sickened me. They were diabolical in nature, with total disregard for others. As the door swung open, their laughter came to an abrupt halt as they turned the lights on and noticed Quinn gone.

nticipation coursed through my veins. As soon as they walked in and switched the lights on, they could tell something was amiss. Even though I was hidden, it's like they knew I was there, watching my every move while I held my breath. Pure, unadulterated mayhem ensued as I watched from a front-row seat. They started screaming obscenities and looked like they were on the verge of opening fire and asking for names later. In a blink of an eye, Titus and three other deputies caught them off guard and were on them faster than lightning, putting them in choke holds. "I don't know who the fuck you think you are or who you're dealing with," Dylan hissed as spit flew from his mouth, "but you better get your filthy hands off of me, or there will be hell to pay!" He was gyrating around, trying to free himself, but Titus's hold remained strong.

All four were mad as hornets, trying desperately to reach for their weapons, to no avail. I was pleasantly surprised at the precision and agility the deputies displayed, not giving the hoodlums a second to gain control. I let out my breath as I boldly stepped from behind the whiteboard, screaming with all the pent-up anger I was feeling—for taking my Dad from me and kidnapping Quinn, not to mention the abuse I had sustained both physically and mentally. "You fuckers are going down, and I hope you rot in jail!" I walked up to each one and looked them in the eye, hoping they could see into my soul and realize the pain they had caused. And then I sucker-punched them in the gut with all the fury that had been building up for weeks.

I took great pride in hearing them gasp for air. It wasn't my finest moment, and I wasn't proud of myself for stooping to their level, but, damnit, *it felt good*! Really, really good.

Titus remained cool and collected, flashing me a hint of a smile, while a glimmer of admiration twinkled in his eyes. He pulled out a bullhorn attached to his belt I hadn't even noticed and yelled into it. "Okay, guys, we've got them controlled. Bring in the help, so we can get these assholes booked and detained." In no time at all, another four deputies who had been waiting in the wings ran through the door with their guns drawn. My eyes must have been deceiving me, because, right smack in the middle of them was Osborne in all his glory.

"Oh, thank God. Bro, it's about time you showed up. Now tell them to release us immediately," Marcus sputtered, trying to catch his breath as the deputy tightened his grip. The place was swarming with deputies, but not a peep was uttered as they all collectively held their breath, waiting to hear Osborne's response. I was hoping and praying he was going to do the right thing. This was his chance to semi-redeem himself.

He puffed out his chest, spat out the toothpick from his mouth and snarled. "Shut your mouth, Marcus. You don't have the right to call me your 'Bro.' Not the way you have been acting. Causing havoc and trying to set innocent people up to take the fall. I almost fell for your warped, delusional games, but not anymore. I'm on to you, and I'm done cleaning up your messes just because we're twins. Even Dad would be ashamed of you. Both you *and* Uncle Dylan." With that, he turned his back and flipped them off.

Applause broke out, and the deputies yelled, "You tell him who's boss. Let these fuckers spend eternity in jail for all we care!" I had witnessed the disgust on Osborne's face, but I also noticed a tinge of sadness and regret in his eyes. It was a hard pill to swallow to admit your own flesh and blood could be this ruthless and deranged.

The next hour or so was a whirlwind of activity, as the four were cuffed and loaded into a van bound for the county jail. I stayed behind with Charlie, Lux and Luke to oversee the collecting of the evidence and the lifting of fingerprints. It wasn't that I didn't trust the deputies to do their job. But I didn't. They were going to have to earn that trust, after all that had transpired. Good luck to them, because that was going to be a big hurdle to overcome, but tonight they had made a step in the right direction.

SIX MONTHS LATER

The leaves were starting to turn the yellow, orange and red that signified the turn of the season. Ever since I could remember, fall had been my favorite season. I often reflected back over twenty-five years ago, how my Mom would enter her famous cookies in the competition at the county fair and win every year. And how as a family we would dress up with a theme for Halloween. My favorite being the Wizard of Oz, when I was the scarecrow leaving straw in my wake. Those were the good ol' days, when I had a family to call my own. My parents were gone now, and it often brought me to tears knowing they both had died well before their time. But they were together and looking down on me. And Quinn. And the life we were building together. They would have adored her, like I did.

Quinn had a couple of bad months with healing and skin grafting, but the badass trouper that she was, she took it in stride and never complained. We were more in love than ever. Planning our future together. I had always visualized us building a life together in Portland, but, after losing my Dad, I decided to take over his practice here. The small-town vibe has always appealed to me, and raising a family here is an ideal setting. I can't imagine not having Luke around my children. His grandchildren.

Another reason I'm staying in Mount Sierra is to be close to Luke. He's getting on in years, and his old war injury acts up more times than not. I owed him my life, after all; it's the least I could do. It wasn't much of a sacrifice because his cabin and land still remained my happy place. So much so that Quinn and I were putting the finishing touches on our own house we were having built on an acre of Luke's land—the same spot my Dad's house had sat on. It made me feel closer to him, and I knew he would have loved the idea of me being close to Luke. I could hardly wait to raise my children here and teach them how to ride horses.

Quinn and I were engaged to be married, and a wedding was in the works for the spring of next year. We had already taken the leap of faith and moved in together, so the next step was just a formality. About two months ago, we took a trip to the local animal shelter and rescued a golden retriever we named Cinnamon. It was in honor of my Canela, who had been so instrumental in my recovery twenty years prior. Canela was Spanish for "cinnamon," so it seemed the most fitting of names for the most perfect pup.

Luke's arraignment came and went, with all the charges dropped. Osborne had done a complete 180, and I can't believe I'm saying this, but he's somewhat likable. I know, I know. That's a stretch, but he has been supportive and helpful in so many ways to seeing justice served when it comes to his shady relatives. He even offered up an apology to Luke and me for being so rude and unreasonable. We accepted after much trepidation. After all, life is too short to hold a grudge. I know all too well how those could fester and take on a life of their own. Come to find out, through the years, he was being fed a bunch of lies that he had taken at face value, causing him to act erratically. I guess we all live and learn.

The evidence, including the fingerprints taken from the lair, were enough to put Dylan, Marcus and the two ninjas, Harry and Paul, away for life. Luke and I had front-row seats at their trials, when we weren't busy testifying. It brought back a lot of memories for me, reliving the trial of the Mount Sierra killer. Most of them were not good, but a couple of good things had come out of it. Justice had been served, and I fell in love with the law. Courtrooms, with all their earthy wood smells, reminded me of power. And justice. It was intoxicating then and still takes my breath away.

Marcus tried to use an insanity plea, but it had been turned down due to the magnitude of his crimes and his understanding of what had taken place. I guess it's true that schizophrenia can go into remission of sorts, too. All four were sentenced to life without parole. In the state of Oregon, the death penalty had been abolished in 2034, so they were left to rot in jail. I was glad, because being executed would have been the easy way out for them, and they needed to pay for their crimes. Osborne grew some balls and decided to be a true man of the law. His testimony was compelling, and I came to understand him better. He had been a pawn in his Uncle Dylan's life for years before he decided enough was nough and he finally learned how to stick up for himself, no natter the ramifications. With a straight face, I could even ay I was proud of the man he had become.

As I peered out into the woods, I couldn't help but reflect on how they have made me the man I am today. With their darkness and their ever-present secrets, they had been my avior and offered healing powers. I'm glad I will have a panoramic view from this day forward. I plan on doing lots of meditation there in the future, but, for now, it's time to get ready for a bonfire with s'mores and great company. Charlie and Lux will be joining Luke, Quinn and me, with a special guest appearance by the one and only Deputy Harold Osborne. Cheers to new friendships, forgotten rivalries and what the bright future holds for us all.

THE END

ABOUT THE AUTHOR

Donna Scuvotti is retired and lives in Northern California with her husband of twenty-five years, three dogs and a very dog-savvy cat. She enjoys spending time with her family and taking her lab, golden retriever and weimaraner to the park, on walks or her happy place, the beach.

Deadly Vendetta is her second book and a sequel to *Just Jonathan*. At the present time she's busy working on a third book with the release date yet to be determined.

When not writing, her passion is traveling. She and her husband plan to take some more exciting adventures in the near future.

Thank you for reading *Deadly Vendetta*! If you'd like to be notified about upcoming releases, sales and other promotions, join Donna Scuvotti's mailing list at . . .

info@donnascuvottiauthor.com.

(Your info will never be shared.)

If you enjoyed this book, please consider leaving a review at your favorite online book review site and kindly tell your friends. Reviews and word-of-mouth recommendations are the best way to help readers find great new reads, and to support independently published books and the authors who write them.

Made in the USA
Las Vegas, NV
17 November 2022

59695515R00204